CHERISHED

BOOK THREE OF THE BEHOLDER SERIES

CHRISTINA BAUER

COPYRIGHT

Monster House Books
Brighton, MA 02135
ISBN 9781946677280
First Edition

CONTENTS

Dedication   v

CHERISHED

Chapter 1   3
Chapter 2   11
Chapter 3   25
Chapter 4   39
Chapter 5   47
Chapter 6   54
Chapter 7   69
Chapter 8   78
Chapter 9   80
Chapter 10   86
Chapter 11   99
Chapter 12   115
Chapter 13   125
Chapter 14   133
Chapter 15   142
Chapter 16   150
Chapter 17   163
Chapter 18   168
Chapter 19   175
Chapter 20   182
Chapter 21   193
Chapter 22   205
Chapter 23   211
Chapter 24   228
Chapter 25   235
Chapter 26   240
Chapter 27   252

Chapter 28   261
Chapter 29   268
Chapter 30   277
Chapter 31   279
Chapter 32   285

ALSO BY CHRISTINA BAUER

CROWNED   295
ANGELBOUND   297
FAIRY TALES OF THE MAGICORUM   299
DIMENSION DRIFT   301

Sample Chapter - CROWNED   303

APPENDIX

If You Enjoyed This Book...   317
Acknowledgments   319
Collected Works   321
About Christina Bauer   325
Complimentary Book   327

DEDICATION

For All Those Who Kick Ass, Take Names
And Read Books

CHERISHED

*I*n the last three months, I hadn't raised the dead, animated any skeletons, or cast a single kill spell. For me, that was an achievement. After all, I was a Grand Mistress Necromancer turned farm girl...And I loved my new life.

Mostly.

Sometimes.

All right. In complete honesty, I was dying to cast a silencer spell right now. The reason was simple—Gail and Lizzie Dunkel had joined me for a wagon ride into town.

"Who do you think we'll meet in the village?" asked Lizzie brightly. She and her twin sister flanked me on the driver's bench. The pair both had big blue eyes, tanned skin, long blonde hair, and curvy figures. They even wore matching green gowns. I was their opposite: long dark hair, brown eyes, porcelain complexion, and slim build.

"Perhaps the widow Feyer or the Hartmann boys," replied Gail. The two went on to list other farm families we might encounter. Their chatter was high-pitched and soothing, like a pair of happy birds. Still, I ached to cast my spell. Why? Without it, the sisters would eventually ask me to join their conversation.

In my life, magick came easily. But small talk? Not at all.

My horse Smokey took a familiar turn into an orchard. Bright morning sunlight gleamed off the trees.

"What beautiful apples," sighed Lizzie.

"They look delicious," added Gail. She rubbed her stomach. "How I'd love to stop and try one." She stared at me pointedly. After all, I was holding the reins to Smokey.

Even so, we weren't stopping. The fruit looked too waxy and perfect, which meant this orchard had been hit with freeze blight. Sure, the apples looked gorgeous. But once you bit in, you'd find the colorful shell was filled with foul white goop. Yes, there was still an apple in the milky slop, but it wasn't anything you'd want to eat—more of a small, gray and disgusting lump. *Most decidedly not delicious.* I gently flicked my reins so Smokey would move a little faster.

Lizzie fluttered her lashes at me. "Can't we please stop, Elea?"

I pretended not to hear her question.

Gail nudged me in the ribs. "You *do* talk, don't you?"

I straightened my spine. What was I afraid of, exactly? Not so long ago, I rode through far more dangerous woods than these, all in the hopes that bandits would attack me. Plus, I raised thousands of Necromancers from the dead. I even exiled none other than Viktor, a fearsome mage who could wield the hybrid magick of both Creation Casters and Necromancers. Back then, I feared no one—I was a Grand Mistress Necromancer on a mission. Now, I was merely an *ex*-mage trying to chitchat with some other farm girls.

Small talk. How hard could that be?

"We aren't stopping." I nodded to the trees. "Those are covered in freeze blight."

The girls began gasping and waving their arms in panic.

I ground my back teeth. As it turned out, small talk was rather hard.

"Freeze blight," cried Lizzie. "Oh, no! It couldn't have hit our shire."

"This is terrible," added Gail. "There will be no food this winter. We're all going to die."

Lizzie gripped my upper arm. "You're just teasing…Aren't you?"

A long pause followed in which I silently cursed my friend Philippe. This had all been his idea. He'd urged me to transport the Dunkel sisters in what he called his Elea Stops Frightening The Locals plan. I'd tried to argue my way out of it, but for some reason, it was impossible to win a verbal battle with Philippe. Now, I was stuck answering Lizzie's question.

I kept my features carefully level. My Necromancer training taught me to mask my emotions. "I'm sure we'll all be fine." Mostly I said this because I could always cast spells that would kill the blight and speed the harvest. But I'd only do that if things got really dire. One rotten orchard wasn't enough to break my vow against magick.

Here was my issue. My parents left me Braddock Farm. It was all I had to remember them by. I wanted to honor their legacy and become a farm girl once more. My best chance to do that was in giving up on magick altogether. "Perhaps we should talk about something else?" I asked.

"I love this idea," said Lizzie. "How delightful that you wish to join our conversation." Lizzie looked so please, I almost felt guilty for not wanting to chat with her. *Almost.*

"Let me think." Gail tapped her tiny pointed chin. "Ah, I have it. Elea, what's your favorite way to bake a barley loaf?"

Barley loaf? That's a thing?

"I don't bake."

Lizzie stared me, slack jawed. "Surely you've made apple tarts?"

"No."

"Bran muffins?"

"No."

"Spiced pie?"

"No." *How many things did most farm girls bake?* For my part, I ate whatever Mabel and Sam had ready. The pair had been watching over my farm while I was out adventuring this past year. They'd stayed on after I returned, mostly because they were excellent farmers. Mabel kept a perpetual pot of stew over the hearth.

"What about porridge?" asked Gail.

Relief washed through me. I was about to answer that, *Yes, I know how to make porridge,* when Lizzie elbowed her sister in the rib cage. "Hush, Gail. Everyone knows how to make porridge." She leaned forward on the driver's bench in order to catch my eye. "What do you make that's *special?*"

"Nothing you'd like to hear about, I'm afraid." I was trying to keep my stories about Necromancer spells to a minimum. My tales tended to frighten everyone except Philippe.

"Please," said Gail. "We know you aren't a witch *these days.*"

"I've never been a witch," I said slowly. "I'm a Grand Mistress Necromancer."

"Right," said Lizzie. She and Gail shared a long look. I got the feeling I'd made a social blunder somewhere along the line, but I couldn't think where. No self-respecting Necromancer tolerated being called a witch. Witches were hacks who performed black magick at travelling faires. Mages like me spent years mastering our skills, and we never used our powers for evil.

"Well," said Gail. "Tell us what things you made as a Necromancer."

My mood lifted. *Fine. If they want the truth, they'll get it.*

"I'm quite good at animating skulls."

Lizzie popped her hand over her mouth. "Skulls."

The shocked look on her face was just too precious. "That's right. And I always cover mine with gemstones. It makes for a nice effect, especially when the eye sockets glow while they're talking."

More silence. *I may have pushed that too far.* It was all part of my Zuchtlos nature, which was what Necromancers called someone who was impetuous. I decided to steer the conversation onto safer ground. "Philippe said nice things about both of you, by the way. I'm so glad he suggested we spend time together."

Another long and meaningful stare passed between the sisters. I almost wanted to offer to let them sit side by side. After all, they had to lean forward to gawk around me.

Lizzie's eyes narrowed. "Do you fancy Philippe? Is he courting you?"

I should have seen that question coming and been prepared for it. But I didn't and I wasn't, so I blurted out the truth. "I don't fancy Philippe and we aren't courting."

"Are you certain?" asked Gail. "He's awfully sweet on you."

Gail wasn't exaggerating. Philippe often proclaimed his

undying affection for me, but I had other suspicions. Namely, I thought Philippe would rather be living with his sister, Amelia. However, Amelia had recently been reunited with her lost friend Veronique, a woman that Philippe detested. So he was hiding out nearby until Veronique took off.

"Believe me," I said. "I have no designs on Philippe as anything other than as a friend."

"If you say so." Gail giggled, and it reminded me how she and Lizzie were nineteen, which wasn't much younger than my twenty-two years. Still, our ages felt centuries apart. I hadn't giggled in years.

Lizzie fanned her face dramatically. "Most girls would die for a chance at that man."

"You're not wrong," I said. In fact, Philippe was exactly the kind of fellow that I *should* fancy. He was handsome, charming, and kind. Unfortunately, my heart was still set on Rowan, the man who was engaged to Philippe's sister.

What a disaster.

I decided to close out this topic. "If you doubt me, we can settle the issue once we get to the village. I'll stop by the tavern where Philippe is staying. He can explain things directly."

Gail squirmed. "Visit Philippe alone? But we've no chaperones to protect our reputations."

"Don't worry. I can kill almost anything, including Philippe."

Lizzie and Gail stared at me yet again, wide eyed. I was going for some kind of record here: Most Social Mistakes By A Necromancer.

"Wh-what?" asked Lizzie.

Obviously, I needed to change the subject once more. I

cleared my throat. "But that's enough about Philippe. Do you have any news about this weekend's faire?"

The Dunkel faire was an annual tradition. It always took place on the fields behind their main house, and the next celebration was this Saturday. This was yet another potential social catastrophe which Philippe had manipulated me into.

Gail beamed. "Oh, the preparations for the faire are coming along quite well. We already have set up the tables and—"

All of a sudden, a wave of energy coursed over me, caressing my skin into gooseflesh. The rest of Gail's words were lost to my consciousness.

Someone is casting magick nearby.

The spell felt like hundreds of embers searing my skin. That could only mean one thing. *A detection spell from a Creation Caster. Interesting.*

All Creation Casters knew magick, but most could only perform a handful of low-level spells. Senior Casters were extremely rare. Sadly, an evil mage named Viktor had transformed most Senior Casters into Changed Ones, which were part-animal mages that could cast hardly any spells. Rowan and I had sent Viktor into exile; most Changed Ones were thrilled with that accomplishment.

A handful still served Viktor, though.

A sinking feeling crept into my stomach. Something told me this new mage was one of Viktor's followers. Not good.

I pulled the wagon to a stop and scanned my surroundings. We'd passed the orchard some time ago. Now, tall stalks of green barley lined either side of the road. The shadows within them seemed too dark for daylight.

Something was wrong here.

And because I was Zuchtlos, that wrongness felt absolutely exciting to me. My shoulders squared. The world came into clearer focus. *An evil Creation Caster was definitely close by.* A battle of wits and magick could start any second now.

For the first time in ages, I giggled with joy.

2

I scanned the barley fields while Gail kept talking about the faire. "And we have dozens of torches and lanterns," she said. "The festivities can last all night long, if we like—"

"Hush," warned Lizzie.

"Why?" asked Gail.

"Because *she* has her arm up." Lizzie's voice trembled as she pointed to my left hand.

Oops. I hadn't even realized that I'd raised my arm in order to cast.

All the color drained from Gail's face. "Is something wrong?"

I spoke in a low and calm voice. "Listen to me carefully. Climb into the back of the wagon and stay down." There was no point in all three of us sitting exposed on the driver's bench. My open cart had tall wooden slats along the sides. If Gail and Lizzie crawled in back, they'd be well hidden, so long as they stayed quiet.

"But why are we leaving the bench?" asked Lizzie. "It will ruin our dresses."

I fought the urge to roll my eyes. "Because I said so."

A petite girl stepped out from the line of barley stalks. She looked to be in her late teens, had pixie-like features and spiky red hair. Her garb was the fitted brown leathers of a Creation Caster.

Gail gripped my shoulder. I couldn't help but notice how she and Lizzie were still not moving off the bench. "Who's that?" asked Gail.

"And why is she dressed so strangely?" added Lizzie.

"She's a Creation Caster. Get into the back of the wagon." They still didn't listen to me. It was becoming irritating.

The girl smiled in a predatory way. "I'm Wren, and I'm looking for someone." Her eyes glinted, and I noticed that they were all black and bulged in an odd way. It reminded me of something, but I couldn't name what.

Gail pointed to my face. "She's a Grand Mistress Necromancer! Take her and leave us alone!"

"I'll do something else entirely." Wren leaned back her head and opened her mouth. A swarm of red wasps flew past her lips and sped toward the wagon.

That was when I realized what Wren's eyes reminded of: *an insect's.*

Not a surprise, really. All of Viktor's followers had their bodies altered in order to take on the characteristics of an animal or insect. They were called Changed Ones and could only cast a limited number of spells—ones that Viktor had approved for them. Most Changed Ones, like my friend Linden, hated their alterations and followed Rowan.

But Wren clearly wasn't like Linden. She beamed with glee as the red wasps whizzed toward us.

My mind raced through options for battle. I wasn't wearing any totem rings preloaded with spells. To use my magick, I had to speak an incantation. That would take time, but there was no avoiding it.

My heart thudded faster at the idea of casting a spell. It had been far too long.

Closing my eyes, I pulled Necromancer energy into my limbs. The magick was all around me. The power of life departing hid in the dying stalks of barley and stayed buried inside bones underground. The right kind of stones held the concentrated remains of those long gone.

Necromancer power quickly gathered inside my soul. A pleasant chill moved up my torso, like inhaling clean air after choking on smoke. I concentrated the energy into my left hand. Once the bones glowed blue with power, I spoke my incantation.

"Protect the weak
Embolden the strong
Encircle my party
Secure from wrong"

The moment the words left my lips, a blue haze of power appeared around the wagon, reminding me of a giant bubble of soap. The form looked fragile, but this spell was so powerful, the sharpest blade couldn't break its surface.

The red wasps slammed their bodies against my protection spell. Angry buzzing filled the air as the magickal insects stung the spell's surface. They didn't break through, though. I exhaled. *We're safe.* Even Smokey was held safely within the bubble of my spell.

Lizzie pointed to the shifting sphere around us. "Did you cast that?"

"Yes."

Gail stared about in awe. "It's keeping the wasps out."

"That would be why I cast it." I pinched the bridge of my nose. "Will you please get into the back of the wagon now?"

Gail screeched beside me. "There's one on my hand! How did it get through?"

I turned to face her. Sure enough, a red wasp the size of a crabapple was crawling up her arm. With each step, it's eight long legs twitched and a pair of thin wings fluttered.

When I spoke next, I took care to use my most soothing voice. "I thought this protection orb would keep them out, but it took some time to cast." I gestured to the horde of wasps that buzzed angrily around our magickal bubble. There were so many now, I couldn't even see Wren anymore. "You must stay calm and keep still. That way, the wasp won't sting you."

Gail's blue eyes widened. "It's going to sting me?"

"That's not what I said."

Gail cocked her arm, ready to slap the wasp. Sure enough, the giant insect jabbed its sharpened back end into her skin. Gail screeched and then fell quiet. Her head slumped forward, but other than that, she didn't move.

"What's wrong with my sister?" asked Lizzie.

I pressed my fingers to Gail's throat. A steady pulse beat there. "She's in an enchanted sleep. Just don't swat any of the—"

"Wasp!" I turned to see Lizzie smack one of the massive insects on her neck. Its stinger pierced her skin. Like Gail, Lizzie immediately hung her head and began to snore.

Needless to say, our trip to town wasn't going well.

I cracked my neck and sized up my opponent. Wren was

barely visible through the throng of angry insects. I could see enough of her to know one fact, however. She was smiling.

Oh, how I'll enjoy erasing that grin.

Closing my eyes, I pulled a fresh wave of power into my arm. So much energy flew through my body, my teeth chattered with the force of it all. I focused the magick into my hand and spoke my next incantation.

"Battle of hundreds
Dark and light"

Blue smoke appeared on my palm. A sense of satisfaction warmed my chest. The spell was almost ready. Once the mists were dark enough, I finished my casting.

"Bring me warriors
Teeth that bite"

The enchanted mists shot up from my palm and quickly crossed over the protective sphere. After that, the haze spread throughout the mass of wasps around us. Blue smoke soon blotted out what was left of the sun.

My spell was only getting started.

The haze solidified into hundreds of sets of tiny white teeth. These were all bat's jaws, which made them the perfect enemy to enchanted wasps. The razor-sharp mouths bit into the insects. Each time, a small poof of red smoke appeared as the bat jaw closed and another wasp was destroyed. By the time the mist cleared, I couldn't see a single wasp in the sky. I let out a satisfied breath.

The spell was over, but Wren's grin was still firmly in place. That was rather disappointing.

"That settles it," Wren said. "Casting that counter-spell proves you are indeed Elea of Braddock, Grand Mistress Necromancer and Tsarina of all the mages who follow the Sire of Souls. You sent my master, the Tsar Viktor, into exile."

I pulled fresh Necromancer power into my body until my bones glowed blue once more. I was ready to cast again. "What do you want?"

"I've come to help you."

"Really?" I shook my head. "Is that why you sent the swarm in my direction?"

"I was told to confirm your identity. I wasn't told to make it pleasant."

I glanced from left to right. Gail and Lizzie still snored quietly beside me. *Ah, well.* The sooner Wren gave her so-called help, the sooner I could wake them up and get this day over with. "I'm listening."

"First things first." A greedy look lit up her eyes. "Do you have any totems?"

"Why would you care about that?"

A totem was an object that a Necromancer pre-loaded with a spell. Our magick was powerful, but it took a long time to cast. Placing a spell on a totem ring was an easy way to get around that. But it was Necromancer-only magick. Wren was a Changed One.

"I hear you can cast hybrid magick," said Wren. "Maybe I could use one of your totems. Viktor shared all kinds of totem his with his top advisors. Perhaps we could make a deal today."

"Deal for what? I have sworn off magick altogether. Casting against you was the first time I've used magick in months."

"So?" That greedy look was still firmly in place.

"I've no totem rings."

"Wrist cuffs maybe?"

"I've no totems, period. How about telling me why you're *really* here?"

Wren looked deeply disappointed. "That means asking another question."

"Ask away."

"Are you mated to the Caster King, Genesis Rex? You may have met him as a traveller named Rowan."

"What?" On reflex, I set my right palm against my chest. My scarab ring always hung there, hidden on a chain under my clothes. Rowan had a matching one just like it. I suppose you could call it a mating band, but it wasn't anything real. Right after Rowan helped me escape from the Midnight Cloister, we went through a fake bonding spell complete with mating bands. Our goal was to unite our powers in order to fight Viktor. Sure, we saw each other's souls, but that didn't mean it was a real mating—or whatever the Creation Casters called it.

Not that I knew what they really called it. I'd never learned much about Caster life. My world was Necromancy.

Suddenly, it seemed rather dangerous that I'd never learned much about the Creation Casters. It was something to work on after this disastrous trip to town.

A smug look softened Wren's features. "Well, are you his mate or aren't you? It's similar to what a Necromancer might call marriage."

"No, he…" *What is Rowan to me, anyway?* "He used to be a friend. That's all."

I stifled a frown. If all we shared was friendship, then why did I offer him my virginity? Not that he took me up on it anyway.

"You clearly care for him," said Wren. "So you'll be interested in my news."

I'd fight her on the *"care for him"* part, but I was interested in what she had to say. "Go on."

"The golden army has arisen." Wren's buggy eyes locked on me as if I knew what that meant.

"And why would that be important?"

"It means a lot to Genesis Rex." Wren's smug grin grew a little larger.

My blood began boiling with rage. When I spoke again, my voice came out as a low snarl. "Stop speaking in riddles." I forced my bones to flare sapphire-bright. Wren stopped smiling; I considered that a small victory.

"It's an old Caster prophecy from one of our greatest Seers, Wakati Ujao." She stared at me as if the name should mean something.

It didn't.

Sure, I knew that Necromancers had Seers. That said, I hadn't thought about the Creation Casters having them as well. Now that Wren mentioned the fact, it made sense that Casters would have their own oracles.

Wren's large eyes bulged even farther from her head. "Wakati Ujao was a very powerful Seer."

I sniffed. "I'm not impressed. Seeing the future is a dodgy affair at best." In the past, there had been a number of Necromancer Seers who claimed our people would never be defeated so long as we wore our dark robes. Everyone wore black, yet Viktor still wiped out virtually all the Necromancers. "Let me guess. This Caster Seer of yours had a prophecy of her own."

"That's right." Wren nodded vigorously. Whoever this Wakati Ujao was, Wren certainly believed her. "She said that there would be a long night of suffering for the Creation Casters. Loved ones would vanish. You wouldn't know if your family was alive or dead."

"Your master Viktor made sure of that." Viktor had abducted the Senior Casters and transformed them into Changed Ones.

"Viktor is a hero to my people. He took Senior Casters in order to improve them. Look at me. I was once a Senior Caster with no focus to my work. Now, I have great power over wasps."

I pinched the bridge of my nose. "I suppose there's no use in saying this, but I will anyway. Viktor didn't help you. He's only convinced you that he did. There are thousands of spells out there. Being limited to wasps isn't doing you any favors."

Wren lifted her chin. "Viktor warned me that most people wouldn't understand my new perfection. And of all those small minds, yours is the absolute worst. You sent my master into exile."

I grinned. It was a big sign of emotion for a Necromancer, but I was ready to indulge myself. "I most certainly did. Twice. And with the help of your Genesis Rex."

"He's not my King. The prophecy says that there will be a long night of suffering for the Caster people under a false ruler. Then, a golden army will appear and usher in a fresh age of plenty. A new Genesis Rex will rise to lead the army himself, and that false King..." She shrugged. "I'm sure you can guess."

I had the distinct sense I was being toyed with, and I didn't like it one bit. "No, I can't."

"The false King will be slowly drained of his life force until the new King is ready to claim his throne. In case you still can't guess the obvious, that means a painful death for your Rowan."

I was so shocked I dropped my arm. All the glow vanished from my bones. "That's the silliest thing I've ever heard. Rowan is the strongest man I know."

"Maybe one time, he was."

A chill crawled up my neck. Was Rowan sick? As soon as the icy sensation moved across me, I used my Necromancer training to beat it down. I shouldn't care what happened to Rowan. He broke my heart and was engaged to another.

"Why do you tell me this? If he's ill, Rowan has other people to care for him." *Like Amelia, the woman who's his fiancée.*

"But no one as powerful as you."

She had a point. I wasn't going to validate it, however. "So, this prophecy requires another Genesis Rex. Who is this would-be King?"

"He calls himself Shujaa." The way she said the name, it was clear she thought the fellow hung the moon and stars. "Viktor chose him to be his successor, you know. He gave Shujaa a great totem to ensure he'd be the most powerful among us."

Which explained why she was totem hunting with me.

"Shujaa is a great leader," continued Wren. "He had raised the golden army by using his powerful totem. And the false King Rowan is already dying a little more each day, just as the prophecy foretold."

I huffed out a tired breath and tried to look unmoved. It wasn't easy. The idea of Rowan dying was making my pulse race so quickly, my head was getting a little woozy. Still, I somehow kept my features level. "So why are you here?"

Other than to break my heart with worry over Rowan.

"Aren't you going to rush off to Rowan and help him? What kind of mate are you?"

"I'm not his mate, and I'm no longer a Necromancer. As I told you, I'm a farmer now, and I don't cast magick. And Rowan?" I swallowed past the lump of sorrow that had lodged in my throat. "He's out of my life."

Wren nodded. "It's good that you won't be bothering yourself with Rowan, but there's still the matter of your title —Tsarina."

There were so many things wrong with that statement, I didn't know where to begin. Yes, I was technically the Tsarina, but only because I'd raised a ton of Necromancers from the dead after I exiled Viktor. All the newly raised mages simply started calling me Tsarina—no one asked if it was what I wanted. All the same, I had returned to my farm while my old Mother Superior, Petra, figured out how to align everyone under a different ruler. Right now, both Petra and the newly raised Necromancers were living at my old cloister, the Zelle.

"Have you been listening?" I asked. "I am not even a practicing Necromancer anymore, let alone Tsarina."

"The Necromancers seem to think differently." Wren sighed. "They need better leadership. You are hereby being given fair warning. Shujaa will hunt you down and take your crown."

"If your Shujaa really wanted to be Tsar, then all he has to do is be a decent mage and ask nicely. Besides, Necromancers don't even have a crown."

"The point is the same. Your people adore you and you abandon them. Someone must kill you and become the true Tsar."

"Fine. Let this Shujaa come after me." I cracked my neck. "I'm not worried."

"You're not going to visit your Cloister and claim your crown?" Wren's buggy eyes looked genuinely perplexed.

"No, no, and no." I threw up my hands. "Look, I understand that you and Shujaa want to rule everything you see, but some of us just want a nice harvest." My eyes narrowed. "And why do you care if I claim my role as Tsarina? Doesn't it make it harder for Shujaa to become Tsar if I'm in the Zelle and surrounded by thousands of my Necromancers?"

Wren opened her mouth, but I raised my arm palm forward and stopped her before she started up again. "I take it back," I said. "I don't want to know. I'm not in the world of magick and power any more. My life is my farm. It's my only legacy from my parents, and I will continue their work. Consider your message delivered." I pointed over the barley field. "Now leave."

But Wren didn't go. *By the gods.* I really needed to work on my terrorizing skills. Between Wren, Lizzy, and Gail, no one was afraid enough of me to do anything.

Wren lifted her chin. "Take my advice. Go to the Zelle and officially become Tsarina. It's your only hope to stay alive. You can't stand up to the hybrid power Shujaa wields from Viktor."

My mouth hung open. Actually, the only way for me to fight hybrid power was in working with Rowan, but I wasn't going to point that out to Wren. Logic didn't seem to be her strong suit. I glared at her again. "I'll give you three seconds to transport away before I cast another kill spell. Make no mistake. This one won't just go after your wasps."

Finally, Wren raised her right arm. "Until next time." The veins of her hand pulsed red with power. Tendrils of red mist wound around her feet. Within a few seconds, the haze surrounded her entire body. The cloud darkened and then vanished entirely.

Wren was gone as well.

Right after Wren disappeared, Lizzie and Gail opened their eyes and blinked excessively.

"What happened?" asked Lizzie.

"There was a girl," cried Gail. "And some insects!"

"What nonsense." I had already erased the protective bubble, so all I needed to do was click my tongue and send Smokey moving forward once more. "You two fell asleep while we were riding along. That was nothing more than a dream. I hope you find the village more entertaining than my company."

"But I've a bite mark on my arm," murmured Gail.

"And I've one on my neck," added Lizzie.

"You both had those before you set foot onto the wagon," I said smoothly. "I just didn't want to say anything about it before." I waved my arm about at some imaginary mosquitoes. "So many bugs this time of year."

Now, it's a strange fact of human nature that mortals will do almost anything to avoid the reality of magick in their lives. I swear, if there weren't mages walking around, humans might not realize magick existed at all.

The Dunkel sisters paused for a long moment before slowly nodding.

"I think I *did* drift off," said Gail. "And perhaps I had been bitten back at the farm."

"Me too," added Lizzie. "I'm certain of it."

After that, the pair launched right back into a discussion of the weekend faire. I didn't hear a word. All I could think about was Wren's warning. A mage battle with Shujaa would be a welcome change of pace, but the news that Rowan might be sick? That couldn't be true, could it?

Only one way to find out.

Tonight, I'd break my vow against magick once more. Sure, I'd sworn never to cast spells now that that I was a farmer again, but this was a special circumstance. I'd only speak a single incantation in order to spy on Rowan. Hopefully when I saw him, I could confirm that Wren was lying and Rowan was healthy as ever. It was a good plan, but it was also a worrisome one.

Because the thought of seeing Rowan in the flesh? It sent excitement and warmth spreading though my torso.

And that was far more dangerous than Shujaa or Wren.

3

*L*izzy, Gail, and I arrived at the village without any further visits from enemy mages. After that, we spent an eternity at the milliner's shop. The sisters carefully reviewed every needle, thread, fabric swatch, and skein of ribbon. I waited by the door and silently practiced incantations. Yes, I could have asked them to leave early, but after all, I'd almost gotten the pair of them killed. The least I could do was wait until they finished looking around.

At last, it was time to take the Dunkel sisters home. All during the ride back, the two chattered happily as they looked over their purchases time and again. It was sweet to see them so excited. And if I were being honest, I felt a little jealous as well. After everything I'd faced, it was hard to imagine achieving that level of joy about anything that didn't involve vanquishing an evil mage.

Oh, well. Give it time, Elea.

My parents died while I was still an infant. I didn't know what they looked like, but I knew they wanted me to have

Braddock Farm. The place was my birthright, future, and sole connection to the past. I simply had to make it work. A small voice in my head said that after everything I'd faced, farming was an impossibility for me. I ignored that voice. It simply couldn't be right.

All in all, night was falling by the time I approached my own front door. These days, it was actually Sam and Mabel's front door, as they were living in the main house.

As I walked up the front path, Mabel swung the door open before I got a chance to knock. She was a plump girl with brown hair, round cheeks, and an abundance of beautiful freckles. Positive energy seemed to vibrate out of her in waves. "Elea, you're home!" She called over her shoulder to her husband. "Sam, did you see that Elea is here?"

A deep voice reverberated through the small house. "Aye." Sam was a tall man with a wiry frame. His dark hair was cropped close to his head. While Mabel was all rounded curves, Sam's body was formed with hollowed-out angles. He rarely said anything beyond "aye" and "nay."

Mabel guided me inside the main room. As always, it struck me how much—and how little—the place had changed since I'd left five years ago. In some ways, my old home looked the same: a fire still burned in the stone hearth. A simple wooden table sat in the center of the room, surrounded by spindly chairs. The walls remained lined with shelves that held all sorts of jugs and boxes.

But after five years with Mabel and Sam living here, things had changed as well. The house all seemed brighter somehow. Long sprigs of dried herbs and flowers dangled from the ceiling. That was Mabel's doing. Meanwhile, Sam loved to work with wood, and his carvings of animals and castles were everywhere.

I picked up a jar of purple dust. This was new. "What are you working on?"

"It's a powder to control the freeze blight. Sprinkle a little of this on the ground, and the plant is protected. We can't have that trouble spreading past the Ackers' orchard."

I reset the jar on the shelf. "I could cast a few protection spells, you know."

"Please. Don't break your vow against magick over freeze blight. We can manage well enough with our own mortal knowledge."

The idea of science and learning were becoming quite fashionable with many non-magickal folk. *Good luck to them.* When Mabel was ready for the protection spell, she knew where to find me.

Mabel bustled over to the stove. "How about some stew?"

"Yes, thank you." I took a seat across from Sam at the main table.

"There's a gift for you on the table," offered Mabel.

"I see it." A lock of yellow-blond hair sat at the table's center. It was tied up like a sheath of wheat with a red ribbon. I frowned. There was only one person who stopped by the house and left locks of hair behind.

"Was Wyatt here?" I asked.

"Aye." Sam didn't look up from the piece of wood he was whittling.

"And he left a lock of his hair as a keepsake for me again?"

"Aye."

"It's a wonder he's anything left on his head."

Sam looked up from his whittling. His cheeks sucked in as he considered what I'd said. Sam was definitely the "quiet but deep" type of man. At last, his rumbling voice sounded again. "Aye."

Wyatt was my neighbor and a general pain in my backside. The last time I'd seen him was when I came back from adventuring. At the time, Wyatt had been driving wagon in order to transport his brother's wife. Wyatt was single then and remained so now.

Ah, Wyatt. When we were younger, Wyatt had worked to run me out of town by proclaiming me an evil witch. When that failed, he tried to be my suitor. If only there were another eligible maiden with land adjoining Wyatt's property, then he'd give up on me in a heartbeat. Unfortunately, as long as I was single and he could expand his holdings with our marriage, I seemed doomed to have him pursuing me in one form or another. It was annoying.

Mabel set the bowl of stew before me and sat down by my side. "Here you go."

"Thank you." I scooped up a big bite. Like always, the meal tasted of sawdust and gravy. In other words, it was delicious. That said, I'd spent the last five years in a Necromancer Cloister eating nothing but bone marrow pudding, which was incredibly foul stuff. Mabel would need to be a horrible cook indeed for me not to enjoy her meals.

Mabel absently rubbed the great bump under her peasant's gown. The baby was due soon. "Sam and I have been talking, and we want you to move into the house."

"Not a chance." I was living in a loft I'd fixed up in one of my smaller barns, and that was fine with me. "You need a place for you and the baby. There won't be time to build before you deliver." I hadn't told them this yet, but I was planning to gift them a small parcel of land in honor of their child. There, they could build their own house with plenty of bedrooms. Sam and Mabel wanted a large family. They'd been wonderful tenants and the gift was well deserved.

"I see," said Mabel. A gleam appeared in her big brown eyes.

I stopped with my spoon halfway to my mouth. "You see what? Is something wrong?"

"No, something's right." She glanced over to Sam. "What do you think? Has our Elea found a young man that she fancies?"

Sam looked up from his whittling again and scanned me carefully. I held my breath as he contemplated his answer. "Aye."

Mabel beamed. Like always, her many freckles seemed to dance across her cheeks when she smiled. "That's why you don't mind staying in the barn. You'll soon be staying with him, won't you?"

The world seemed to freeze around me. Mabel and Sam thought I had a young man that I liked. Was my affection for Rowan that obvious? Words began tumbling from my mouth. "I'd planned to contact someone tonight with a spell. Yes, he's a man. But I don't fancy him."

Which was a total lie. Just discussing my plans to see Rowan had my insides fluttering with excitement. All of which was beyond foolhardy. Rowan was engaged to someone else. Sure, Rowan said he had his reasons, if I'd only listen. And to be honest, there were days when I did want to know if there was a plausible reason why he was engaged to Amelia and yet, that situation wasn't a problem for him. Because the gods knew it was a large issue for me.

A shudder twisted across my shoulders. The last time I trusted a man, it was Tristan and he saddled me with a curse. I was able to break the spell, I shouldn't take risks like that anymore. If someone seemed to be trouble, then I needed to cut them out of my life.

"Whatever you say." Mabel patted her stomach once more. "Maybe by this time next year, you'll be the one expecting."

"Aye," added Sam.

"Only…" Mabel paled. "It's not Wyatt, is it?"

"Never never never never NEVER." That was a lot of times to say the word "never," but Wyatt was all that repulsive and more.

Suddenly, I was in a great rush to leave the knowing gazes of Mabel and Sam. I stuffed the rest of the stew down my throat, said some quick goodbyes, and headed for the barn.

The moment I stepped inside the wooden space, Smokey tossed his head and whinnied. It was as if he suspected I might be about to do something stupid and desperately wanted me to stop. My black cat Lucy stalked along the edge of the hayloft—which had been cleaned out and refitted as my bed—and she watched me blandly. By contrast, she seemed positive that I was about to do something stupid, only she couldn't be troubled to care. The rest of the barn was empty. In other words, I wouldn't upset anyone with my casting.

Time to contact Rowan. This wasn't because I cared about him or thought there could be some insane explanation for his engagement to Amelia. All I needed to do was confirm Wren's lies and see that Rowan was healthy as ever. After that, I'd never need to see Genesis Rex again.

Maybe.

Closing my eyes, I pulled in Necromancer energy from the world around me. Power pulsed through my bones. My left hand grew cold as my bones glowed blue with magick. Soon, I had enough energy to cast a transporter spell. Normally, I'd need to know Rowan's exact spot in order for this incantation to work. But since Rowan had once cast spells on my mating band, the ring retained some of his magickal signature. I could use that power to find him easily enough.

"Sire of Souls, I call upon thee
Give my magick strength
Make my path open and free"

With my right hand, I pulled at the chain that held my mating band beneath my dress. Once the ring was gripped in my fist, I continued my spell.

"Take me to the mage whose power I touch
From far to near, less to much"

A blue haze of magick formed by my feet. My entire body vibrated with energy. After that, everything became black as pitch. My body felt torn in a thousand directions at once. Pain radiated through my bones.

Oh, no. It didn't matter how many times I cast a transporter spell. I never got used to this pain.

The next thing I knew, I was standing in a darkened room. All the hurt vanished from my body. The space was tall and circular with walls that were made from bamboo stalks. The windows were teardrop-shaped and made by smooth gaps in the bamboo, like some greater force had pulled them apart. Outside these window-holes, a lush green jungle was visible. Moonlight glinted off the wide emerald fronds. Heat pressed in around me. The air felt thick with the promise of rain.

As my eyes adjusted to the dimness, I saw Rowan standing in the shadows. There was no mistaking his outline: a hulking man wearing fitted leathers. His brown hair hung a little longer than when I'd last seen him, while his emerald eyes seemed to pierce through the darkness.

He was looking straight at me. A realization slammed into my soul. Somehow, Rowan knew I was coming.

Tendrils of energy wound around us and through us. Rowan and I always had this crazy connection. My heart began pounding with extra force.

Rowan's deep voice rumbled in the darkness. "What happened?"

My mind loathed the way Rowan had betrayed me. How could he become engaged to another woman? But seeing and hearing him right now...My body craved him like air. "What do you mean?"

"One of my Seers said you would come here. He told me you were in trouble." Rowan reached by his throat and pulled out a chain that had been hidden under his leathers. His own mating band hung at the end of it. There was no mistaking the scarab pattern as it gleamed in a shaft of moonlight. "And I sensed it when you called on my magick in order to cast your transport spell."

I stared at the ring. *He keeps it by him, just like I do.* My knees got a little wobbly at the realization. "I met one of Viktor's Changed Ones, a girl named Wren. She said you were ill."

"I'm fine." The energy between us turned so thick, it was almost a palpable thing in the room. "Tell me what threatens you."

"Oh, that. Wren said that someone named Shujaa is going to try to kill me." I shrugged. "Good luck to him."

"Are you certain of that name?" Rowan stepped into the moonlight, and by the gods, I'd forgotten how handsome he was. It shouldn't matter that his shoulders were broad and his chest firm. But my body felt jittery to see him again so close.

Good thing my mind is in charge.

"Yes, the name was definitely Shujaa."

"What else did this Wren tell you?" He took a step closer. Now he was near enough that I could feel his body heat radiate over me. I wanted nothing more than to lean into his embrace. It was beyond stupid and the definition of Zuchtlos. *Rowan has other women to worry about, like his fiancée Amelia, who just so happens to be my ex-best friend.*

I hugged my elbows. "Wren said that she was a messenger for Shujaa. She found me to warn me. Shujaa plans to kill me and take my crown."

Rowan's deep voice rang with humor. "And I know how you value that particular item."

I fought back a grin. "The Tsarina doesn't even have a crown."

Ugh. I think that came across as flirting. Why can't I control my emotions around this man?

Rowan's mouth curved up into one of his lopsided smiles. "In that case, we certainly can't have you losing something that doesn't exist."

I forced on a more serious face. "Wren also offered some so-called advice. She said if I went to the Necromancers, I could defeat Shujaa. Trouble is, he wields some hybrid magickal totem from Viktor, so I doubt that would work."

Rowan's smile disappeared. His face took on that unreadable look that frustrated me to no end. "I see."

"That's it? You see?"

"Wren is right that you should leave your farm. But you should come here and stay under my protection."

"And we would fight together?"

"No, that's too risky. Shujaa was once a Creation Caster. I've cast wards protecting my castle. Shujaa will never breach the walls while I live."

Words starting tumbling from my mouth without any particular analysis from my mind. "But he could still attack your castle, am I right? What if he does? In that case, you and I may need to fight him. We've battled hybrid magick together before."

Why was it so important to me that he admit we'd fight together? Some small part of me already knew the answer to that question all too well. I'd been around Rowan for less than a minute, and I was already craving the unique connection that we shared when we battled side by side.

"It won't come down to you and I fighting Shujaa."

I did my best to look like I didn't care. "If you're certain."

"Still, it's true that you aren't safe. And there's little I can do when you're on another continent. I have few Senior Casters who are powerful enough to transport that far and guard you. Plus, I'm busy with many other concerns."

"As am I," I said. "I'm running my farm."

"Which is important. Though, it's not as important as your life. I can't sacrifice my people to keep you safe."

"I'm not asking you to." My voice dripped with anger. "I'm not your responsibility."

A long pause followed. When Rowan spoke again, his voice was gentle. "Would it change anything to say I can explain?"

"Some lines can't be uncrossed."

"But my culture isn't yours. When we exchanged mating bands, you saw my soul. Am I capable of such terrible deceit as to become betrothed to another?"

"Souls are tricky things. I once thought my friend Tristan

was incapable of deceit."

"I'm not him."

"I came here to make sure that you were safe and well."

"I told you, I'm fine."

Maybe it was the mating band around my throat, but I knew one thing.

Rowan was lying.

"You're ill."

"I'm angry. Shujaa was one of our finest Senior Casters before Viktor wooed him away." Rowan raked his hand through his loose brown hair. "Now, the man is a bloodthirsty killer."

"Wren kept pushing me to become Tsarina. Why would Shujaa want that?"

Rowan glanced away. "I cannot tell you."

I frowned. "You're keeping secrets from me. Again."

"Only because I wish to protect you." Rowan stepped closer until our bodies were almost touching. By the gods, it was distracting. I needed to walk away, but couldn't get myself to move. "Promise me something." Rowan's voice was a gentle murmur. "If Shujaa gets anywhere near you, you'll transport to my castle."

"I don't run."

"Consider it an opportunity to learn more about Caster culture. If you're here, I will open everything I can to you. We've no written words, but we have record keepers called Hadithi. They memorize our history. If you come to Nyumbani, you can ask them any question you like."

"That's more double-speak." I shook my head. "I can ask any question, but there are no guarantees that they will answer."

"What about your fellow Necromancers at the Cloister?

Or even your neighbors. I told you that I knew Shujaa. The man is ruthless. No one will be safe so long as you're outside my realm. If he attacks here, I can protect you easily with magick. If you're anywhere else, you place others at unnecessary risk."

Rowan's words struck home. I couldn't put my friends and fellow mages in danger. I pictured Lizzie's and Gail's innocent faces. What if the next time, Wren did worse than put them to sleep? "I'll consider it."

"Not good enough. I know you, Elea. You'll never forgive yourself if some non-mage got hurt or killed because of this. Think on their safety. Promise me."

"Fine." I exhaled. "I give you my word." I shook my head. "I hope it doesn't come to that. I vowed to give up magick, and I've already broken that promise too many times today."

"But if Shujaa attacks, you *will* come here."

"I'll need to transport to my old Mother Superior first. She should know where I've gone." I hadn't seen Petra since I'd returned to Braddock, but I'd no doubt she had tracking spells that would alert her if I left my lands for too long. The woman was stuck in the Zelle Cloister, trying to convince thousands of Necromancers that I wasn't their Tsarina. She had a right to hear my plans directly from me.

"That sounds wise." Rowan's face relaxed, and for the first time, I noticed the dark circles underneath his eyes. I'd never known him to get tired.

"You are ill."

"It's been a long day, that's all."

More lies. I was about to say just that, when someone stepped into the room. I turned around to see another man in warrior's garb. A leather helm covered his face. "Greetings, my King," he said. "Our little Seer told me I'd find you here."

My brows lifted. Was this the same little Seer who'd warned Rowan that I was in danger?

The man gestured to me. "Ah. I see the great Elea of Braddock has deigned to visit at last. No wonder my King waits in the shadows. The little Seer reported that at last, the Tsarina would arrive. So my King seeks out a quiet place to meet."

There was so much to unpack about those short sentences. Rowan had gone to the little Seer and asked when I would visit. After that, Rowan found a secluded and dark spot for us to speak. That information shouldn't make me as happy as it did. After all, the man was engaged to my best friend.

Ex-best friend, actually.

This was a mess.

Rowan moved to stand at my side. "Elea, this is Kade, one of my guard."

Kade tilted his head. "That's how you wish her to know me?"

"Unless you think differently."

Once again, I got the feeling there were a lot of things happening that I wasn't aware of. "What's going on? Clearly, this Kade means more to you than a guard."

Kade folded his arms over his chest. "Much as I'd love to discuss personal matters, a delegation has just arrived that needs our attention. The Changed Ones have struck again. A was burned to the ground. Some of the strongest people have vanished. The ones who escaped have found their way to your castle. They now require food, shelter, healing...and their King."

Changed Ones were attacking other Casters? "I thought most of the Changed Ones were peaceful."

Kade glared at me. Even through his helm, I could see the

glint of rage in his green eyes. "What you think is uninformed at best, dangerous at most."

I kept my face calm. I wouldn't be distracted my insults. "My visit tonight was because a Changed One visited me, a woman named Wren. She said someone named Shujaa is part of some prophecy to save the Casters."

"That's what the people think," said Kade. "But he's really the one running raids on our people."

I frowned. "How can they think Shujaa is their savior if he's burning down villages?"

"Shujaa is clever," said Rowan. "There are never any witnesses linking him to the attacks."

"And most Casters are fools," added Kade. "Besides, they don't think that Shujaa is the one who will lead the golden army. The people think it's—"

Rowan's voice took on a warning tone. "That's enough."

I set my fists on my hips. "I wanted to hear what he has to say." I turned to Kade. "Go on."

Kade simply stared forward without saying a word.

The energy in the room had turned downright hostile. I wouldn't learn anything more tonight. And I couldn't stand the thought of victims of the Changed Ones waiting around on my account. "I'll take my leave now."

Rowan took my hand. His touch sent shivers through me. "Don't forget your promise."

"I won't."

It took a force of will step away from Rowan and begin the incantation to transport back to my farm. I couldn't shake the sense of dread that weighed down my bones. I'd seen my share of disasters.

And this situation with Shujaa? It had *catastrophe* written all over it.

4

*M*y little wagon lumbered along the dirt road. The setting sun cast a pinkish glow atop Smokey's mane and around his twitching ears. I sighed. The last time I drove my wagon, I was taking the Dunkel sisters to the village. For this trip, I was alone. Things wouldn't stay that way for long, however. I was headed for the Dunkels' faire.

A ball of dread weighed down my stomach. If I thought making small talk with two girls was rough, I was about to meet virtually every soul in the shire.

Damn that Philippe, always forcing me to be social.

It was only four days ago that I took the Dunkel sisters to town. Since then, I'd minded my farm and cast not a single spell. I felt rather proud of that. It was the true way to honor my parents and their legacy.

A press of magick swept over my skin, making my arms prickle into gooseflesh. All my senses went on alert. Had Wren returned? Almost a week had passed since my encounter with the Changed One. There had been no further sightings or incidents.

Still, I pulled on the reins. Smokey stopped. I scanned the darkened fields. Was Shujaa following me? Excitement tingled across my skin. I raised my left arm, ready to cast a spell.

One second passed.

Two.

Three.

Nothing happened.

The awareness of magick disappeared. I forced my hand down. *Another false alarm.* That made the third one today. I was sensing Shujaa around every corner. Sure, I'd promised to transport away at the first sign of danger, but "first sign" was a relative term.

I could easily squeeze in a quick mage battle before leaving. My eyes turned misty. How wonderful to get into another mage battle, and perhaps even a serious one this time? Fighting Wren had been far too easy.

A chill of realization prickled across my skin. It was time to be honest with myself. There was no mistaking the pulse of excitement that now moved through my veins. I let out a long breath. *Fine.* I was woman enough to admit that I was having trouble adjusting to farm life…And honoring my parents. Had it only been two months since I'd sent Viktor into exile? It felt like a year had slogged by.

It felt like even longer since I'd last seen Rowan. Confronting him did nothing to ease the constant ache in my chest from missing him.

I shook my head. There was no point thinking about Rowan. He was engaged to someone else and that was the end to it. And as for Shujaa, I was starting to doubt that a fight was coming. Powerful mages could transport anywhere they wanted at will. Chances were, if Shujaa wanted to attack me, he'd have done so already.

Long story short, I needed to stop looking for magick and focus on my new life. Sure, it was hard not to cast spells right now. But I'd eventually adjust to farm life. Enemy attacks and heartbreak would become distant memories.

That said, I needed to be patient. It was only a matter of time until I fully became a farm girl again.

Night fell as Smokey and I crossed the empty countryside. At last, my wagon approached a rolling hill covered in tents, tables, and hanging lanterns. About a hundred people meandered across the green. Voices and laughter echoed out into the night. The full moon cast everything in blue shadows.

Philippe waited for me at the base of the hill, just as we'd agreed. He was leaning against a large oak tree, looking handsome and suave in his gray velvet longcoat and silk breeches. His tall leather boots gleamed in the dimness. I slowed my wagon beside him.

"Good evening, Philippe."

He stepped forward and bowed slightly at the waist. The man had excellent manners. "Good evening, my lady. I was beginning to worry that you wouldn't join me."

"I promised that I could come."

Philippe hoisted himself onto the driver's bench beside me. Like always, he was handsome in a roguish way with his fair hair and a gleaming smile. The man reminded me of a blond pirate. He winked. "You usually make good on your word."

I lifted my brows. "Usually?"

"Always." His grin widened. "Eventually."

"You know, it could be a mark on my reputation to be seen driving with you alone."

"Please." Philippe rolled his eyes. "We're within spitting distance of half the village. That means your reputation is quite safe." He gave me a sly look. "It's not like you're talking about visiting me in my rooms at the tavern."

My eyes widened. "Who told you about that?" I hadn't seen Philippe since my visit to the village with the Dunkel sisters.

Philippe chuckled. "Oh, everyone."

"Lizzie and Gail must have gone gossiping after I drove them into town. I'll cast a spell to give them extra foreheads. That will teach them."

"Please. Don't go casting odd spells on my account. Personally, I thought the story was rather hilarious. Now, urge on your racehorse to the stables, or we'll never get to the faire."

I flicked the reins gently and Smokey took off. Even though the stables were large, the place was already half-full with wagons and horses. Folks wandered about, getting their mounts settled before heading off to the faire. I stowed the wagon outside, so I now unharnessed Smokey and brought him into one of the clean stalls. The Dunkels were known for taking good care of their animals.

Once everything was in place, Philippe approached me and offered his arm. "Are you quite ready?"

I nodded. "You'll notice that I took your fashion advice this time." I gestured across the yellow monstrosity that was my gown. "Bright colors. Although I must admit, I feel a bit awkward."

When I was a Necromancer, I always wore our traditional black robes. Before that, I lived on a farm where I donned peasant dresses. These days, I had my choice of fancy gowns, thanks to Philippe and his questionable relationship with the seamstress in the village. This yellow dress was one of my less ornate options. Still, it felt incredibly bawdy. I pulled at the high neckline.

"Stop fidgeting," said Philippe. "You look lovely."

"I feel like a banana."

"Have you ever seen a banana?"

"I've read about them. The Zelle Cloister has quite a library." I pulled at my neckline again.

Philippe exhaled a dramatic sigh. "In order to stop your ceaseless fidgeting, I suppose I must compliment you yet again." He stopped and grasped my shoulders, forcing me to face him. His palms were warm and soft against my upper arms. His gaze locked with mine. "You are so beautiful, Elea, it hurts sometimes to look at you."

Philippe's face was so sincere that I felt a weight of guilt in my bones. Why couldn't I care about him? "Thank you."

The side of his mouth quirked up in a smile. "Although, truth be told, the dressmaker did select an atrocious color for this frock."

I couldn't help but grin back. "Ha! I knew she was making me ugly gowns as an excuse to flirt with you."

Philippe smirked. "Why, are you jealous?"

"No, merely wishing I wore black."

At those words, Philippe's eyes lost some of their light. I knew that he'd been hoping something more would develop between us. Over the last few months, I'd done my best to keep an open mind, but I still hadn't felt anything more than friendship toward him.

Sadly, my heart was set on Rowan, and it was a very stubborn organ.

If my comment had upset Philippe, he recovered quickly. His sneaky smile returned in a flash. "It may be atrocious, but I still like yellow far better than black. As I've said a dozen times, you'll blend in more if you look cheery and appropriate. When you wear black, you resemble a matron of death."

"I *am* a matron of death."

"But you've sworn off magick."

"I'm trying."

Philippe lifted his brows. "Anything you care to share?"

"Not tonight."

"Excellent. You're far too intense for your own good." Philippe turned toward the crowd and set my hand on his elbow. "Let's move on. There's no point in revisiting this verbal battle since I have already won it."

"There was a verbal battle?"

"On whether or not you look lovely. You do, I won, and now we're moving on." Philippe's pale blue eyes twinkled in the moonlight. He really was an adorable rogue. Why couldn't I have feelings for him?

I shook my head. "You do realize that you've this way of tricking me into doing things. Don't think I haven't noticed."

"Good. Now join the faire with me, like a good little matron of death."

I couldn't help but chuckle, and together we left the barn and headed toward the maze of tables lining the hillside. There were folks selling wax candles, linen tunics, wooden spoons, and leather boots. The scent of roasting meat filled the air.

Philippe and I made a slow stroll through the different tables. We weren't a yard from the first vendor when a ripple of excitement moved through the crowd. I'd seen this happen before. In the past, it had always been because the village sheriff or town mayor had shown up. Now, it was all about Philippe.

Within seconds, we were surrounded by a cluster of young

girls. It was hard to tell them apart, what with their carefully combed hair, spotless gowns, and eager faces. They began a high-pitched chorus of greetings.

"Philippe, so nice to see you."

"Fine weather we're having."

"Would you like to try my apple tarts?"

"Come this way. I'd like you meet my mum."

Philippe sighed dramatically once again. It was a move he used to excess, but these young ladies never seemed to mind. "I'm sorry, my sweets. Elea has made me promise to devote all my attention to her this evening. She's a rather jealous creature. I'm sure you understand."

The girls all glared at me as if I'd invented the plague. The fact that I was a Necromancer didn't help matters, either. Even so, Philippe's gentlest request was as good as a compulsion spell. The young ladies all curtsied and marched off into the night. We resumed our slow stroll.

"Have you spotted the Dunkel girls?" I asked.

Philippe winked. "I'm not sharing your company so quickly. I had to ride in all the way from the village to secure merely a few small hours in your presence."

"You're the one who's been off trying to find messengers." I scanned his face carefully. Philippe loved his sister deeply. She'd written him daily, but the messages had recently stopped. I knew it was bothering him. "Did you get any word from Amelia?" I wished my voice didn't have the acidic edge of jealousy.

"Last I heard, Veronique was still with her." The way he said Veronique's name, it was clear why he hadn't run off to Amelia the moment her letters stopped.

"Perhaps you should visit her."

"We're not speaking of Amelia right now. We're walking around the tables."

I grinned. "You're a horrible taskmaster, you know."

"Of course."

A prickly sensation ran up my back. Once again, I felt the sensation of hot embers of magick burning into my skin. It was a spell to detect a magick user, just like the one Wren had cast before.

Had Wren returned? Or better, had Shujaa arrived at last?

I pretended to inspect a table of painted eggs. How many times had I imagined Shujaa attacking this week? Too many.

Thoughts of mystery mages aren't going to ruin my evening.

I lifted a particularly pretty egg from the tabletop. The artist had poked a hole in the bottom to drain out the insides and painted a lovely farm scene on the exterior. I turned the dainty object over in my hands. *Now, this is real and beautiful.* Farm life, where the most magickal thing was the power of what you could make with your hands.

I was about to set the egg down when a low voice sounded in my ear. "Good evening, Elea. I'm Shujaa."

I glanced about, frantic to see who was speaking. No one was there. Was the mage invisible? The sensation of burning embers became stronger than ever before. My head turned woozy. Perhaps the mage wasn't invisible as much as wielding a potent spell to cause disorientation. But that kind of magick was rare. Only Senior Caster could hope to wield it.

Perhaps Wren had been telling the truth. Shujaa wanted my crown, such as it was, and he was willing to do anything to get it. That meant a fight was coming.

I gently reset the painted egg onto the tabletop. There were far more interesting things to focus on. I was about to cast again. Huzzah!

5

The woozy feeling grew more intense. The nearby lanterns and torches seemed to blur into the night sky. It felt as if the ground were rolling beneath me in great waves. Raised voices overlapped one another in strange ways.

It took a force of will, but I focused on where I'd heard the man calling himself Shujaa. I needed to lessen the effected of his disorientation spell, and that meant putting some distance between us. I couldn't fight if I couldn't think straight. It took all my focus, but I was able to make my legs move in the opposite direction. The scene around me quickly became normal once again.

Partly.

Yes, there were still tables all around. The lanterns and torches appeared normal once more. But my neighbors were all staring at the extremely large warrior who'd entered our faire. Shujaa was well over six feet tall and wearing some kind of metallic armor that gleamed purple in the firelight. A matching metal helm covered his face.

Not a good development. A purple hue meant hybrid magick. If I had to bet, I'd say that was enchanted armor from Viktor. And more than that, the armor was most likely the totem that Wren had spoken about. A totem of that size would be able to store an enormous amount of magick.

Wren stood at Shujaa's side. His great bulk made her look even smaller. I wasn't fooled, though. You didn't wear that much armor without a good reason. Viktor forced his Changed Ones to trade all their magick for one concentrated set of spells. For Wren, it was her power over wasps. For Shujaa, I'm guessing it was his proximity spell that disoriented anyone who got too close. Why would Viktor have done that? It was a question I set side to ponder later on.

A chorus of worried voices sounded from the crowd. No one was moving, really. It reminded me of whenever someone's cart got stuck in a gulley. Folks came around, watched, and made comments. Few offered to help. In this case, everyone was somewhat concerned about the strange warrior and odd-looking woman. But no one was alarmed. Not yet. After all, it was a faire, and sometimes odd folks stopped by.

Then Wren raised her right arm, which was a sure sign she was pulling Caster power into her body. Sure enough, the veins in her arm glowed with bright crimson light.

The crowd gasped.

Wren and Shujaa glared.

I did what any self-respecting Necromancer would do, especially one who didn't want to cast a spell in front of her neighbors. I took in a deep breath and screamed at the top of my lings. "Run for your lives!"

My words snapped my neighbors out of their reverie. Some folks started to run. Others began packing up their tables.

Philippe stole up beside me. "What's going on?" He eyed Wren's lit-up arm. "Forget it. I understand. I'll help evacuate the locals."

"And stay away from the tall guy. He has some kid of permanent spell on him that muddles your senses." I began pulling Necromancer energy into my body, but didn't focus it into my arm. I really was trying to keep with Philippe's Elea Stops Frightening the Locals plan. But having that much power twisting through my body made my bones vibrate and organs ache. I called to Philippe. "But be quick about it, if you please."

"I will." Philippe stepped away, paused, and then came back. "Only, promise me you won't kill anyone or cast any decent spells until return. You know how I love to watch you work."

"Philippe." This time, I had to speak through gritted teeth. Philippe got the idea quickly enough and ran off.

Wren began mumbling under her breath. Red smoke appeared around her palm. The crimson haze quickly expanded until it encircled her body. When the cloud vanished, Wren had transformed herself into a massive red wasp. If a tiny bite from one of her insects could put someone to sleep, then I had a pretty good idea what her larger self could do: kill me.

Philippe had worked quickly, but he hadn't gotten everyone out of viewing range. Still, I couldn't risk waiting any longer. I focused the power of my magick into my left arm. The bones of my hand glowed bright blue. A sphere of sapphire-colored mist appeared above my palm. It was time to speak my incantation.

"Fast as wind

Sharp as a knife
Bring me skull seekers
Protect my life"

Skull seekers combined the worst of a hungry ghost and a whipping comet. They were speedy, and their teeth could bite through almost anything. My blue sphere split into four separate orbs of light, mist, and power. After that, they congealed into what looked like long comets of blue light, only with skulls at their centers. A long tail of sapphire-colored mist trailed behind them.

Wasp-Wren took to the air, her huge wings buzzing so loudly it was an effort not to cover my ears. My skull seekers whipped around me like planets around a sun. I pointed out different seekers as I spoke. "You two, attack the wasp. The others, go after the warrior. Now!"

The seekers took off into the night sky. The first pair tried biting into Wasp-Wren, but her exoskeleton was too tough. That was shame, really. Skull seekers have pointed teeth that drip with poison.

The other pair went after Shujaa. As they closed in, their attack arcs became jagged and random. When they were within arm's length, the two went berserk and started attacking each other. Evidently, Shujaa's power of disorientation worked on my spells. This wasn't good.

The seekers I'd sent after Shujaa began cackling maniacally as they bit into each other's vapor trails. This was worse. I crossed my fingers.

Please, let them be immune to their own poison. I'd never tested the spell to see what would happen if the skull seekers attacked each other.

Wasp-Wren swooped in close to Shujaa, and her two skull

seekers followed. Soon, they too were happily chomping into each other's vapor trails.

Then they stopped.

I was about to cheer. Hopefully, this meant they'd recovered from Shujaa's disorientation magick and were ready to fight again. The four skull seekers shivered in midair for a moment. After that, they imploded in a spray of blue smoke.

By the gods. I'd never had a spell go wrong like that before.

I still had some power left in me, but not enough for a major casting like skull seekers. I'd have to go with some traditional fireball spells. I focused the power I had left into my hand until my bones shone brightly again.

> *"Show my strength*
> *Focus my ire*
> *Smite my enemies*
> *Bring me fire."*

Another haze of blue smoke appeared on my palm. It quickly solidified into an orb of blue flame. With my right hand, I pushed the sphere toward its intended target. Shot after shot went at Wasp-Wren or Shujaa. None hit their mark. Wasp-Wren was too speedy in the air; she easily dodged each volley. Shujaa hardly seemed to notice the fireball hitting him. His armor was simply that good. All that happened was that the metal glowed purple for a moment or two. I'm not sure I even left a bruise.

After each missed fireball, Wasp-Wren flew at me again. Her goal was clear: she was trying to herd me toward Shujaa. All I needed was to get closer to that man's sphere of disorientation, and I was done for. I gave up on the fireballs and cast almost every other spell I could think of.

Spine ripper ghosts.

Skeletal servants.

Bone bombs.

I even tried a transporter spell, wondering if I could just send Wasp-Wren and Shujaa away. True, it was a long shot. Most mages learned how to block these early on. But at this point? I was panting with exhaustion and ready to try anything. Except giving up, of course.

Suddenly a figure in a long cloak walked onto the hillside. The hood was pulled down, so I couldn't see their face.

"It is I, Petra, come to help Elea."

But it wasn't Petra. It was Philippe doing his very best impression of an old lady speaking. I sped to his side and hissed at him in a voice only Philippe would hear.

"You're not helping me," I whispered. "You're going to get yourself killed."

"On the contrary, dearie." Philippe raised his cloak-covered arm toward Shujaa and Wasp-Wren, who had actually stopped advancing toward me.

I blinked.

Stared.

Blinked again.

Philippe was right. The threat of Petra really had ceased our battle completely, and this meant two things. First, Shujaa and Wasp-Wren were afraid of Petra. And second, Philippe was going to be completely impossible for at least a week, considering how his non-magick trick was working. In fact, Wren had transformed back into her human self.

Still, I didn't have anything else that had worked so well. I had no choice but to play along. "You've pushed your luck," I said to Wren and Shujaa. "Now Petra is here, and you know what that means."

Shujaa's deep voice sounded from under his helm. "You're going to accept your role as Tsarina with her aid."

It wasn't *exactly* what that meant, but at that moment, red mist began to appear around Shujaa's and Wren's feet. The haze grew larger.

They were casting transporter spells.

Leaving.

I couldn't believe it. Shujaa thinks I'm about to be Tsarina, so he leaves the field of battle. Is he leaving to plan an attack on my people? Or is he pleased that I'm supposedly ruling the Necromancers? I didn't understand what was happening in my own world. A weight of worry settled onto my shoulders.

Petra always said that knowing the politics of the magickal world was like wielding fire. People who didn't understand how to handle it got themselves burned. I'd made it through this battle safely enough, but next time? Unless I understood more about what was happening, I was certain to get burned. Badly.

6

I slowly turned about, surveying the ruined hilltop. Bits of wooden tables and smashed produce were everywhere. Moonbeams shifted across the torn-up green. Wren and Shujaa had just transported away.

Philippe pulled his robes over his head, hood first. He turned to me and grinned, his white teeth gleaming in the moonlight. "Wasn't I wonderful?"

"If I say yes, will you drop the subject forever?"

"Heavens, no. We need to find a bard. Someone should write a song about me." He made a dramatic show of looking left and right. "Where's a wandering minstrel when you need one?"

"Where did you get that cloak?"

"You don't want to know."

"No, I really do."

"The young widow Buckens doesn't live far from here. She and I have a, uh, friendship where I sometimes dress up as—"

"You know what? I've changed my mind."

"Thought you would." He propped his right leg up onto an overturned wooden box and leaned his elbow onto his knee. It was a pose appropriate for the statue he was no doubt imagining someone carving of him. "Would you like to hear the full tale? I'll leave out the adult parts for your virginal ears."

"I'm twenty-two."

"Anything happen lately I should know about?"

There was no question what he was referring to. I had never slept with a man. Once, I thought it might happen with Rowan, but he turned me down. In retrospect, he was about to get engaged to Amelia, so I appreciated his discretion. Since then, men had certainly shown their interest, including Philippe. But the time was never right.

It most certainly was not because I was still waiting to see if Rowan would somehow come back into my life. That door was closed. Completely.

Most days it was, anyway.

I realized Philippe had been staring at me for a while now. "What were you saying?" I asked.

"I'll take that as yes in the 'still a virgin' column." He fixed the lapels of his longcoat. "Let's get back to my story. As I was saying, your enemies appeared, and I did the gentlemanly thing by making sure everyone was evacuated."

"Thank you."

"I returned to find you casting all sorts of interesting things, but I must say, the fight seem rather lopsided with two on one."

"I would have killed them both eventually."

"Of course, but I figured it might help things along if the opposition thought it was an even match of two on two." He arched his hand over his eyes, like a sea captain searching for land. "So I visited yon widow and asked her for a cloak. She was very obliging, and so I donned said garment, returned here, and singlehandedly scared away the fearsome mages."

I'd correct him about the singlehandedly part, but there really was no point. I never won verbal battles with Philippe. "You should get a statue made in your honor."

"Exactly what I was thinking." He winked. "But in all seriousness, you need to talk to Rowan."

I worked hard not to gasp. "Absolutely not."

"Please. I saw what that brute was wearing. Purple armor. Now, blue Necromancer power plus red Creation Caster magick equals purple hybrid magick. That suit of armor glowed when your fireballs slammed into it. That means it's not just a pile of metal, it's one of your Necromancer totems. And only one person can make Necromancer totems that hold hybrid magick. Viktor."

My eyes widened. "So you knew why I was having trouble in the fight, and yet you still came back?"

"I did. You'd have flattened them easily if it hadn't been for whatever Viktor put in that armor."

"There's more to Shujaa as well. Every Changed One gets their natural Caster magick focused into a single set of spells. For Wren, it's wasps. For Shujaa, he confounds anyone who gets near him. At first, I thought the man was invisible."

Philippe took his leg down from the box and folded his arms over his chest. I knew the man well enough to know what that meant. Philippe was done playing around, and I should take the rest of his words seriously. "When it comes to hybrid magick and Viktor, only one person can fight it. Two, actually. You and Rowan."

I laced my fingers behind my neck. "That won't be easy."

"True enough. But I'll be there. I need to visit Nyum-bum."

"The Caster realm is called Nyumbani, Philippe."

"That's what I said. In any case, it's beyond time for me to check on my sister."

My mind reeled through different options here. Was there any way of stopping Shujaa without involving Rowan? I couldn't think of anything.

Philippe gave me a roguish grin. "Believe me, I don't relish saying this. He's the only impediment to my stealing your heart."

I couldn't help but crack a smile. "Serves me right for trying to win against you in an argument. I suppose I'll have to go."

"Excellent. I knew I'd win in the end."

"But I must see Petra first." After all, she was trying to manage the thousands of Necromancers who see me as their Tsarina. I couldn't go to Nyumbani without letting her know, face-to-face.

Philippe paused. "Does that mean you'll cast a transport spell right now?"

"I'll try." I rubbed my neck and even that movement was an effort. *What a battle.* Every muscle in my body felt drained.

"You look horrible." Philippe narrowed his eyes. "Get a good night's sleep and transport in the morning."

I let out a long breath. "Maybe you're right. Transport spells are tricky even when I'm well rested. But right now? I'm so tired I could curl up on the burned-out grass and take a nap. Plus, it gives me a chance to say goodbye to Sam and Mabel. I have a farewell gift for them, you know."

Philippe's gaze became fixed on something over my shoulder. "On second thought, it might be better for you to transport right now."

"Why's that?"

He tapped his square chin. "I've got an idea. How about

you take my word on something for once? Transport, my dear." His snarky grin looked forced.

Something is wrong.

The smart thing to do would be to cast my spell. But I didn't. Instead, I turned around to follow Philippe's line of sight. My mouth fell open in shock and horror.

The darkened countryside was alight with torches. And farmers, let's not forget those. There must have been thousands of them, carrying pitchforks and clubs. Their angry shouts echoed in the air. Even from a distance, the chants of "Kill the witch!" were clearly audible. At the front of the mob was a figure with yellow-blond hair who looked a lot like Wyatt.

By the Sire of Souls. My own neighbors were racing here to kill me.

I gripped Philippe's arm. "You have to get out of here."

"Moi? They aren't after me, Elea." He picked up a burned-out torch from the ground. "I can easily blend in as one of the crowd. Grr."

"Right." I pressed my palms to my eyes. It didn't seem possible: being murdered by Wyatt. Yes, the fact that I just finished flattening this hill with magick didn't help any, but I doubted my neighbors would have gone for their pitchforks without his inspiration.

"They're moving quickly." Philippe's eyes glinted with determination. "You better cast that spell."

I nodded, raised my left hand, and reached out with my mage senses for Necromancer power. The surrounding area was completely drained. I'd used up too much energy in my last fight. The roar of the crowd grew louder. They were getting closer. Bands of worry tightened around my chest.

Closing my eyes, I reached out farther in search of magick.

The mob's roars grew into ear-piercing shrieks. The ground trembled with their footsteps.

At last, I found a well of magick. There was a small quarry on the far side of the Dunkel lands. The stones there held the perfect kind of energy for my needs. *Thank the Sire.* Pulling that power into my body, I focused the magick into my left arm. The bones in my hand quickly glowed blue as I spoke the incantation.

> *"In mountains of snow*
> *By forests of ice*
> *Take me to my Cloister*
> *My heart's paradise"*

Energy tore through my veins. My limbs felt ripped in every direction at once. A blue haze formed around my feet. The spell began.

The mob crested the hill where I stood. From the corner of my eye, I saw a group of girls break off from the crowd to surround Philippe. Unbelievable, the power that man had over women.

Well, most women anyway.

All the other faces were twisted with rage, and none more so than Wyatt's. As the spell took hold, I took care to blow him a kiss. He grimaced with rage as he leapt for me, torch in hand. Darkness enveloped me just as his fingertips brushed my throat.

Another failed attempt from Wyatt.

Normally, transport spells hurt like anything. But this time? Seeing Wyatt so enraged seemed to lessen my pain. The next thing I knew, I was back in the familiar surroundings of the office for Petra, my Mother Superior at the Zelle Cloister.

The place appeared unchanged. It was still a cave-like room hollowed out from a mountainside.

Petra sat at her massive wooden desk, scribbling away on parchment with a quill. As always, she looked rickety with age. Her dark mage robes contrasted with her pale, lined face, and long white hair. As my spell completed, she looked up. There was the barest widening in her eyes as she saw me appear.

"I wasn't expecting you." Her voice warbled.

"I would have warned you of my visit, but there wasn't time."

"Not to worry. You're welcome to barge into my office unannounced whenever you wish." The barest glimmer of laughter shone in her eyes for a second or two. For Petra, that was as good as a belly laugh.

I soaked in every line of her familiar face. Images and happy memories flickered through my mind, like practicing incantations together, singing vespers with the other Sisters, and searching through spell parchments in the library. Every impulse inside me wanted to run up and embrace her. But as soon as the emotion filled my heart, I felt ashamed. Petra spent five long years teaching me to lose all my emotional ties, like a true Necromancer. I'd only been gone from the Cloister for less than a year. Already, I was out of control.

With a force of will, I made sure my face became a mask of calm. "It is good to see you, Mother Superior."

She set her pen down. "And you as well, Elea." She focused on the door and raised her voice. "I know you're all out there, listening at keyholes."

I lowered my voice to a whisper. "Who is?"

"Everyone," answered Petra. "All the Necromancers you raised from the dead. They've been haunting my doorway, waiting for the big moment when you'd deign to visit me. And they are listening to every word we speak right now."

"You don't ward the door?"

Petra lifted her shoulder. It was the barest of movements. "Why ruin their hopes of being the first to catch your visit?"

Her words sent a chill down my spine. It was strange to think of people waiting for me to appear. "What do you wish to do?" I asked.

"Why, let them in for a moment, of course." She rapped on her desk with her bony knuckles. "Well, she has transported here last. You might as well enter."

At those words, the door to Petra's study flung open and a half-dozen Necromancers sped into the stone office. All wore the long black robes typical of our order. However, each of their faces had the image of a skull embedded on their skin. It was a kind of tattoo that showed the bones beneath their flesh. And it was the unmistakable sign that these were some of the Necromancers I'd raised from the dead.

A sheen of sweat broke out on my skin. Sure, I knew that I'd brought people back to life, but I'd only seen these folks from a distance, say through a window or across a darkened battlefield. Back then, they were only a blank-faced mob. Up close, I couldn't help but soak in the differences. A young girl with a dimpled smile. A older man whose nose had been broken. A teenage boy with a face flushed with excitement. Each had their own history that had brought them to this point. All of them looked at me with such hope. The question was out there but not spoken.

Are you here to be our Tsarina at last?

A long silence followed. I felt as if I should say something, but I couldn't think what. My mind was stuck on a single thought: I'd brought these people back to life. It was overwhelming. And even more amazing, these were just six of the thousands I'd affected. How many stories did they have? What did they *really* want from me?

Petra gestured between us. "Tsarina, I'd like you to meet some of your loyal subjects."

I was about to say, *I'm not their Tsarina*. Before the words could cross my lips, the six Necromancers fell to their knees and spoke in unison.

"Greetings, Tsarina."

"Hello." I was amazed at how calm my voice sounded.

A young girl looked up. "May the other Necromancers enter?"

"Others?" I was glad my voice still sounded so calm.

She gestured to the opened doorway. My breath caught. The outer hall was packed with more mages. There were so many more faces, and all of them were filled with hope that I'd lead them.

I shook my head. "Another time perhaps. I'm here to speak with Mother Superior."

The girl rose. "But you'll stay, won't you? We've been planning a ceremony of welcome for our new Tsarina. We've had it ready to go at a moment's notice, for whenever you returned to us."

Shujaa's face appeared in my mind. If I lingered here, he'd might attack again. I needed to travel to Nyumbani and team up with Rowan. "Thank you for the offer, but I'll have to enjoy that another time."

Petra's eyes narrowed a fraction. That was her scheming look. "The Tsarina and I have much to discuss. As you can see, she is here and we are making plans. All is well. You must excuse us now."

The Necromancers sped from the room. They couldn't

have moved faster if I'd placed a velocity spell on them. Within seconds, the mages were gone, the door was closed, and I was alone with Petra.

I'd just left one mob because they were trying to kill me. Now, I'd almost been caught by another one trying to make me into their leader. It was turning into quite a day.

Petra gestured toward the high-backed chair before her desk. "What brings you here?"

I sat down on the cold wooden seat. It felt familiar and somehow comforting. Memories sped through my mind— images of all the hours I'd spent in this chair before Petra's desk, trying to figure out how to end my curse from Viktor. Those worries seemed centuries ago now. "Why did you call me their Tsarina?"

"It's easiest until I find a suitable replacement."

"But don't you think—"

"If you question my judgment so much, you can come here and rule."

She wasn't wrong. "I'm being hunted by a Creation Caster and Changed One named Shujaa. He says he wants to kill me in order to become the Tsar."

"So why not become the Tsarina? Surely, you'd be safe with thousands of loyal Necromancers around you."

"Shujaa wields hybrid magick from Viktor. If I stayed here, I'd only put all of you at risk. The only way I can really take this warrior down is by working with Rowan."

"How do you know for certain? Perhaps if you came here, this Shujaa would lose interest and never show his face again."

I frowned. "You seem to know a lot about it."

"Not at all." Petra arched her right brow. "But I believe there is more to this situation than merely the threat of Shujaa."

Leave it to Petra to suss out all my secrets in five minutes or less. "There's also a Caster prophecy that may apply to Shujaa. It says that there will be a time of suffering for the Casters when their powerful mages will be taken away."

"Viktor did that."

"Yes. The prophecy goes on to say that family members will also disappear."

Petra began tapping her desktop with her fingernail. "They call that Shadow Family." Her voice took on the familiar lilt of her giving me a lesson. "The people of our continent, Ausdauer, are divided into those who have magick and those who don't. Necromancers and Forgotten Ones. It's not the same for the Creation Casters of Nyumbani. Everyone has magick, even if they can only cast a small spell or two. They all can sense each other in ways we can't. Shadow Family is when someone's gone, but you don't know if they're alive or dead. It's very upsetting for the Casters involved." She stopped her tapping. "What else did you learn?"

I tried not to frown, but it wasn't easy. I hated this part of the prophecy. "It is said that a true King will rise to save the Caster people. Shujaa believes himself to be this true King."

"Nonsense. He's a Changed One, isn't he?"

"Yes, how did you know?"

"Let's say I've heard a rumor or two about him. In any case, most Casters hate Viktor. Only a handful of the Changed Ones stayed loyal to Viktor after you sent him back into exile the second time."

I shouldn't have added this in, but I couldn't help myself. "Rowan helped me send Viktor into exile. Twice."

"And now Shujaa thinks he's the rightful King."

"Supposedly he'll raise a golden army, just like the

prophecy says. And as Shujaa becomes more powerful, Rowan will become sicker."

Petra leaned back in her chair. "And now we come to the heart of the matter. *This* is why you wish to go to Nyumbani. How many times have I told you: good Necromancers avoid emotional entanglements?" Petra's eyes narrowed the barest fraction. "You care for him."

Now, Petra and I hadn't discussed Rowan in any depth before. But knowing my Mother Superior, she'd have sussed out that he was important to me somehow. And no doubt, she'd taken it upon herself to become an expert in our relationship. Petra wanted me to rule the Necromancers as Tsarina. In her mind, that meant every detail of my life was her business.

There was no point lying to her. "Rowan and I have been on a number of adventures together. He saved my life many times. If the man is sick or an army is attacking him, then yes, I do want to help him."

"So why come here today? You're not asking for my counsel, are you?"

"No, I came here to inform you of my decision." I gripped my hands in my lap to hide how they shook. "I'm going to Nyumbani."

Petra stared at me for a long time. "If you must go, then there are things you must know."

"About what?"

"Yes, I've had word of this situation from our Seers."

"We have Seers again?" Viktor and his agent the Vicomte had killed off virtually every Necromancer. We hadn't had a Seer in our number for years.

"If you'd shown any interest in your people, then you'd know this already. After all, you were the one who raised them from the dead." Petra fiddled with some papers on her desk. If I didn't know her better, I'd say she was acting guilty. "Based on their visions, you may go to Nyumbani, team with Genesis Rex, and kill this Shujaa."

Seers. I still couldn't believe it.

Suddenly, Petra's unreadable features took on a darker meaning. I knew my old Mother Superior. If Seers were here, she'd have spent months hounding them for any scrap of insight in how to get what she wanted. And she wanted me as Tsarina. "What did they tell you, exactly?"

"That when this moment came and you insisted on leaving, that you should indeed go to Nyumbani."

I slumped back in my chair. It had been quite a day, and my patience was through. "Don't play games, Petra. I know you. There's more to this than you're telling me."

"Sit up straight and mask your emotions."

I wouldn't be distracted from my point. "What else did the Seers tell you?"

"You won't like it."

"Tell me."

"Genesis Rex is a liar who will say and do anything to win your heart and power. You must go, kill Shujaa, and come back to these lands as quickly as possible. Don't count on anything but the most minimal help from this Rowan. Even if he wanted to, he's too sick to share his power with you anymore."

I sucked in a shaky breath. "What's wrong with him?" Surely, the Seers had to be mistaken on this point. Rowan was always the picture of health.

"Why should you care? Your Rowan is deeply in love with his Amelia. He thinks nothing of you beyond how to use your magick to secure his own throne."

My skin cooled over with shock. Petra had been my guiding star. She was the one person who'd helped me become a Grand Mistress. No one else would dare defy Viktor. Plus, after her years of Necromancer training, Petra shouldn't even be able to lie to another Sister. "No, Mother. Rowan is fine. Something else is at work here."

"There is." Petra's voice lowered with anger. "In a matter of months, you've destroyed years of your Necromancer training. Now, you're being distracted by frivolous emotions that are not even returned. And to top off all this insanity, you are throwing away your gifts. Is this how I trained you?"

Her words cut into me like so many knives. When I spoke, my voice quavered. "Mother."

"Enough of this foul emotional display. I thought you a far better mage and woman. Now leave my presence and do your duty as a Necromancer. Go to Nyumbani and kill Shujaa, but that is all you must do. Don't believe anything else this Rowan has to say. He can't be trusted." She waved her hand. "Neither can you, apparently. If there's any consolation, it's that Rowan won't live too long. Soon he'll be dead, and you can move on from this madness. I hope you return to me as less of a disappointment."

I couldn't believe what I was hearing. Petra had been the image of patience and kindness for five years. She could be stern, certainly, but never anything like this. And saying Rowan would die soon? It was all a mistake. *It had to be.* I rose on shaky legs. "I'd better leave."

Petra pulled a totem ring off her finger. "You can use this to transport. You look dead on your feet."

"Thank you, Mother." I picked up the band from her palm. The ring had been carved with the image of a skull. "You made this for me?"

"Of course. I'm not all emotionless cruelty, Elea. I've been worried about you and wish nothing more than to keep you safe. After all, you're the closest thing I'll ever have to a daughter."

I could only stare in disbelief. In all the years I'd known Petra, those were the most open words of affection she'd ever offered. "You mean the same to me, Mother."

"Then you'll come back to us?"

I looked at her beloved and wrinkled face. Petra was only person who'd ever been a consistent source of love and support in my life.

"I won't fail you, Mother."

"Excellent. I would expect nothing less."

I set the ring on my finger. Despite my vow, every mage sense I had told me that Petra was still hiding something. Still, this woman was the only family that I had left.

I'd never felt more confused in my life.

ransporting with someone else's totem ring was a mixed experience. The good part was that I only had to speak one word—*"transport"*—and I could begin my magickal journey. Plus, since the spell was preloaded onto my ring from Petra, the trip wouldn't drain me of any magick, either.

But the bad side? The spell still hurt. Terribly. I'd no sooner spoken the word *"transport"* than waves of darkness and pain enveloped me. I'd suffered before during transporter spells, but going to Nyumbani would be my longest journey ever, and as the Necromancer saying goes, *"The farther the trip, the greater the pain."* Agony now shot through every pore of my body until I couldn't remember a time before this all-consuming anguish.

Then it ended.

Bright light overwhelmed my vision. For a few seconds, all I could make out was a yellow and green haze around me. Heat seared against my skin. After all this time, I was still wearing my yellow dress, and the heavy silk quickly turned sticky with sweat. Once my eyes adjusted to the sunlight, I found myself standing in a garden. It was a round space framed by strange trees. They reminded me of a cross between a palm and weeping willow, but with wide red leaves that cascaded to the earth. Round plots of colorful flowers covered the ground: yellow, red, and green. Everything was planted into a swirling shape.

A road led out of the garden, across a moat, and ended at the entrance to a castle. In some ways, the structure was typical. The castle had multiple stories and turrets like the ones back home. However, this particular castle was made entirely of trees, stones, and moss. Four great silver trees stood at the four corners of the structure. Heavy branches sprouted out from the tops of these pillars, creating a framework for the building. The rest of the exterior was made from artistic swirls of stones, moss, and tiny white flowers. It was beautiful.

A presence closed in behind me. Turning around, I saw Rowan. He stood tall with a halo of sunshine gleaming through his brown hair.

Somehow I managed to speak. "Rowan."

He gave me the barest of nods. "Elea."

"How long have you been here?"

"Only a few minutes."

"How did you know when I'd arrive?"

"My little Seer told me."

"Oh right, the Seer. That's good." Rowan had mentioned how few magick users still remained among his people. It was good that at least one Seer remained. I scanned the gardens once more. We were alone.

Rowan gave me one of his crooked smiles. "If you're

wondering why no one else is here, I'll let you in on a secret. I didn't want to share your company."

I tried to ignore how those words made me lightheaded. Petra said this man was a manipulator and a liar. And although Petra was acting strangely, I still needed to be cautious. I straightened my spine and focused on the task at hand. "I'm here because of Shujaa."

Rowan nodded. "You kept your word. Thank you."

"We need to kill him."

Muscles tensed in Rowan's throat. "Shujaa is a threat to my people and my rule. I need to handle it alone."

I lifted my chin. "He wields magick from Viktor. If you really want to kill him, then you need my help."

"There are ways around that totem armor of his. I already have a plan to defeat him. Please." His gaze locked with mine. "I don't want you placed at risk."

A sense of warmth and comfort spread through my chest. My Zuchtlos nature loved how Rowan wanted to protect me. But the logical part of my Necromancer mind said that something still didn't make sense here.

I shook my head. "What's this plan of yours? If you want me to step aside, then I need to understand the full story."

"The full story." Rowan's gaze turned intense. "I can do that."

Once again, I noticed the dark circles under his eyes. Rowan really was ill. The thought made me shiver.

"I can tell you the full story," continued Rowan. "But it's an old tale. A story of Nyumbani. Would you like to hear it?"

With Rowan looking sick, I couldn't refuse him anything. "Please."

"The tale goes like this. Two birds once sat on a branch. One was a blackbird while the other was a white dove. Now, the blackbird couldn't fly. Meanwhile, the dove could soar, only she'd never tried. You see, neither bird had ever left their shared branch."

I frowned. "Then how did they eat?"

Rowan gave me a sly look. "It's not that type of story." A small grin rounded his full mouth. "Are you going to listen or make comments?"

"Both."

Rowan chuckled. "Fair enough. Then one day, the dove asked the blackbird to fly away with her. Of course, the blackbird knew that the moment his dove took to the air, she might love flying so much that she'd never return. He also realized that if he confessed to being flightless, she'd never leave their branch. So the blackbird did a terrible thing. He told a lie. He asked his dove to fly away, and promised to follow along right afterwards. But the dove was rather clever."

"I'm guessing she was brilliant."

"And you would be right." Rowan all-out laughed. I loved the deep and rolling sound of his voice. "At this point, the dove said to the blackbird: 'What aren't you telling me? I need to understand the full story.' And the blackbird said: 'I'm not telling you anything. I'm giving you a choice, and I need you to trust me.' And so, the dove flew away."

I hadn't realized it, but I'd been hanging on Rowan's every word. It really was a good story. "What happened next? Did the dove ever return?"

"It's not that kind of story. It pretty much ends there."

I rolled my eyes. This was an obvious sign of emotion, but I simply couldn't help it. "That was the worst tale I've ever heard." I set my fist on my hip. "And the moral is fairly obvious. I already asked you the same thing that the dove did. What aren't you telling me?"

"And my answer will be the same as the blackbird's. I'm not telling you anything. I'm giving you a choice."

"So my knowing your plan for Shujaa is really you giving me a choice?"

"Yes. And I need you to trust me on that."

An image appeared in my mind. Rowan and Amelia getting engaged as I looked on, stunned. "That's not easy. Not after what's happened between us."

"I can explain."

"You have a reason for your relationship with Amelia? I don't believe it."

"Yes, I do. The court is holding another engagement ceremony tomorrow night."

"To you?" *How many wives did he need?*

"Not me. Please attend this event, and I swear, everything that happened with Amelia will make perfect sense. I could tell you, but I know you better than that. You'll need to see this with your own eyes."

"The first engagement ceremony I saw broke my heart." I scrubbed my hands over my face. "This is all very confusing."

"I know. I want things to be different between us. You've no idea how much. Once this situation with Shujaa is truly over, then I'll be able to tell you everything. Believe it." Rowan stepped so close he loomed over me. I wished this particular movement of his wouldn't make my willpower turn into jelly, but it always did. I needed to stop him before I did something stupid.

Correction. Before I did something *more* stupid. Simply talking to Rowan was probably a mistake.

Suddenly, the leaves of a nearby tree rustled suspiciously. Rowan turned toward the direction of the noise. "I know you're out here, Jicho."

A young boy's voice sounded in reply. "Am I in trouble?"

I noticed how the child didn't address Rowan as Your Majesty. This seemed odd—our Royals were very particular about their titles—but Casters were a rather informal bunch.

"You're not in trouble," explained Rowan. "Come down and say hello."

There was the thud of someone jumping down. A second after, a boy stepped out from behind the curtain of red palm leaves. He looked about nine years old, with a shaved head and the sleeveless red robes of a Seer, the kind that draped across him to tie at his shoulder. Our Necromancer Seers wore this same style too, only in black.

Rowan turned to me. "Elea, I'd like you to meet Jax. He's the little Seer I told you about before."

The boy lifted his chin. "Call me by my traditional name. I'm Jicho."

"All right, Jicho." I knelt before him to get a better look in his eyes. "Does everyone here have two names...Or is this a game you play?"

The boy turned to Rowan. "She really doesn't know anything, does she?"

"Not about our Caster ways." Rowan's sly smile returned. "You'll have to take very good care of her and answer the questions you can."

Jicho puffed out his chest. "And I'll protect her too, just like you said."

What a sweet boy. "Are you to be my guide and guard, then?"

"Yes, the King says I'm to take you wherever you wish to go." Something in the gleam of Jicho's green eyes felt familiar. "And I can answer all your questions."

"All?" asked Rowan slowly.

"Well, not *all* of them." Jicho lowered his voice to a child's whisper, which was really no whisper at all. "I'm sworn to secrecy on some things."

I gave him a solemn nod. "I understand." My eyes narrowed as I thought through this turn of events. Jicho couldn't answer all my questions, but he could take me to someone who would. "So you can guide me anywhere?"

Jicho grinned a gap-toothed smile. "Yes."

"In that case, I'd like to see Amelia."

As plans went, I'd had crazier ones. Sure, when Amelia and I had last parted, our friendship was in a bad way. She'd just figured out that Rowan and I had feelings for each other, so she'd turned her back on me. I hadn't heard from her since. That said, Amelia was a very logical and reasonable person. If I could see her, then I could explain the truth to her: I had no idea that Rowan was courting her at the same time he knew me. Amelia was a good soul. Once she knew the truth, I was certain that she'd tell me whatever I needed to know.

I stood and offered Jicho my hand. "Shall we?"

Rowan raised his arm, palm forward. "Hold on. What's the goal of this meeting?"

"To explain to Amelia that I had no idea who you were."

Rowan tilted his head. "That's all?"

"And to find out what you're hiding, of course."

Rowan sighed. "So, you intend to interrogate Amelia about me."

"Unless you plan to be more forthcoming." I set my fist on my hip. It was a broadly emotional move, but Rowan brought out the worst in me. "Why can't I see her? Are you afraid she'll turn on you when she finds out that you kept me in the dark about your engagement?"

Rowan's gaze locked with mine. "I was honest with Amelia."

I frowned. "She didn't act that way."

"It's her story to tell." He sighed. "And believe it or not, I'm happy for you to hear it from her, if she's willing to share the truth. You may visit Amelia with my blessing, but on one condition."

"What?"

"The engagement ceremony tomorrow night...I'd still like you to attend."

A long pause followed while I considered this. "Your ceremonies haven't been pleasant for me." I thought back to the last one I saw. After Amelia and Rowan had gotten engaged, all Rowan would talk about was some Sword of Theodora. He'd even acted like getting engaged wasn't a serious endeavor. "My Mother Superior told me about your attachment to Amelia. She confirmed my worst fears."

"She did, eh?" Anger flared in Rowan's green eyes. "Your Mother Superior is a liar."

"She said the same about you," I countered.

"Wow," said Jicho in a low voice. "You guys are fighting."

Rowan inhaled a long breath. Some of the tension eased from his shoulders. "You're right, Jicho. You should only talk to those you care about in a spirit of calmness and respect." He took my hand, and a shock of warmth and pleasure shot up my arm. "Please trust me one last time, and I'll never bother you again. I humbly ask you to attend the ceremony."

My lips seemed to move on their own. "Yes, I'll be there."

"Good." His gaze turned so intense, my insides started to squirm. "Then we have an agreement."

The moment Rowan looked away, I wanted to kick myself in frustration. Somehow, I had allowed that man to maneuver me into attending this so-called ceremony. And yet, I still didn't have any answers about Rowan's health or how he planned to get rid of Shujaa.

Rowan stepped away. With some distance between us, I noticed how his leathers fit a little more loosely on his body. His collarbones were almost visible through his jacket.

He was ill.

I took a few steps toward the castle and paused. "I will find out what's really happening."

"You will try." Rowan gave me another crooked smile.

Jicho rushed up to my side. "You better take my hand. That way, no one will give you any trouble."

"Thank you, Jicho."

I took his smaller hand in mine and headed off toward the castle. One thought echoed through my heart. *No one will give me any trouble?* If I was going to find out what was really happening, then I'd need to be the one causing trouble. Not a problem.

8

*J*icho and I headed off for the castle, leaving the gardens behind us. I could feel Rowan's gaze on my back every step of the way. Once we were well out of earshot, I decided to try my luck with getting answers out of Jicho. It was a long shot, but even those paid off sometimes.

"Tell me," I said. "What's wrong with Rowan?"

"Nothing. He can still cast a lot of spells. Plus, the rest of his powers will come back when he feels better."

There was the slightest hitch in my step. Did Jicho just say what I thought he said? Rowan was sick? And not just the kind of sickness where he was physically tired, but one where he was losing his magick, too?

I decided to push my luck and ask another question. "What's this history between him and Shujaa?"

Jicho shook his head violently. "I'm not telling you anything. Rowan is my brother."

My mouth fell open. "He's your brother?" Somehow, I

never pictured Rowan as having family. He was always just Rowan. "Who else is in your family?"

"Uh, I probably shouldn't have even told you about me. I can't say anything else." Jicho scrunched up his face. "Sorry about that."

"You're loyal to your brother. I respect that." *And you're telling me a ton of things without meaning to, anyway.*

We walked along in silence for a time before Jicho spoke again. "So, do you think you can help Rowan by chatting with that Amelia lady?"

"Absolutely."

"If you say so. She's pretty crazy." Jicho pointed to one of the towers on the corner of the castle. "She's up there."

The tops of towers were where you placed prisoners who didn't belong in a dungeon. It seemed odd for Amelia to be there, especially if what Petra said was true. Who places their true love in a prison?

"Lead the way, Jicho."

"All right, but you might be a little crazy, too."

I smiled. "Oh, I definitely am."

As Jicho and I closed in on the castle, my thoughts raced through everything that happened in the last few days. There was the battle with Shujaa...Talking with Petra...This prophecy of the golden army...Plus the way Rowan's health and powers were failing. Everything fit together in some larger picture, but for the life of me, I couldn't see the pattern.

Even worse, my soul told me that the stakes of his hidden plan were a matter of life and death, and not only for me. The image of Rowan's weary face was seared into my mind. If his magick was dying, Rowan was, too.

By the Sire, I would discover the truth or else.

9

*J*icho soon led me across the moat and past the castle's main doorway. Inside, the place was as lovely as its exterior. The walls and floors were framed with silver trees. Smooth gray stones, green moss, and small white flowers filled all the spaces in between. No matter where I looked, there were guards in shiny Caster leathers with the emblem of three white columns on their shoulders. All the men and women were bristling with weapons. A sense of excitement filled the air.

Something was happening.

I had an idea for how to get more information out of Jicho. I felt vaguely guilty for continuing to push the boy, but it wasn't like I wouldn't use the knowledge to help Rowan. "The guards all look like they're in their best leathers. Are they expecting someone?"

Jicho sniffed. "Maybe."

"Do they think the golden army is coming soon?"

Jicho paused. "You've heard of the golden army?"

"Yes." I looked at their perfect uniforms and gleaming weapons. "That's definitely what this is all about. They're getting ready to show off for when the golden army arrives."

"That army isn't coming." Jicho's lower lip trembled as he spoke. "It's just an old story, and these guards are all traitors."

"Jicho, I'm—"

"You know what? You're a mean lady, and I'm not talking to you anymore." Jicho grabbed my wrist and yanked me in a new direction. "Amelia's this way."

A weight of guilt settled onto my shoulders. "I'm sorry, Jicho. I didn't mean to upset you."

"I said, I'm not talking to you." Jicho dragged me to the base of a winding staircase. "Crazy Amelia is up there." He leaned against the wall and folded his arms over his chest. "I'll wait for you here."

I knelt before Jicho and tried to catch his eyes. He wouldn't look at me. "I really am sorry."

Jicho screwed up his face into a frown and looked away.

"Does this mean you won't be my guide anymore?"

"Just go up and ask if she'll talk you." Jicho kicked at the ground with his sandal. His frown did seem a little less prominent, though. I took that as a good sign.

"I'll do that," I said. "And I'll return as soon as I can."

I hiked up the cramped stone staircase that wound inside the tower. With each step, anxiety made my pulse speed faster. I hadn't seen Amelia since the night she got engaged to Rowan. In my mind's eye, I could still picture the look of hurt and betrayal on her face when she discovered that Rowan and I had feelings for each other. At the time, she'd made it pretty clear she never wanted to speak to me again.

Not wanting to be friends anymore? I couldn't blame her for that, really.

I gripped the folds of my yellow dress as if the motion could keep my feelings under control as well. I couldn't allow what happened with Amelia to make me lose focus now. Someone was out to kill me. Rowan was sick and losing his magick. Shujaa and his golden army were coming to take the throne. And since Amelia was engaged to Genesis Rex, that meant she was in danger, too. Amelia would just need to set her feelings aside and give me the information I required.

I scaled up one floor, then two. At each level, there was a stout red door leading to a room in the castle's interior. At the end of the staircase, I reached a small landing and one last wooden door.

This was it—the tower room.

A single guard in faded leathers waited by the door. It was Kade. His green eyes locked on me as I approached. "You again."

"Greetings, Kade." Suddenly, I wished I could have changed out of my yellow dress from the faire. I didn't look very much like a grand Mistress Necromancer. It also wasn't clean. I stiffened my spine. No matter how I looked, I was the Tsarina of all the Necromancers, as far as he knew. "I'm here to see Amelia."

He sniffed. "She doesn't want to see you."

"You haven't even announced me. Tell her that Elea of Braddock is here. I'm the Tsarina of all the Necromancers." Amelia didn't need to hear that part, but I thought it might impress Kade a little more and at least make him announce me.

"I know all your titles." Kade rested his hand on the pommel of his sword and gripped it so tightly, his knuckles flared white. "And you're not welcome in my Lady's chamber."

That got my anger up. "Amelia is her own person. She can make her own choices about whether to see me."

"And why would she want to see you?" The way Kade asked the question, the words came out as a snarl.

"Because I'm very concerned about Rowan's safety...And about hers as well."

"You." The thick muscles in Kade's neck tightened. "You, of all people, are concerned about Rowan."

"That's what I said. Now, I don't know why you're acting this way, but at least announce me. Amelia can decide for herself if she wishes me to visit."

"She knows you're here, and she doesn't want to see you. Jicho told her you'd be stopping by days ago. And besides, my Lady already has company. Veronique and her brother Philippe are inside."

I rubbed my chin. *So, Philippe is already here.* That was good news. Philippe could be relied on to do two things: flirt and gossip. If there was any information to be gotten, Philippe would be sussing it out right now. He'd surely tell me everything, even if Amelia wouldn't. I inhaled a deep breath, ready to call out his name, but Kade was too fast. He moved behind me in a heartbeat. A second later, his right hand covered my mouth while his left gripped my casting arm.

"I told you," snarled Kade. "She knows you're here and doesn't want to see you. Don't make me toss you down the stairs."

My eyes widened. Kade wasn't tossing me anywhere. I started to pull Necromancer energy into my arm. I knew a few spells that would break down the door while knocking Kade out for at least an hour.

"Don't use your magick," warned Kade.

I paused as I thought through this turn of events. Was

Kade one of the Senior Casters who could work a major spell on me?

"I know what you're thinking," said Kade. "You're wondering if I'm a Caster like my King. Well, I can't wield major magick, but I've something even better. *Knowledge.* In fact, I happen to know that if I pinch your shoulder in a certain way, then I can send you tumbling to the floor faster than maybe." His low voice sounded familiar.

In fact, he sounded a lot like Rowan.

I released the power from my casting arm.

Kade let me go. "Glad to see that we understand each other," he said.

"You—" I began.

"Don't give me any trouble for restraining you," interrupted Kade. "I'm supposed to guard this door."

"That's not what I was about to say. *You* are Rowan's brother. Am I right?"

He stepped back to his post. "What makes you say that?"

"You've Rowan's body type and green eyes. Most of all, you aren't wearing your best leathers—" I gestured across his faded uniform "—which means you aren't getting ready to show off for the golden army. You're loyal to Rowan in a time when that loyalty might be risky. You must be family. It's a logical assumption."

Sometimes, my Necromancer training in logic was a wonderful thing.

"Yes, I'm Rowan's brother and his top guard, too." Kade tapped the faded emblem of three white pillars that had been sewn onto the shoulder of his leathers. "All this stuff about a prophecy and a golden army, it didn't start until three months ago. You know, when *you* came into his life?"

"I find it hard to believe that I'm somehow responsible for Shujaa."

"Maybe not, but you're still trouble for Rowan." Kade stared at the closed door with so much intensity I wondered why I didn't see the resemblance before. "Anyway, forget about Amelia, too."

"Will she be attending the ceremony tomorrow night?"

Kade's body almost vibrated with menace. "Not if I have anything to do with it."

"In other words, Amelia wants to go." I scanned Kade more carefully. For a guard and a Royal, Kade certainly had a lot invested in Amelia. Yet another piece of information to add into the jumble of facts. Hopefully, things would start to make sense soon.

Kade folded his arms over his chest. "I can handle her."

"Can you?" I couldn't help but smile. "Amelia can be very hard to contain when she wants something."

"Good thing I'm the best guard in the realm, then."

"In that case, I'm sure everything will be fine."

In truth, Kade was in deep trouble; he just didn't know it yet. Amelia was a master with anything mechanical. There wasn't a door or a lock that could hold her back. And since Kade couldn't cast major spells, there weren't a lot of other options for him. "Until we meet again, then."

"Be careful," said Kade. "You never know what'll be waiting for you on the stairs."

The way he said the words, I had the feeling he wanted me to trip and kill myself. Well, he'd have to get in line. Many people have wanted me dead over the years.

None had succeeded yet.

10

I hadn't gone ten steps before I found out what Kade meant when he said, *"You never know what'll be waiting for you on the stairs."*

Because there was someone waiting for me: a woman in red Seer robes. Like Jicho, hers were tied at the shoulder, toga style. She had long brown hair, an athletic build, and bright green eyes. Her skin was smooth and tanned, like Rowan's had looked when I first met him. This mystery woman didn't look much older than I was, but the way she held herself said she was someone important.

Well, now. Brown hair, green eyes, and regal bearing? No doubt, here was another member of the Imperial family. I paused on the steps.

"Greetings," I bowed my head slightly. "I'm Elea. Let me guess. You're Rowan's sister."

"No, I'm his mother. Call me Zoriah." Her voice had the deep rumble of age.

"You look so young, if you don't mind my saying so."

"I don't mind." Zoriah waved her hand dismissively. "I'm a strong Seer, which is why I don't age like other mortals, including Rowan. Now, I'd like to talk to you about him."

I looked around the cramped staircase. "Here? Half the castle could be waiting and listening around the next turn in the steps."

"Not here, you idiot girl. We'll talk in my greenhouse."

Now as a rule, no one called me an "idiot" or a "girl" without consequences. But this was Rowan's mother. I had to be careful. Plus, I was in serious need of information. Perhaps Zoriah would be more forthcoming than the rest of Rowan's family.

I forced my face into the picture of Necromancer calm. "Lead the way, then."

Zoriah sped down the rest of the staircase. I followed close behind. The moment we stepped back out into the main hallway, I found Jicho still waiting for me by the wall. He paled when he spied his mother. Zoriah didn't even acknowledge Jicho; she simply marched through the side hallway and out into the gardens behind the house. I stayed to Zoriah's left. Jicho jogged along at her right.

"What are you going to do with Elea?" asked Jicho. His voice warbled a bit with worry. *Poor child.*

"We're just about to have a friendly chat," answered Zoriah. "Why don't you run along and tell Rowan all about it? That's what you do best, isn't it? Spy for him."

Jicho frowned. "Rowan's the King. I owe him my feal… feal…" His face reddened as he tried to get the word out. I had the distinct impression that being around his mother flustered Jicho.

"Fealty, child. That's the word you were failing to say." Zoriah kept up her fast pace. We reached a heavy wooden door at the back corner of the castle. Zoriah pushed it to reveal an open green that stretched across a rolling hill until it ended in a line of palm trees. Without a word, Zoriah began marching across the green and toward the jungle beyond. After a few minutes, she seemed to notice that Jicho hadn't left. "Run along, child. I've no use for you."

Jicho stopped. "I hate you."

"Good," said Zoriah. "That will make your future pleasanter for me."

Zoriah kept on going, but I stopped and knelt so I could meet Jicho's gaze straight on. "It's probably best if you leave your mother and I to talk."

Jicho leaned in and whispered in my ear. "I won't be far. Remember when you first arrived in the gardens? Rowan didn't even know I was in the trees before. I only shook the branches once I wanted him to find me."

"Thank you, Jicho. That sounds like an excellent plan."

Zoriah had made great headway toward the jungle. She yelled over her shoulder at me. "Come along now. This is no time to play with children."

"I'll be right there," I called.

Refocusing my attention on Jicho, I gave him what I hoped was a confident grin, took to my feet, and followed Zoriah once again. I hadn't been in Nyumbani for a full day, and I already knew one thing for sure.

I truly hated Rowan's mother.

Zoriah and I trekked through the jungle for a long time. Well, it may actually have been a short time by the sundial, but it was a slow slog for me. My silk slippers were absolutely useless in the jungle mud. Within minutes, the bottom half of my yellow gown became soaked with gunk and shredded on prickly shrubs.

At length, the rainforest opened up into a small clearing. A stout rectangular building filled the space. It had a peaked roof and walls that were made of small squares of mottled yellow glass. Everything was held together in a metal lattice-work. I'd seen things like this back when I was snooping around Royal residences with Philippe, but I never expected to find anything like this in Nyumbani.

Zoriah pulled open the glass door. "Come along quickly. You'll let out the chill."

I stepped inside and closed the door behind me. The space was filled with rows of plants. More greenery hung from the arched roof. In the center of the space stood a tall fountain. The cool air wrapped around me, turning my skin into gooseflesh.

Zoriah eyed my arms. "Are you uncomfortable, girl? I thought you'd like it in here. It's more like your mountain Cloister, isn't it?"

"It's only the surprise I mind, not the temperature." I rubbed my upper arms for warmth. Zoriah was playing games, changing things on me without warning and then watching my reactions. Rowan's mother or not, I was in no mood for this. "What do you want?"

"Merely to show you this fountain," explained Zoriah smoothly. She stepped toward the large stone sculpture. The thing was as tall as me. All the stone was chipped and ancient looking. I stepped closer. The wide outer basin held a knee-deep pool of water. In the fountain's center, there stood two figures, a man and a woman. The details of their faces had been washed away with time, but their arms were raised with palms facing each other. Between their hands came a spray of water, which arced down from either side of their hands into the basin.

"It's lovely," I said. And I meant it. Even though it was hard to see any detail, there was a sense of peace in the pose of the couple.

"It's an extremely old fountain and made with ancient magick. Watch this." Zoriah lowered her head, and the veins in her chest and neck turned black. My breath caught with surprise. I'd known some Seers could cast magick, but that was so rare, we didn't even have any books on the subject back in our library at the Zelle. When Zoriah lifted her head again, her eyes had turned completely back except for her pupils. Instead of being dark, these now were filled with small red lightning bolts of power.

Zoriah focused her gaze on the statue. When she spoke again, her voice rang with magickal power. "Break apart." The stone creaked as the man and woman lowered their arms. Even though their palms were now separated, I could see that the water still flowed between their hands.

"It's interesting," I said. "What does it mean?"

"Those are the original *truly* mated pair of Casters."

At the mention of *"mated pair,"* my chest tightened. Now I knew why Zoriah had brought me here alone. She wanted to discuss my relationship with Rowan. My mating band from Rowan was still hidden under the neckline of my yellow gown. The thing seemed to weigh extra-heavily on my skin. It took all my Necromancer training to keep my features carefully blank. "As I said, it's a lovely statue."

I started to turn away, but Zoriah gripped my arm. "You can make these two figures do anything," she said. "And yet, the water will still move through their hands in a circuit.

That's what happens with a *true* mating." Her mouth thinned into a bitter line. "But over the years, we Casters have gotten away from that. Now, anyone who shares a pair of mating bands calls themselves a mated pair. But that's not a true mating."

The hairs on the back of my neck stood on end. "What's a true mating?"

"The water here is meant to represent magick. In a true mating, that energy is shared equally. But if it's a false pairing, then whoever is the stronger mage will take power from the other."

My eyes widened. The last time we'd fought Viktor, Rowan had given me some of his power. He could only give to me, but I could never return the energy? Was that because we weren't a true mating?

Zoriah watched me closely. I hated the satisfied grin on her face. The lightning in her pupils flashed more brightly than ever. "Interesting history, isn't it?" An eternity seemed to pass before she turned her attention back to the fountain. "As you were," she commanded.

The statues returned to their previous pose as Zoriah lowered her head. Within seconds, the veins in her neck and chest disappeared. When Zoriah met my gaze again, her eyes were back to their regular shade of green. Nothing flared in her pupils. Her grin widened. "You know why I'm telling you this, don't you?"

"Not at all." I'd never admit my feelings for Rowan to this woman.

"I hear you and my son worked together to defeated Viktor. The first time, you found some powerful magick to help you share your energies equally. The gods Oni and Yuri gave you a spell."

"How could you know that?"

"I'm a Seer, you silly little fool."

My skin broke out into fresh goose bumps, and it wasn't from the cold.

Zoriah pulled me closer. "And the second time, he gave magick to you, didn't he?"

"This is none of your affair."

"He is my son. It's very much my affair."

"Enough." I nodded toward the fountain. "I understand what you're trying to say. Rowan gave me magick, and we're therefore not a true mated pair." I gave her my most unaffected Necromancer stare. "If that's all you brought me here for, then it was a waste of your time. I've no interest in Rowan in anything other than a fellow warrior." I tried to step away, but her iron grip on my arm tightened.

"A false mating is nothing to be ashamed of," said Zoriah.

"I'm sure you'll tell me why." Perhaps the fastest way to get this over with was to let her have her say. It wouldn't do to get in a mage battle with Rowan's mother on my first day in Nyumbani.

Not that I wasn't tempted.

"I was locked into a false pairing as well. Rowan's father is named Aaden. Did Rowan tell you that?"

"No." I would add that Rowan didn't tell me much of anything, but I was sure that would please Zoriah to no end.

"As you've no doubt noticed, I'm one of the few Seers who is strong enough to cast spells. I'm also the only offspring of our last Genesis Rex. My mother was a lovely and trusted house servant."

I couldn't help it. "So you're a bastardess."

"I'm from the Imperial line. Aaden was a common Caster."

Her cheeks reddened. "In fact, Aaden could hardly sense any magick. The man never cast a single decent spell."

"Most of the people on my continent can't even sense magick."

"And you call them Forgotten Ones, because the gods forsake them. And that's what they should be: forgotten. But my father became obsessed with Aaden. How noble he was. How kind and clever. My father called for a ritual battle to determine the next Genesis Rex and forced Aaden to fight him. And you know what happened on the battlefield? My own father hardly didn't his sword or cast a single spell. Aaden merely had to swipe his blade and my father was dead. It wasn't a fight so much as a suicide. Aaden became Genesis Rex and I had to become his bride. I was forced into a mating I didn't want. And you know what happened with our mating? I never gave Aaden so much as a taste of my power. He only could transfer to me." She rounded on me. "Don't wish such an unequal life on yourself. Rowan adores his Amelia. Even if you could manipulate him into a mating, it wouldn't be a true one. It would never be equal."

It took all my Necromancer training to stay calm. Inside, I wanted to weep, scream, or both. "I fail to see what this has to do with you."

"My, oh my. Now, you are getting so very upset. I thought you Necromancers were far more controlled than this." Zoriah's green eyes lit up with an evil sort of excitement. It hurt my heart to see the beloved shade of Rowan's gaze turned against me in such a way. I could only imagine how she had hurt Rowan, too.

"I'm returning to the castle now." I twisted in her hold. "Let me go."

"Don't be so defensive," cooed Zoriah. "I brought you here

to help both you and Rowan get beyond the mating issue. It's a matter of safety. Life and death."

I sniffed. "Safety. Really."

"Yes, I showed you this fountain for a reason. If you ever do decide to assist Rowan in battle, then you'll only drain his already-low reserves of energy. He's very ill, you know."

I stepped closer to her. Even though this woman was foul, maybe this was my chance for more information. "What's wrong with Rowan?"

"*You're* what's wrong with him. You coming here will kill him."

All the air seemed to get sucked out of my lungs. *I would kill Rowan?* "That can't be true."

"It is." She shrugged. "I've seen it time and again in my visions." She finally released my hand and stepped over to a tall table dripping with hanging vines and small yellow fruits. I knew I should run for the door, but Zoriah now had me trapped in other ways. I stood speechless as she began to examine the leaves on a nearby plant. "Don't worry so much, girl. Our realm is better off without Rowan, believe me."

I stared at her, my mouth hanging open. I thought of how Mabel and Sam loved their unborn child, and that baby wasn't even in the world yet. How could anyone be so calm when talking about their child dying?

"Why do you hate Rowan so much?"

Zoriah moved from examining the tiny leaves to eyeing the round yellow fruits. "Ah, this one is just right." She grabbed a red satchel, plucked the fruit, and set it inside the bag. "So hard to find perfection, you know."

The fact that she avoided my question made me even more eager for an answer. "Tell me why you hate Rowan."

Zoriah looked up from her bag. "Don't you know who killed my husband?"

"No. Who killed him?"

"Why, Rowan of course."

My breath caught. "That's not possible."

"We accept challenges to the throne once every year. The Tsar Viktor challenged my husband, and Aaden accepted. Viktor was about to win, too. But as my husband lay dying, he asked any Caster to kill him and take his throne, so Viktor wouldn't rise. Rowan was the only one who would do so. My son is no true King."

Righteous anger pulsed through my veins. "That's a terrible thing to say. If Rowan hadn't done as his father asked, you'd be ruled by Viktor right now. Believe me, you don't want that."

"Who are you to tell me anything? I had a vision. If my husband was murdered by one of his own people, then the Caster nation would fall into dark times, just as the ancient prophecy predicted. And hasn't that come to pass? Are our lands not in chaos? And it's all because Rowan defied me. He ruined us all. And now, the prophecy is the only thing that can possibly save us."

I eyed her carefully. "I'm not sure your logic holds out there. The prophecy says that there will be a long night of suffering for the Caster people under a false ruler. Then, a golden army will appear and usher in a new age of plenty. You are the one who placed Rowan into everything."

"How dare you question my Seer powers? I speak the truth. Now, all we can do is pray for the golden army to free us all."

I stared at this perfect-looking woman who was filled with so much ugliness. "You know what I think? You're in league with Viktor somehow. You asked me here to try to frighten me away from Rowan. But your plan has failed. I'm staying by Rowan's side, and I'll help him fight you."

"No, your staying here will kill him."

"That's not true."

"Really? I'm the strongest Seer in Nyumbani's history. Better than even Wakati Ujao, the woman who spoke the prophecy of the golden army. I've spoken to the Mother of Creation herself. The goddess showed me your face. She gave me your name. And she told me what you came here to do. You say that you'll help Rowan, but in truth? You'll only destroy my son and take over our lands. Well, listen to me carefully. You'll have to kill me to do it. I can stop you. I've seen that."

I took a half step toward the door. "I don't know what you're talking about. I have no such plans."

"So you say." She returned her attention to her plants. "You'd better get ready for tomorrow night's celebration. I've asked my servants to set out an especially beautiful gown for you." She leaned in and sniffed one of the yellow fruits, plucked it, and set it in her satchel.

For the first time, I took a closer look at the plant she'd been tending. My brows lifted in surprise and recognition. I scanned all the fruit in the greenhouse. I'd recognize that waxy look anywhere. "This is all wrong."

"Nonsense." Zoriah tapped another yellow fruit with her long fingernails. "What are you talking about?"

"Freeze blight." I spun about, scanning all the plants. "Everything in here is infected."

Zoriah rounded on me. Every inch of her shook with rage. "Liar!" Her voice rose to a screech. "Leave my greenhouse immediately!"

She didn't need to ask me twice. I sped from that green-house like my life depended on it. Who knows? Maybe it did.

Once I stepped back under the cover of the jungle, I leaned against a moss-covered trunk and tried to catch my breath. A rustling sounded from the branches nearby. A heartbeat later, Jicho dropped to the ground beside me. He gave me a sympathetic look. "Did mother get to you?"

"Yes, she did."

"She scares everyone, you know. She's been that way ever since..." He shrugged and stared at his feet.

"Ever since your father died, you mean?"

"No, ever since Storm ran off. He was her favorite son. He was everyone's favorite prince." Jicho's lower lip trembled. "I like Rowan better though."

"I do too, Jicho." It was a foolish thing to say, but it did seem to comfort Jicho. When I next spoke, I took care to make my voice especially gentle. "Why don't you show me to my room?"

"If you like."

We didn't say another word as Jicho led me back into the castle to my bedroom. My chamber was a mixture of living trees, moss, and stone, just like the rest of the castle. I also had large bureau and an even larger bed made from a hollow stump stuffed with furs. The place was lovely, but after meeting with Zoriah, I couldn't soak in the beauty.

Jicho left, and I tried to relax and sleep. It wasn't easy. I had a big day behind me and an important ceremony to face tomorrow. Although I tried, I couldn't sleep a wink. All I could do was keep running through the same awful facts. Rowan was sick. And his mother thought I was here to kill him and take his throne. And the real reason I was here was because I needed to kill Shujaa, only Rowan didn't want my aid.

I shivered. I hated the whole concept of Seers. When they had a strong vision, sometimes there was nothing you could do to avoid the fate they predicted, no matter how awful it might be. Was I really here to kill Rowan, even if it was unintentionally? I groaned. This situation was turning into a battle of wits and information, not spells and fighting.

Sadly, that was the kind of battle I rarely knew how to win.

11

It took me a long time to fall asleep, and when I did, it was the kind of rest one got on a battlefield, which is to say: it wasn't any rest at all. I fidgeted under my covers and twisted my nightgown around me. All the while, the air in my chambers became thicker with anticipation.

Something was coming.

Suddenly, a searing heat surrounded me, making it hard to breathe. I sat up with a start. My heart thudded in my chest. Despite the warmth, I had the sense of cool fingers poking against my skin.

No question about it; someone was casting a spell. And since the magick felt icy, this person was definitely a Necromancer. My chamber walls burst into perfect sheets of red flame, and then, I understood. Only one Necromancer visited me at night and did so in fire.

Tristan, my one-time friend.

The man who'd sentenced me to a curse.

The person who changed my life forever and never asked my permission to do so.

I twisted my hands in my thin coverlet. With every passing day, it became harder to see Tristan as a friend. After all, the man had saddled me with a curse without my consent. Sure, he'd said it was for my own good—being cursed meant learning to be a Grand Mistress Necromancer, and ultimately, it was my only protection from Viktor.

But having the choice taken away from me still stung.

Tristan stepped through the wall of flames. He looked as he did the last time I saw him. He was tall and swarthy with loose black hair, dark eyes, and pale skin. It struck me that he was like a dark-haired version of Philippe, only without the aristocratic air. The last time I'd seen Tristan, he'd been wearing a long coat and breeches. Now, he was in Necromancer robes.

"Elea!" Tristan stepped toward me with his arms outstretched. "It's so good to see you."

I leveled him with an icy stare. "One moment." I slid out of bed and pulled on a thin cotton robe. "What do you want?"

He tilted his head. "Is that any way to greet a friend?"

"That depends." My words were clipped and angry. Until this moment, I hadn't realized the depth of rage I'd held toward Tristan. "Are you here as my friend...Or have you come to introduce a new terror in the name of doing what's best for my welfare?"

He sighed. "You know I love you."

"So, you're here for some new terror."

Tristan shook his head. "You've changed."

"You should know. You were the one who changed me. Wasn't that your aim all along? Now, I'm no farm girl. I'm unable to even take a ride to town without a mage battle breaking out, and worst of all, I love the fight."

"This isn't about magick." Tristan's eyes widened with sympathy. "It's all about your feelings for Rowan, isn't it?"

"You haven't earned the right to discuss my private life."

"Don't forget, if I hadn't inspired you to become a Grand Mistress Necromancer, then you'd never have met Rowan."

I eyed him carefully. In their afterlife, most Necromancer ghosts would float around in the Ocean of Calm. A select few got to keep their mortal bodies and live in the palace of the Sire of Souls. They were the elite who'd earned an eternity of quiet contemplation and study. "Who are you? Why aren't you floating around the Ocean of Calm...Or reading scrolls in the Eternal Libraries? Either way, you should be dead and know nothing of the realm of the living. How can you be aware of a single thing that's happened to me?"

Tristan finally lowered his arms. "We can go in circles about this for hours, but I really am here to help you." He reached into his pocket and brought out a totem ring. "This is loaded with enough spells to take you to see what's happening right now with Shujaa."

I stared hungrily at the totem ring. Petra's rings were all decorated with carved skulls. This one had a large blue stone. Someone else had made it. "Whose magick is that?"

"I cannot say."

"Will you at least tell me why you're doing this?" I locked gazes with him. "And try to be honest with me, for once."

Tristan met my steady gaze. "I want you to take your rightful place as Tsarina of the Necromancers. To do that, you need to finish things here."

My throat tightened with worry. "Meaning I need to wait until Rowan dies and then move on."

"You need to prepare yourself for the fact that your Rowan won't live much longer, no matter what you do. It's the will of Oni and Yuri, the Sire of Souls and the Lady of Creation. They are the ultimate power in our world. If they wish Rowan to die, then that is what will happen."

My eyes stung with held-in tears. No matter what, I wouldn't let Tristan see how his words affected me. "If Rowan is doomed, then why even give me that ring? Why show me what Rowan's enemies are up to?"

Tristan raised his arm, and the ring sat on his outstretched palm. "Because I want *you* to live. You need to survive and return to your people."

I swiped the ring from his hand. After all, hadn't I wanted information? Who cared what motivations were really behind Tristan's actions? I turned the dainty object over in my fingers. "How do I activate this?"

"Place it on your finger and think the word 'transport.' Only, be careful—the magick has limitations."

That was no shock. All magick came with boundaries. "What are they?"

"The ring will transport you to Shujaa and then right back here to your chambers. While you spy on him, he won't be able see or hear you."

I tilted my head. "I'll be like a ghost?"

"Exactly. This totem ring combines ghostly invisibility with transport."

My brows lifted. "That sounds rather tricky." I'd never even heard of a spell this complex before, let alone something that was activated with mental commands.

"The limits are as follows. Don't speak to anyone or the magick will shatter. They'll be able to see and hear you then." The way Tristan explained this, it was like I was a Cloister

Novice once more. Had he always been this much of a know-it-all?

"I won't forget." The totem ring was tiny—more something you'd give to a child than a grown woman. I slipped it onto my pinky and looked over to Tristan. "I won't forget *a lot* of things."

"Suit yourself." Tristan shrugged. "In the end, you won't have any choice in the matter. You'll need to bury the hatchet and move forward with life as Tsarina."

Anger corkscrewed up my spine. How could Tristan dismiss what he'd done so easily? I wanted to kick his face in, cast a bone melter spell, or both. Instead, I thought the word *"transport."* Blue light flared out from totem ring on my pinky. The chill of Necromancer magick cooled my skin. Both Tristan and my chambers vanished.

The next moment, I found myself standing outdoors. I shook my head in awe. Whoever cast the spell on this new totem ring was truly a master. Not only did it transport me without pain, but it did so instantly. As angry as I was with Tristan, I would need to find out the secrets of this particular casting. Painless transport was something I could use.

I scanned my new surroundings. The totem ring had sent me to the burned-out remains of what was once a Caster village. Moonlight cast everything in a bluish glow. The charred remains of circular huts dotted the landscape. Ropes of shock tightened around my chest.

There were Changed Ones everywhere.

Men with human torsos and jaguar legs stalked through the burned-out huts. Ladies with serpents for arms dug through the ground. Warriors with alligator skin prowled along the edges of the crowd.

They were all looking for something. After they tore

through a ruined hut or storage pit, they would come out again with an armful of clothing or furniture. Everything got dumped onto a small bonfire in what used to be the village center.

I'd heard of villages being attacked by Changed Ones. Some of the Casters had gone missing—Petra said that they were called Shadow Family. It was all part of the prophecy of the golden army. Perhaps this was one of the villages that had been attacked.

If so, then why had the Changed Ones returned?

Shujaa stepped out of a nearby hut. On reflex, I scanned the scene to find a safe place to hide. That was when I caught a glimpse of my body. Or rather, I saw what wasn't there. Looking down, I found myself to be as transparent as a ghost. There was no need for me to hide. All the same, I noticed how everyone kept a safe distance from Shujaa. His powers to disorient must work at all times.

So I didn't need to conceal myself, but I'd keep a safe distance all the same.

Shujaa marched toward the bonfire. The flickering light reflected off his armor. Wren was next to step out of the shadows. She stopped a few arm's lengths away from Shujaa. With her spiky hair and short build, Wren could easily be mistaken for his child. I remembered the wasps inside her, though. Wren was a grown woman and a killer.

"Would you like me to hold one of your gauntlets?" she asked.

Shujaa chuckled. "You're forever trying to steal yourself a bit of a totem."

Wren laughed along with him. "Would it be so bad if I had just one gauntlet? Really?"

"Most of the power comes from the helm, not the

gauntlets." Shujaa's gravelly voice lowered. "But if you touch any bit of the armor that Viktor gave me, I'll cut off your hands. Do we understand each other?"

"Of course." Wren laughed again, but the sound was forced.

Shujaa kicked at the ground. "My Changed Ones took down this place a month ago. I was told that everyone who escaped already went crying to the King. Now, our scouts tell me that there are still good candidates around. Why do they think someone is still here?"

Wren opened her mouth. A wasp flew out and landed on her finger. "The information came from one of my wasps. You stung someone here yesterday, didn't you?" She petted the wasp with her pinky. "It was a villager who returned to her hidey hole."

"And she's a good candidate?"

"The right age and very little magick. She'll be perfect."

Shujaa stared down at the mud and his eyes widened. Leaning over, he picked up burned-out scrap of tapestry. "They did needlework in this village?" A note of awe lightened his deep voice.

"I suppose they did." Wren's gaze slowly travelled between Shujaa and the scrap of fabric. She giggled. "I heard an outrageous story about you and sewing, you know."

Shujaa touched the stitching reverently. "What story?" His voice had a far-off sound.

"The tale goes like this. It says you were once a scrawny lad, and you admired tapestries, of all things." Wren pointed at the fabric Shujaa clutched. "But then at the age of thirteen, the gods blessed you with great height and a warrior's taste for battle."

Shujaa shrugged. "That story happens to be true." He

stepped over to the fire and tossed the scrap into the flames. "It was many years ago, though." He stared into the flames for a moment before focusing on Wren once more. "Speak of it to me or anyone else ever again, and I'll stuff you with nails until you burst. Understood?"

Wren paled. "Yes, my future King."

Bile crept up my throat. Shujaa stood in the remains of a village that his Changed Ones had destroyed, but his largest concern was that no one would ever find out that he liked tapestries as a child. And this was the man who wanted to be King. The thought sent a shiver across my shoulders.

A woman's scream broke the night air. Across the clearing, a group of Changed Ones tore up the bamboo beams that made up the flooring from one of the huts. A second later, they dragged a young woman out of the ground. She looked to be about my age with brown hair and blue eyes. Her leathers hung loosely on her frame. Two of the jaguar Changed Ones dragged her over to Shujaa and Wren. She kicked and howled the entire way.

"Let me go! You're nothing but Viktor's pets. Abominations!"

My stomach twisted with worry. What were they going to do to this girl?

The Changed Ones held her up to Shujaa. The girl stopped struggling. She eyed his purple armor and gasped. "It's you... The prophecy."

Shujaa grinned, and his face again seemed to gleam with moonlight. "I am your rightful King."

"But what are you doing with these monsters?" the girl asked. "You're the one who's going to save us."

"You're right," said Shujaa in his deep voice. "I will save you and fulfill the prophecy. But before I can do that, I have other tasks I must complete first. The Changed Ones are a means to an end. Someone needs to burn down the villages and find good candidates from my army. It can't be me, now can it? My people can never suspect that I am allied so closely with the Changed Ones and Viktor. Plus, I certainly can't be seen doing this."

His helm glowed with purple light. Anxiety tightened across my chest. Whatever magick Viktor had loaded into that armor, it did more than simply protect Shujaa from fireballs and other forms of attack.

Purple light gleamed off the helm, highlighting the dark runes carved over its surface. The words were in Necromancer code and read "Viktor Eternal." I hugged my elbows. You didn't name something after the Eternal lands unless it was a totem of massive power.

The girl had stopped struggling. Instead, she merely stared at the helm, her face slack with awe.

Tendrils of violet smoke wound down Shujaa's arm. He grasped the girl by the throat, and she collapsed onto her knees beside him. His gauntlet flared with purple light as he held her upright. All the while, the girl simply stared at Shujaa with glassy-eyed calm. She was too close to Shujaa now; the disorientation must have taken over her mind.

A spirit then appeared by Shujaa's free hand. This time, it was a man who was kneeling on Shujaa's right side. Since the ghost was transparent, his spectral body was hard to see in the moonlight. My eyes soon adjusted to the play of shadow in the see-through body. After that, every part of my soul turned numb with shock.

Rowan's ghost was kneeling beside Shujaa.

Now, it was possible for a Necromancer to detach a spirit from a living person's body, but it wasn't easy magick. I began to see why Viktor needed an entire suit of armor to hold all the spells he'd intended. According to Shujaa, the helm stored the most powerful magick of all. I didn't even want to imagine what spells were loaded in that thing.

Shujaa wrapped his right hand around Rowan's spectral throat. Rowan's spirit struggled against the grasp, but his motions were sluggish and random. Even as a ghost, Shujaa could disorient someone. As Shujaa gripped Rowan's neck, the gauntlet glowed with purple light.

It took everything in me not to scream.

Now Shujaa had both the girl and spirit-Rowan kneeling on either side of him. It was an image I'd never forget.

Suddenly, crimson lines of power and light appeared on Rowan's ghostly skin. Like tiny streams, Rowan's red Caster energy poured up to his neck and into Shujaa's grip. The gauntlet glowed more brightly than ever before as it became charged with Rowan's magick and strength.

Bile crept into my throat. This was the same kind of thing that had happened when Rowan and I had sent Viktor into exile. Rowan gave me some of his magick, and I changed that into hybrid power to send Viktor away. Now, Viktor had left behind this armor and Shujaa to wield it. Tears welled in my eyes. The same tactic Rowan and I used to defeat Viktor was now being turned on us.

Rowan was growing ill and losing his life force, just as the prophecy predicted.

This is precisely how it was happening.

Why hadn't Rowan told me anything about it? Did he realize what Shujaa was even doing to him?

The purple light moved across Shujaa's chest. It then slammed into the girl and transformed her. Small golden beetles appeared on her wrists and neck. The creatures multiplied. Soon the girl was entirely encased in a shifting mass of tiny golden insects.

The beetles solidified into a smooth casing that covered the girl entirely. She appeared taller and more fit. Her skin took on a metallic sheen. Her body became encased in golden armor with only her head visible. And every one of her features—eyes, nose, and mouth—were now gone. Her face was as smooth as a skipping stone.

Shujaa had used Rowan's magick to transform someone into a golden warrior.

And he'd used a totem from Viktor to do it.

My Necromancer mind wanted me to analyze what all of this meant. Shujaa had said he'd been hiding his true identity as the leader of the Changed Ones, so who did the Casters think he really was? But my Zuchtlos nature only wanted one thing: Shujaa's hand off Rowan's throat.

It wasn't even a contest, really. I drew Necromancer power into my body, focused it into casting arm, and raced straight for Shujaa. There wasn't enough time to speak a formal incantation, but I did get enough power in my arm to enhance my punch. I cocked my fist and rammed it straight into Shujaa's jaw. The man went flying backward. He lost his grip on Rowan's ghostly throat as well as the newly transformed golden warrior.

All the Changed Ones turned to me, their faces slack with shock. I was now visible, and that was fine with me. I still had some power left over in my body, so I could use the pause to speak my incantation.

"Sharp as a razor
Forced from bone"

Blue smoke materialized around my palm and then solidi-fied into a large ball made of bone. I finished my incantation.

"Give me a weapon
Strong as stone"

The ball burst apart into a thousand bits of bone. The razor-sharp parts went flying into everyone. The Changed Ones roared as the bone bomb tore into their skin. The golden warrior stood tall and unmoving. None of my bones caused so much as a scratch. I saved that thought for later; these golden warriors wouldn't be easy to fight.

I focused on Shujaa. Wren circled nearby as he curled on the ground, howling in pain and rage. Rowan's ghost was nowhere to be seen. I took that as a good sign. Spirits of the living always went back to their host's body as soon as they were able.

Shujaa pointed his gauntleted hand in my direction. "Wren, take care of this!"

Wren rounded on me. Tears streamed down her filthy face. She raised her right arm; the veins in her hand glowed red. My mind raced through all the waspy Caster counter-spells she might try.

Instead, there were no wasps involved at all. Red smoke curled around my feet. Wren was casting a transporter spell. I didn't know where she was sending me, but I didn't want to visit. I thought the word to activate my own totem ring from Tristan.

"Transport."

A moment later, I found myself back in my chambers at Rowan's castle. I wanted to race and find Rowan. Was he all right? I took a step toward the door, but my legs turned wobbly beneath me. My vision blurred as the intense need for sleep overwhelmed me. This wasn't an effect of Shujaa's this time. All the casting and transport had simply taken its toll.

It was all I could do to collapse onto the bed and pass out.

I awoke to the sound of Jicho calling my name. "Elea? Elea?" Sunlight streamed through the open windows. Long shadows crept across the floor. It must be late afternoon.

The door rattled as Jicho knocked on it again. "Are you all right?"

Sitting up, I yawned and rubbed my eyes. "I'm fine, Jicho. I was just very tired and slept in today." I slid out of bed and adjusted my robe. There was no sign of dirt on the garment. It was like I hadn't been at the Caster village last night. "You can come in, if you like."

The door swung open. Jicho stood on the threshold in his red robes. "Do you want a tour of the castle?"

"I'd like to see Rowan."

"He's not here today. Another village was attacked by Changed Ones last night. They killed all the guards and everything." Jicho shivered. "Rowan went to check things out and look for any survivors."

"Is he safe and well?"

"Oh, he's fine. I saw him myself before he left."

"I can help him." I strode over to one of the bureaus and pulled open the doors, hoping to find a pair of fresh Caster leathers. No matter what, I would never wear that yellow dress again.

Jicho leaned against the doorframe and grinned his gap-toothed smile. "He said you'd say that."

I stopped. "Let me guess. He wants me to stay here where it's safe. I should rest up and prepare for the engagement ceremony tonight."

Jicho let out a low whistle. "Are you a Seer?"

"No, I just know your brother."

Jicho's grin widened. "So, what do you say to that tour?"

Now that I knew Rowan was safe and nowhere I could see him, my legs felt wobbly again. It had been a rough past few days. Still, I couldn't pass up the chance to talk some more with Jicho. He gave me all sorts of information before without meaning to. "That sounds like a great idea."

Jicho narrowed his eyes. "You look tired."

"I'm fine."

"Rowan said that if you looked tired and still wanted to follow me around, then I should tell you something."

Now it was my turn to narrow my eyes. "What?" Rowan was far too sneaky for his own good.

"He's cast an aegis on me. I can't talk about things that give away secrets, even if I don't mean to."

"Oh."

Jicho wagged his finger at me. "I told him every word of our talk yesterday. Rowan said you were playing Necromancer mind games. So I told him to cast an aegis on me. Now I can't tell you anything, even by mistake. I can't even—" The words stopped in his throat. A soft red light glowed on his tongue. He pointed at his mouth. "See? Isn't it wonderful? Rowan's the most powerful Caster in all our history."

My shoulders slumped. "I don't doubt it."

"So, do you still want that tour? Remember, you can't trick me today. It has to be a real tour." Jicho bobbed a little on the balls of his feet. "And you look awfully sleepy. There are these big old bags around your eyes and everything."

I'd been found out and we both knew it.

"Come to think of it, I am rather tired. I think I'll rest today and go to the ceremony later. Will you accompany me there?"

"I'm not old enough yet, and people might think we're...You know."

"We're what?"

A little blush lightened his cheeks. "They might think we're courting."

"Ah, I see." He was so cute I wanted to pinch his cheeks.

"But Philippe can take you there. And I'll see you when you arrive and all. Rowan says you can be seen with Philippe since no one will believe he's serious about courting anyone. Rowan would take you, but you don't have..." Jicho screwed up his face like he was trying very hard to remember something. "An official standing in the Imperial family yet."

"I understand. Philippe will be fine to walk me to the engagement ceremony."

"Did you notice he said 'yet?' Because I noticed that he said 'yet,' and I also noticed that I can tell you he said 'yet,' which means that's not affected by the aegis and he really wants you to know that."

In this moment, it was impossible not to smile at Jicho. "I noticed."

"Good news. Bye then." Jicho slammed the door shut, and I heard the drumroll of his light footsteps racing down the hallway. I'm sure he had many things that he'd rather do today than give me tours of the castle.

I stared down at my hand. My ring from Petra was still there. It still had a transport or two left in it, and you never knew when those would come in handy, so I kept it on. The ring from Tristan remained as well. I decided to stow that somewhere safe. It was used up, so when I had time, I could look into reloading it with more painless transfer spells. The magick would be easier to replicate than build from scratch. I might even try loading some other spells on there, too.

I had a feeling that I'd need a lot more spells before this adventure was over. Shujaa didn't strike me as the type to get punched in the face and forget about it.

$\mathcal{I}$ stood inside my chamber, staring into a shiny stone that acted as my full-length mirror. For the last hour, I'd been sending away servants. All of them wanted to help me wash, dress, or otherwise get ready for tonight's ceremony. As a Necromancer, I'd never needed anyone else's help to dress, so I'd gotten ready solo. Any minute now, Philippe would stop by and escort me to the engagement event.

If I were wise, I'd use this time to plan what questions I'd ask Philippe. I still needed more information. Unfortunately, I couldn't focus on anything but my own reflection. I was dressed in the so-called gown that Rowan's mother had chosen for me. Unfortunately, I'd had bathing togs that covered more skin.

In fact, this outfit was so awful, I now felt guilty for all the terrible things I'd said about my banana dress. At least, that thing was an actual garment with seams and stitching. This Caster gown was nothing but two leather scraps tied around my chest and waist. That was it. No undergarments. No jewelry. And there was nowhere to hide my mating band, so I kept it hidden under my pillow. Not wearing that band really bothered me, and it bothered me that it bothered me, if that made sense.

I worried my lower lip with my teeth. Why had Rowan's mother chosen this particular gown? Did she want me to leave the mating band behind? If so, how could she have possibly known about it in the first place? I'd never told anyone about the specifics of our ceremony, not even Petra.

I frowned. There was also the distinct possibility that Rowan's mother was trying to embarrass me. I pinched the bridge of my nose. *Be kind, Elea.* Why was I ruling out the option that this dress was appropriate and Rowan's mother was simply being thoughtful?

Oh, yes. That's right. Rowan's mother was mean as a snake. She'd selected this gown with a motive. I just needed to figure out her scheme.

A knock sounded. I pulled a light blanket off the bed and wrapped it around my shoulders. "Who is it?"

"Philippe."

Exhaling with relief, I pulled the wooden door open. Philippe stood in the outer hallway, wearing his finest black velvet longcoat, breeches, and high boots. I waggled my finger at him. "Not fair! Why do you get to wear actual clothing?"

He gave me a roguish grin. "What an odd way to start a conversation. May I enter?"

"Please." I stepped back and gripped the fuzzy blanket even more tightly. "Explain yourself. Why are you in a jacket?"

Philippe shot me a pointed look. "I'm fine, Elea. Thank you so much for asking. I've been spending quality time with my sister and her evil harpy of a friend, Veronique."

I closed my eyes and tried to organize my thoughts. Philippe had a point. He hadn't been getting letters from Amelia, which was why he'd crossed the continents to see her. All sorts of awful things could be at work here. I needed to set my wardrobe worries aside. "You're quite right. How is Amelia?"

"She's in one of her more belligerent frames of mind. Veronique has been brainwashing her."

"Veronique? Really?"

"She can be very convincing when she chooses." An intense look flickered in Philippe's eyes. I'd seen that same glimmer in Rowan's gaze before. The look was somewhere between love and desire, but it was gone so quickly, I couldn't know for certain. Philippe was once again his suave self. "Thanks to Veronique, my sister is now convinced that she needs a protector."

"Meaning Rowan." I hated how that thought made my insides churn with jealousy.

"Quite right. Amelia believes that she needs this marriage in order to be safe." He raked his hand though his blond hair. "Honestly, it's Veronique who wants the protector, and she's barraging Amelia with lies in order to get one."

My eyes widened. "Veronique is trying to seduce Rowan?"

"Heavens, no. The man's far too noble for anything like that. On the contrary, Veronique is merely wise enough to realize that being the best friend of a Queen is a rather fine spot in society. Far better than a dungeon, for example. She's just telling my sister what she needs to hear in order to become a belligerent and somewhat crazed brat on the subject."

I pictured how Veronique looked when I'd rescued her from the Vicomte's dungeon. She was skeletally thin and covered in blood. People had gone through far less and done much worse to get a crown. "So what exactly has Veronique been telling your sister?"

"That you knew who Rowan was all along, and by employing your womanly wiles, you seduced him away from his true love, Amelia." Philippe frowned. "I'm afraid my sister is rather angry with you for betraying her."

"What? I have no womanly wiles."

Philippe rolled his eyes. "I didn't say it was a logical story. Did I mention that the two of them are rather insane and spending far too much time together?"

"Even so, Amelia can't be that crazy, can she?"

Philippe winced. That wasn't a good sign.

My voice raised an octave. "Doesn't she remember how I saved her life? Amelia was almost squashed by ta falling beam in the battle with Viktor. I pushed her out of the way and took the hit myself. If I hadn't gotten magically healed, I could have died."

"Be that as it may, you and Rowan have genuine feelings for each other."

That was the truth, and it quieted my anger quickly. "So Amelia is convinced that I'm still trying to steal away Rowan's heart and her safety net."

"Yes, unfortunately."

I shook my head. "I still find that hard to believe. That's not my Amelia." She was one of the most independent people I knew.

"But she's been through a lot. And don't forget, the Vicomte is dead."

"I remember." *I was the one who killed him.*

"Quite right. And although the man was a monster, the

Vicomte spent an inordinate amount of time building up Amelia's self-image only to squash it in the dust, over and over. His death is having a massive impact on her. She's like a drowning woman grabbing on to anything to stay afloat."

A weight of sadness settled into my limbs. It was one thing to suspect that your dear friend hated you and was miserable to boot. It was quite another to have her brother confirm it. "Will either of them be at this ceremony tonight? I'd like a chance to explain myself face-to-face."

"No, that would necessitate them leaving their sanctuary of a tower. They're both locking themselves in there until they achieve their aim."

"What are they doing? Planning the wedding?"

"Not exactly. It seems that lover boy is stalling on setting a date."

It was on the tip of my tongue to ask why, but I was able to stop myself in time. After all, it was none of my business when Rowan and Amelia got married. I needed to change the subject. "In any case, thank you for accompanying me tonight."

"I was looking forward to it. However, I'm starting to wonder if the event is a costume party. How are you dressed under that blanket?"

"It's not a costume party. They merely gave me some... Odd things as garments."

"I've seen the things the ladies around here wear. Or don't wear, as the case may be."

I peeped under my blanket. "So this is normal for Caster culture?"

"Let me ask you one question."

"All right."

"Is your chest bare?"

"No!"

"Then whatever it is, it's extremely conservative for Caster culture."

"You're lying to me."

Philippe chuckled. "Would I lie about fashion?"

I kicked at the floor with my sandal. "I suppose not."

Philippe stepped closer and tugged on the edge of the blanket. "May I please see this dress of yours? You know I'll be honest."

"And if I look awful, what will we do then?"

"I'll say you're sick and can't attend."

"But I promised Rowan."

Philippe rolled his eyes once more. "Drop the blanket, Elea."

It took a force of will, but I let go of my grip on the fuzzy fabric. The blanket fell into a pool around my feet. Philippe's face became unreadable.

"So I look awful, don't I?"

"By the gods." He stepped up and set his hands on my bare shoulders. The touch was warm and centering. "You're even more lovely than before."

At that moment, the door flew open, and Veronique stomped into the room. To my surprise, she looked much recovered from the last time I'd seen her. In fact, she was almost perfectly back to the girl I'd first met on the wagon ride over to the Midnight Cloister: tall, willowy, and loud-mouthed. From her time in the Vicomte's dungeons, only the barest hints of silver scars could be made out on her skin.

Philippe tugged me against his side. "Why, hello, Vee. How shocking of you to leave your tower."

Veronique wore a blue gown that contrasted nicely with

the red splotches that had just appeared on her cheeks. "I...You...Elea."

I debated stepping away from Philippe. After all, this was a lot of touching for a Necromancer. However, it seemed to be upsetting Veronique, so I stayed put and remained calm. "Greetings, Veronique. So nice to see you."

She rounded on Philippe. "You cad."

Philippe merely arched his brows. "Harpy."

I waved at her. "Remember me? The one who saved you from having your soul sucked out by the evil Vicomte? You're welcome for that, by the way."

Veronique kept right on ignoring me and yelling at Philippe. "I see your evil plan. Amelia and I are going after the Caster King, so you're pursuing the Tsarina."

I lifted my chin. "He's not pursuing me." *Not really, anyway.*

"Ha!" Veronique turned to me, her voice rising to a screech. "Are you two betrothed?"

Now, I'd seen Veronique throw her share of screaming fits over all sorts of things: the lack of silk sheets at the Cloister, the poor quality of meals...The list went on and on. But I must admit, I did not see that question coming.

"I'll answer that." Philippe pulled me even more tightly against his side. "Yes. We're engaged."

Veronique's eyes narrowed. "Betrothed or engaged? I know the difference, you liar."

The hair on my neck stood on end. *Betrothed versus engaged?*

"What's the difference?" I asked.

Veronique glared at me. "Don't play games." She focused on Philippe. "If you're betrothed, then where's her ring?"

"She lost it." Philippe looked down on me indulgently. "Didn't you, love?"

Veronique's pretty mouth thinned to an angry line. "You're lying."

"And you'd know a lie," retorted Philippe.

In all the drama, I'd almost forgotten the question I needed to ask. Now, it came back to me with clarity. "You two said something about the difference between betrothed versus engaged. I'd like you to explain it to me. Now."

"You didn't tell her?" Veronique grinned. "Philippe stayed with you for months, and yet, he didn't tell you?" She tilted back her head and laughed. It took everything in me not to cast a bone melter spell on her right then and there. Veronique refocused on Philippe. "This is just like how you didn't tell me about Mimi Sue La Fonte."

"Mimi Sue was a woman of loose morals. I was young and stupid. Can you blame a fellow?"

Things were getting out of control again. I'd forgotten how tricky it was to manage Veronique when she was in a snit. "Enough, you two. What's this betrothed versus engaged?"

"Ask Amelia," said Veronique. "She's going to the engagement ceremony."

Philippe's eyes lit with rage. "You allowed that?"

"I tried to stop her. So did Kade. That's why I came here to find you, so you could help us hold her in the tower. Your sister's not stable, you know. And if she goes to that ceremony? I don't know what will happen." Veronique chewed her thumbnail. "She could snap."

Amelia having a breakdown? It was serious indeed. "Maybe I should go with you."

"Please, no!" Veronique gasped. "If she sees you now, she'll crack for certain."

Philippe moved to stand over Veronique. "If she's close to breaking, you're the one who made her that way."

Veronique's lower lip wobbled. "I was trapped in a dungeon, Phi. Amelia was kept captive for years by the Vicomte. If I've been pushing her, it was only so we'd have some security in our lives."

"Will someone please talk to me?" My voice was rising with anger, which as a Necromancer, I really shouldn't allow. That said, I wasn't sure I cared anymore.

Philippe stepped toward the door. "We will find Amelia immediately." He paused and turned to face me. "Where was I? Right. You look lovely. Now go down the stairs and through your first door on the right. There's a large meeting hall. You can't miss it. I need to preserve my sister's sanity now. Ta."

I stepped into his path, blocking him. "Philippe, what does it mean, engaged versus betrothed?"

Philippe sighed. "Vee here is right. I didn't explain the difference, and that was a lie of omission on my part. But I only did it so you'd fall in love with me."

My exasperation transformed into an intense desire to get them gone. "You know what?" I stepped aside. "You both can leave. Now."

Veronique glowered. "Welcome to my world, Elea. This man is a foul villain."

Philippe's gaze lit up with a combination of anger and something else. "And you're a brainwashing harpy."

With that, the two of them sped down the hallway and out of sight. All of a sudden my dress—or the lack of it—didn't bother me so much anymore. My mind felt foggy as I left my chamber. Every step toward the ceremony felt like I was moving closer to some kind of nightmare.

Betrothed versus engaged? What was I about to discover, exactly?

My head turned foggy with dread. What kind of difference could there possibly be? As I rounded on the first door on the right, I came to a solemn conclusion.

Whatever the difference was, I felt certain that I wouldn't like it.

13

J waited at the entrance of large meeting hall. The engagement ceremony would take place here. For some reason, I couldn't force my legs to walk more than a step or two inside. Instead, I merely admired the view.

The walls were covered in tapestries of scenes from Caster history. In one spot, a past Genesis Rex rode into battle on a massive black bear. Nearby, a circle of Seers lifted their arms to receive visions. Farther off, a Caster hunter prayed over the body of a slain deer. The room itself was packed. Casters were everywhere—men, women, and children alike. The chatter of many voices filled the air.

All of a sudden, Jicho stepped out from the crowd. He was still wearing his long red robes, and I envied him that. "Greetings, Elea."

"Hello, Jicho."

"I have bad news." His round face drooped into a frown. "You have to call me Jax now. Mother says I can't use my traditional Caster name anymore. That's reserved for special people."

An order from Rowan's mother? That wasn't high on my list of things to follow. "How about I still call you Jicho?"

He instantly brightened. "Yes, please do."

"May I ask you a question?" On reflex, I pulled on my wrap skirt as if hoping some additional folds of materials would appear out of nowhere.

"Whatever you wish."

"Are there any Caster leathers around that I can change into? I feel rather awkward."

Jicho stared at me as if I were insane. "But you're the ruler of your people, right?"

"Yes." *As far as you know.*

"So, that's what rulers wear to an engagement ceremony. Mother can be evil, but she's a stickler for ceremony."

"Ah." My heart sank. I was truly hoping I could change outfits. Still, I could put this time with Jicho to good use. "I need you to tell me something. What's the difference between an engage—"

At that moment, the ear-splitting peals of drums boomed through the chamber. I almost jumped, but the crowd didn't seem upset at all. Instead, they settled down to sit on the stone floor. Evidently, the ceremony was about to begin. I leaned in closer to Jicho. "As I was saying, I really need to know about the difference betw—"

"Shh." Jicho pointed to the far wall, and I followed his gesture. I hadn't noticed this before, but there was a stage on the opposite side of the room. It held four thrones. The largest one was huge, made of gold, and set far apart from the others. The remaining three were progressively smaller in size and made from silver, bronze, and pewter. The meaning seemed clear to me.

Four thrones for four brothers: Storm, Rowan, Kade, and Jicho.

At the back of the stage, there stood dozens of Casters pounding out ever-faster rhythms on log drums. The beat reverberated through my chest.

Then, the drums stopped, and Rowan stepped onto the stage.

My breath caught at the sight of him. Mostly because he was wearing nothing but a leather kilt, lace-up sandals, and a golden crown. Sure, he was also wearing a long red cloak, but it was clasped at his throat and tossed over his shoulders, so it didn't hide his bare chest or thighs. Not that I was staring.

Fine. I was looking a little bit.

Perhaps it was more like a lot.

That said, who cared if I gawped at Rowan? I could be conflicted about him and still appreciate his beauty. If the spirit attack from Shujaa affected him, he certainly didn't show it.

Rowan stepped to the center of the stage and raised his right fist. The movement highlighted a red ribbon that was tied around his wrist. I'd seen that before—at the engagement ceremony between Rowan and Amelia. At the time, a red ribbon had been around Rowan and Amelia's hands. And now, he was wearing it.

That doesn't seem to be a good sign.

"My people," announced Rowan. "Tonight, we review our engagements. This sacred ceremony preserves our oral traditions and laws. By honoring it, we hold to the true Caster way." He scanned the crowd. Immediately, his gaze locked with mine. I could almost picture the arcs of emotion moving between us. My pulse sped.

Rowan lowered his arm to gesture toward me. "We have with us a special guest: Elea of Braddock, the Tsarina of the Necromancers. She is welcome to sit on the golden throne of my own brother Storm, the chair that has sat empty for so long."

All eyes turned to me. I supposed I should say something, but I was still trying to think through the implications of Rowan's speech. Storm's golden chair had sat empty? Why was that, exactly? Rowan was King; he should sit there. Unless they were still holding that throne for his brother Storm? My heart sank a little at the thought. Rowan had said that Storm ran away. How sad to be saving his throne for so many years.

There wasn't any more time to analyze. Jicho grabbed my hand and began dragging me through the crowd. Before I knew it, I was walking up a short flight of stairs and onto the stage. My mind became a blank as I strode toward Rowan. Curse the gods, the man was smirking.

How I hated him.

Definitely.

Possibly.

Honestly, I had no idea what to think anymore.

Jicho bowed low at the waist before his brother. "Genesis Rex, I present to you the Tsarina Elea of Braddock."

A dimple appeared on one side of Rowan's crooked grin. It really wasn't fair that a man like Rowan got both dimples and a beautiful body. It meant the gods shortchanged someone else miserably. "Greetings, Tsarina."

There was definitely some kind of formal statement I should make now, but for the life of me, all I could think about was his silly dimple. "Hello."

Rowan gestured toward the golden throne. "Would you like to have a seat?"

My eyes bulged with alarm. "I'll stand." On reflex, I yanked at the edges of my skirt again. What kind of people placed their royalty in kilts and sarongs without underwear and then made them sit on high thrones so everything was visible at eye level? This was thoughtless at best.

"I understand." Rowan gave me the barest of winks, which meant he really did get why I was uncomfortable. I maybe loved him a little for that.

Or liked him a lot.

Or disliked him less.

Really, I had no idea what I felt.

"Thank you," I managed to say.

"You're most welcome. I always like to stand for these ceremonies myself."

"Well, I'm sitting down," announced Jicho. He stomped across the stage and plunked down into the smallest throne. Did I mention that I envied him his long robes? I did.

Rowan turned to face the audience. "Will the Hadithi declare today's engagements?"

For the first time, I noticed how the men and women near the stage wore green robes. They weren't Seers—those robes were black—but they certainly must be here to do something official. One gray-haired man stood, straightened his robes, and began a long speech in his reedy voice. He was using the ancient language of Nyumbani, so I couldn't understand too much. I did catch a bunch of names and dates, however. I guessed this man was some kind of record-keeper, which made sense since Rowan talked about their oral culture. Necromancers wrote everything down.

Eventually, the elder man sat down once more. After that, a young couple rose from the back of the chamber and stepped forward. She was a tall warrior woman with long auburn hair. The man was short and squat with a shaved head.

Once they reached the stage, the pair stopped. For the first time, I noticed how there weren't any guards around. I didn't like it. This close up, I could see the lines of fatigue around Rowan's eyes. He might require extra help in case of trouble. And I really needed to find out what was ailing him.

Rowan focused on the man first. "What is your engagement about, Caster Felix?"

Felix lifted his right arm, and a red scrap of fabric was tied about his wrist. "I was engaged to give sixty cows to the family of Darkfire by this past harvest."

My world stopped. *He was engaged...To give cows?*

I pulled on my earlobe. Perhaps I'd heard him wrong. It had been a long day, and I was in a strange place. I wouldn't be the first person to mishear something in such a situation.

Rowan gestured toward the woman. "Caster Ember, has this man made good on his promise?"

Ember glared at Felix. "No, the fool hasn't delivered a single cow."

My skin prickled over in awareness. I wasn't hearing things. Engagements seemed to be something very different in Caster culture. My mind reeled with the implications. Rowan had said his engagement to Amelia was for something called the Sword of Theodora. Had Amelia promised that in exchange for his protection? If that was the case, how could Amelia have gotten so confused that they were due to be married?

"I see," said Rowan. "Hadithi, and what was the agreement if the engagement had failed?"

The elder man rose again. "She may take him as a slave for four years or as her husband for a lifetime."

Felix pulled on the neckline of his leathers. "I am an important man in my clan. I can't be taken away. Ember must agree to wed me."

Ember scanned Felix from head to toe. "I'll take four years of your labor, and your family will thank me for taking your lazy carcass of their hands."

"My King," pleaded Felix. "This isn't fair."

Rowan's gaze swept across the room. "Are any of your family members here to plead on your behalf?"

All the blood seemed to drain from Felix's face. "No."

Ember folded her arms over her chest. "I'll take my slave now."

"So mote it be," said Rowan.

The Hadithi walked up to Felix and untied the scrap of fabric from the man's wrist. "Caster Felix, you may return to this chamber in four years. If your service has been completed, you may take back this symbol of your engagement." Turning to Ember, he tied the fabric onto her wrist instead. A small cloud of red mist engulfed Ember's hand. For a moment, the fabric's threads glowed red with power. After that, the mist and brightness both disappeared. The spell was cast.

Thus began a long litany of people coming forward. Sometimes one or two Casters, sometimes many more. They discussed the terms of their engagements and the status. I had lots of time to contemplate Rowan's engagement for the Sword of Theodora. As much as I hated to admit it, it was a wise move to secure that weapon. The Sword of Theodora could kill anything.

Including Viktor.

And of course, Shujaa.

The more I thought about it, the more confused I became.

So many questions still remained. If this were merely a kind of trade, then why did Amelia insist they were truly betrothed?

As if drawn by my thoughts, Amelia swept into the room. All the air seemed to get sucked out of the chamber.

One thing I had to give Amelia—her eyes may have had the glazed look of someone dancing on the edge of sanity, but her clothing was flawless. She'd donned one of her puffy pink dresses that was trimmed with every kind of lace and flounce. Despite the jungle heat, her hair hung in perfect red ringlets to her shoulders. Her skin had no sheen of sweat. Her gaze locked on Rowan and me as she raised her voice. "What are the two of you doing here? And why are you both half naked?"

Worry pressed in around me, the feeling as tight as a vise. No question about it. This couldn't end well.

14

*A*melia stood at the back of the chamber, looking doll-like in her perfection…As long as you didn't focus on the crazed twitching around her eyes.

But besides that, perfect. I hadn't seen her in months, but it felt far longer than that. My heart ached to reconnect with my old friend. It seemed I was alone in my fascination, however.

While I was riveted to the sight of Amelia, the Caster audience barely glanced in her direction. Once she stepped into the room, most of the crowd began chattering amongst themselves. It was like Amelia was a familiar-yet-crazy aunt who interrupted things from time to time. She wasn't a threat. In fact, she wasn't even a subject of mild interest.

They certainly didn't treat her as a Queen. That seemed to support the theory that Amelia and Rowan weren't really betrothed, at least from the people's point of view.

Amelia, however, seemed to have a very different opinion. "You!" She pointed to Rowan. "You lied to me." Even from across the room, I could see the muscles twitching in her neck. She really did look a few seconds away from a total snap with reality. Where were Philippe, Veronique, and Kade? Weren't they all rushing around in order to stop this very incident from happening?

The gleam of a key shone from Amelia's hand. That explained things. Amelia was a genius when it came to anything mechanical. I'd no doubt that she figured out some clever way to lock everyone up. Back home, she'd built a door of gears to protect her inventions in the basement. After two months of living around here, I could only imagine what she'd been up to.

Amelia's face flushed with rage. "This is a ceremony of engagement, isn't it?" She stomped her foot. "That's why I'm here. Rowan was supposed to make good on *our* engagement."

The old balding Hadithi rose to stand once more. "I recall this engagement. Genesis Rex promised to ensure your safety. In exchange, you were supposed to provide the Sword of Theodora." His reedy voice deepened. "That weapon was due to be delivered two months ago."

At those words, the room fell silent. All eyes locked on Amelia. It seemed Amelia herself wasn't interesting to them, but the Sword of Theodora was a different matter. I was riveted as well, but for a different reason.

This is the moment. Would Amelia say that their engagement was only for the sword? Or would she insist on marriage again? It didn't matter what Rowan's people thought if he'd gone ahead and lied to Amelia.

"Let me explain something to you all," said Amelia. Her voice was steady and strong. "Our engagement was—"

All of a sudden, another figure stomped into the room. *Shujaa.* Like last night, he wore armor and a matching helm that gleamed with a purple hue. The way he confidently marched across the room, you wouldn't think he'd used evil magick from Viktor to transform some helpless girl the night before.

For a monster, he was certainly perfect looking.

Shujaa's deep voice echoed through the room. "Greetings. I have come to claim my engagement."

The crowd, which had been silent before, now broke into applause. Everyone started speaking at once.

"It's Shujaa at last," called one man.

"Save us," cried another.

"Where's your golden army?" asked a third.

Their voices grew so loud, my head hurt. It didn't seem possible. Shujaa was here, and it was the same situation as last night. The people not only knew him, but they thought this man was the answer to the prophecy about the golden army. What a mistake.

Rowan raised his arms. "Silence!" It took a few seconds, but the Casters finally fell quiet once more. Rowan's deep baritone voice boomed through the empty space. "Who comes before this gathering?"

Shujaa bowed slightly at the waist. "Why, none other than your own brother Storm, of course. These days I go by my traditional Caster name, Shujaa."

My mouth fell open with shock. *This can't be right.* Shujaa was Storm? I glanced over to Jicho, who had turned wide-eyed with fear. He got up from his small throne and raced over to hide behind Rowan. Whoever Shujaa claimed to be, Jicho was certainly afraid of him. But could Shujaa actually be Storm? That wasn't possible, was it?

Across the chamber, Amelia took few wobbling steps toward the exit archway. Shujaa's appearance seemed to upset her as much as it had Jicho. She disappeared from the room without another word. Plus, I couldn't help noticing that she was able to leave without actually delivering the Sword of Theodora. Again. I'd be frustrated to have been denied an answer about their engagement—yet again—but I had bigger things to worry about. Namely Shujaa. Or Storm. Whoever he was.

The reedy Hadithi stood. "Prove your identity. Prince Storm was taken from us long ago."

"Easily." Shujaa whipped off his helm. He had a golden hair, green eyes, and a jaw so square it could have been a block of granite. There was no denying the family resemblance. More cries erupted from the Caster audience.

"It's Storm at last!"

"We knew you'd come back to us."

"Save your people."

Shujaa raised his hands in a movement that asked for silence. The crowd grew quiet. "But I am more than merely your Shujaa returned." His gauntlets flared with purple light and hybrid magic. A heartbeat later, a swirl of violet smoke appeared beside Shujaa. When the haze cleared, a golden warrior stood in its place. The crowd instantly began to "ooh" and "ahh." I rubbed my forehead as if the motion would make this turn of events sink into my brain.

Shujaa was actually Storm, Rowan's older brother.

But whatever the name was, the people clearly loved Shujaa and thought he was the bringer of the prophesized golden army. *Huh.* I wondered if they'd feel that way if they knew what their Shujaa was really doing these days. I remembered the story Wren told about the young Storm loving tapestries and then later being a great warrior. He must have been a very different person at one time.

Shujaa stared at me, and a small grin curled the corners of his perfect mouth.

That made my restraint snap. I rounded on the audience and raised my voice. "You all love Shujaa, but how do you feel about Viktor and his Changed Ones?"

The temperature in the room seemed to drop instantly. Evidently, everyone hated Viktor. Excellent.

"The Changed Ones are raiding your villages. People are dying and disappearing, am I right?" The tension in the air turned even heavier. I was making headway with the crowd. "Well, Shujaa is wielding totems that Viktor created. You can all see how his gauntlets glow purple. The magick he uses to create this golden army is entirely evil."

Shujaa's small grin became a white-toothed smile. "Yes, I stole a totem from Viktor, but only to help my people." He gestured to his golden warriors. "Don't you think this is beautiful? The ancient prophecy is coming to life. The golden warriors are coming! How can we question the will of the gods?"

A sick feeling settled in my stomach. The golden warriors were actually made with Rowan's magick. I glanced over to him, but Rowan kept his face devoid of emotion as he stared forward. I wanted to scream that this was all mixed up, but I didn't know enough about Rowan's people to know if I'd only make things worse. And until I spoke to Rowan, I didn't feel right addressing his people again.

A few elderly Casters came up to examine the golden warrior, but Shujaa waved them off. "You may make your acquaintance with this warrior—and many more—in a very short time. Today, I am here for a different purpose. I hereby claim the engagement that is due any elder Prince. I challenge Genesis Rex for his throne."

The old Hadithi lifted his grizzled chin. "We'd need some time to validate that you are truly Storm."

"I'm Rowan's brother." Shujaa pointed to the gold throne. "Which means that chair is mine. That's all the validation you need."

The Hadithi ran his veined hand over his balding head. "But that means—"

"We all know what it means, my friend," said Rowan slowly. "If Shujaa wants this throne, he must fight me for it."

"To the death," said Shujaa. He seemed to particularly relish those words, and I hated him even more for that.

Rowan's face was stone. "Yes."

"I am stronger now, you know." Shujaa lifted his right hand, and the gauntlet there glowed with hybrid light.

"There is no need for dramatics, brother. I already accepted your challenge." Rowan's eyes narrowed. "But remember, there are no trinkets or totems allowed on the field of battle."

I didn't bother to hide my smile. *Well done, Rowan!* Without Viktor's armor, Shujaa would have to fight Rowan cleanly.

Jicho whimpered and buried his head in Rowan's thigh. My protective instincts took over any scrap of logic in my mind. I'd seen Shujaa in battle. There was no way I wanted Rowan anywhere near him, even without his magick armor.

I stepped forward. It didn't seem right to share that Shujaa was stealing magick from Rowan, but there were other ways I could derail this battle. "I am the Tsarina of the Necromancers. I thought you desired my throne, Shujaa. Why not fight me first?"

Shujaa's eyes glittered with excitement. I had the sinking feeling that whatever I had said just played into his bigger plan. "I think the Tsarina makes a generous offer." Shujaa gestured to Rowan. "Are you certain you can fight me? I hear you've been ill as of late. Perhaps if I fought the Tsarina first, it would give you time to recover."

A murmur rose up from the crowd. They seemed to think this was a good idea as well.

Fine. I'd rather fight this bully.

Rowan's mother stepped into the chamber. She looked timeless in her beauty and made a great show of pausing, staring, and gasping at Shujaa. She then rushed over and threw her arms around his neck. "My sweet boy has returned!"

The crowd cheered with joy as their embrace went on. I couldn't help but think that for someone who seemed so dark and evil before, Rowan's mother now appeared to be the picture of motherly love. "My people, do you remember the Battle of Jangwa? The Siege of Mlima? All the times my eldest son had fought for you? He battled in your name against the tribe of Eusi, the very savages who killed my uncle, the man who led our troops for decades. It was the mighty Shujaa carried our great general's body back from the field of battle. And no one suffered more than Shujaa when his father, our dear Aaden, died at the hands of Rowan. Only after the crown went to the current Genesis Rex" —there was no missing the sneer in her voice as she said the words Genesis Rex— "did Shujaa leave us on a pilgrimage to cleanse his soul of the foul deeds from his own blood relations." She didn't come out and say that Rowan was evil for killing his father, but everyone knew what she meant. I had no doubt if she was confronted, she'd say she referred to another Genesis Rex who did foul deeds, not Rowan.

I really and truly loathed her.

The back door slammed open. Kade marched into the room with Veronique, Philippe, and Amelia close behind.

Even across the chamber, I could see the gleam of the metal key that was still tightly gripped in Amelia's hand. *So that's where she had gone off to.* Amelia must have left in order to release Kade and the others. A little of the tightness left my chest. At least, my friend wasn't totally insane.

Kade stood before Shujaa, and I got the feeling he was definitely not in the "welcome home" camp. "Leave here," growled Kade. "Now."

"But you're too late, my sweet brother. Rowan has already agreed to fight me. We meet on the field of battle in one week. It is my right as eldest brother, after all." He raised his arm. A curl of purple smoke appeared around his right gauntlet. The violet cloud grew larger. Within seconds, the purple mist was gone and with it, so was Shujaa and his golden warrior.

A few seconds passed in stunned silence.

Then Rowan addressed the audience. "My people. Shujaa is not the man you remembered."

They didn't seem to agree. Angry cries rose up from the people.

"He cast a spell, just like the old days," said one.

"He can help us," shouted another.

Kade stepped forward and raised his arms. The crowd quieted again. "I, too, have fond memories of my brother. But when he was taken by Viktor, he was changed. He's not the man you think him."

In response, a low murmur sounded from audience. The people weren't paying attention to anything but blissful chatter about Shujaa. A large group of them had surrounded the Queen, congratulating her with happy tears.

"The ceremony is adjourned." Rowan turned to me and lowered his voice. I was the only one who could hear him speak. "Don't get involved, Elea. I brought you here to show you the truth about engagements. The rest is family trouble, and it's nothing I can't handle." Taking Jicho's hand, he walked off the stage.

There was no way he was leaving now. I followed right after him.

This whole time, Rowan had been telling me the truth. His engagement to Amelia didn't mean they were going to get married. He didn't love her. Even so, there were still so many blanks. Why didn't Rowan tell me about Shujaa and the fact that his own brother was draining his life force?

More then ever, I needed to understand the big picture.

And now? I was getting answers. No matter what.

15

Rowan pulled open a door on the far right of the stage. I rushed to follow him, but someone grabbed my wrist from behind, stopping me.

It was Amelia. Tears were streaming down her pale cheeks. I wasn't sure whether to jump for joy or scream with frustration.

"I'm so sorry, Elea. I've made such a mess of things. Can we talk?"

I watched the door shut and Rowan disappear. Part of me wanted to tell Amelia it was her turn to be patient, but I couldn't forget Philippe's warnings about how unstable she'd become. This was my dear friend, in tears, and asking for my help.

Getting the truth from Rowan could wait.

"Sure. My chambers aren't far, if you'd like to go there."

"That would be perfect."

I walked back through the crowd to the main exit archway,

scanning the room for familiar faces. "Where are Kade, Veronique, and Philippe?"

"I asked them to give us some time alone."

As we started back toward my room, I couldn't help but notice that a certain someone was following along behind us. "You said you asked Kade to leave you?"

"I did. I don't want to fight with him anymore."

"He seems to still be following us."

Amelia glanced over her shoulder, and her entire body shook with rage. "Ignore him. That's what I do."

"But Philippe says you and Kade fight."

Amelia sniffed. "I didn't say it was what I *always* did. Ignoring him is a new strategy for me."

"How is it working out?"

"I just came up with the plan two seconds ago. Give it some time."

We were within a few steps of the door when Kade slipped in front of us, blocking access to the room. He looked so much like a younger version of Rowan, I had the urge to run off and find the real thing. However, I couldn't pass up this chance to talk to Amelia.

"What's wrong?" The way Amelia asked the question, I got the feeling she knew exactly what the problem might be.

"I can't allow the two of you to talk."

"That's fascinating, Kade. Get out of my way."

"If you're talking to Elea, I'm joining you. Rowan gave orders."

"He can't order me around." Amelia lifted her chin. "I'm breaking off the engagement."

"Why don't we all three go inside and discuss this?" I gestured to the door. "You first, Kade."

Kade glowered at Amelia. "Any more tricks?"

"I won't lock you up again, I swear." Amelia smiled innocently.

"Fine." The way Kade spoke the word, it came out as more of a grunt.

The three of us had no sooner entered the room than Amelia gripped my hand. "I need your help. I must have a protector."

I sighed. This must be what happens when you spend too much time with Veronique as your friend. "You can take care of yourself pretty well." I looked over to Kade. Based on the way his jaw was clenching, he seemed to agree with me. "That trick you mentioned before. How did you lock Kade up?"

Amelia lifted her chin. "It was a simple unfolding mechanism made from some glass parts I created in the window. That's not what's important, though. Veronique says—"

I raised my hand, palm forward. "Let me guess. Veronique says you're powerless without a protector."

"Yes. And Rowan's ill. You heard his own brother say it. And that Shujaa—" she shivered. "I know everyone around here likes him, but I don't."

I broke my wrist free from her grip. "This isn't you. You're the one who built your own laboratory. The only girl who helped me find all the hidden Necromancers, even though it risked her life. I don't know who this blubbering fool is that's standing before me, but I want my friend Amelia back."

"No, you don't. Veronique explained everything to me. You want Genesis Rex for yourself. Well, that plan failed. He can't protect either of us."

I'd heard this kind of talk before, but never from Amelia. "You know what I think?" I asked.

"Enlighten me."

"I think that if you *really* believed Veronique, you wouldn't be here. On some level, you suspect that Veronique is using you."

Amelia rounded on Kade. "You told her to say that."

Kade folded his arms over his chest, a movement that made his leathers creak. "I haven't been out of your sight since you arrived, except for when you locked me up, of course." The way he said that last bit, it was clear that he wasn't too angry. *Interesting.* "When would I have had time to plot with her?"

"I don't know." Amelia's eye twitched again. It wasn't an encouraging sign. "You're sneaky, Kade."

He stepped closer to Amelia. Evidently, not respecting personal space was something that ran in the family. "Sneaky? Give me one example." His voice lowered. "One."

Amelia began breathing quickly. "I can't think of any at the moment, but I will."

Kade leaned in to whisper in her ear. "Can't wait."

I set my hands on their respective shoulders and guided the two of them apart. "Now that you two are settled, I'd like some questions answered."

Kade stepped between Amelia and me. "You can ask me first."

Amelia tried to wiggle out from behind him, but he kept blocking her with his massive arms.

Clearly, Amelia wasn't getting any closer to me with Kade there. Rowan had obviously wanted to keep certain things from me, and Kade was here to act as gatekeeper. *Fine.* Sometimes, the questions you couldn't answer told you as much as the ones you could.

I glared right at Kade. "I want to know about the engagement between Amelia and Rowan."

"Go on," said Kade.

"Did she know that there was a difference between and engagement and a betrothal?"

Kade stepped aside. "That she can answer."

At last.

Amelia stared at the floor. "Veronique said that the only way a woman can be safe in our world is to be married to power."

Despite the heat, my skin chilled over. "So Rowan *did* make it clear to you? He said it was an agreement, not a betrothal?"

Amelia pulled out the key from her pocket and stared at it. "That's what he said when it was only the two of us. But later, the Havillands said it was a true engagement, and he didn't correct her. Veronique says—"

"I do not want to hear about Veronique. What about this sword? Can you get it?"

"My grandfather is a nutter. He placed it in some cave. Veronique says that going after it is a waste of time."

"Ugh. She's been filling your head with nonsense."

Kade nodded. "Listen to your friend. Your true friend."

Amelia twisted the key over in her fingers some more. "Vee has been through a lot. She's only trying to protect us both."

I nodded toward her hands. "You've been experimenting again, haven't you?"

"A little."

"You want my advice? If someone's going to take care of you, it needs to be you. I've never met a more brilliant inventor."

"The Vicomte wasn't so sure."

"He was a horse's ass."

Amelia pursed her lips. "But what about Vee? She went

through so much, and now she's back to normal. She knows what she's talking about."

"I agree that Veronique's appears normal now, but how did that happen, eh? You want my analysis?" I went right on without giving her a chance to answer, since I figured she probably didn't want to hear this anyway. *Too bad.* "Veronique appears normal because she's been sharpening her claws on you for two months. By cutting you down and making *you* the one who's terrified, she doesn't have to own her own fear and pain. Waiting for a protector isn't you, Amelia. You're better than this."

"This is exactly what I've been telling Amelia for weeks," said Kade. "Only, she wouldn't listen. She said I was a…" He tapped his square chin. "What did you call me again?"

"Warthog thug wrapped in a leather boulder holder."

I stifled a laugh. "You called him what?"

"He was being very rude."

"Although I did appreciate the reference to boulders. I'm quite the well proportioned man."

Amelia tried to look angry, but she only managed a half-smile. The two of them were clearly falling for each other.

Kade took a tentative step closer to Amelia. "And now Elea says that you're a mechanical genius? How did I miss this? Other than Veronique distracting you from sharing anything of interest about you, of course."

Amelia blushed and gripped the key behind her back. "It hasn't necessarily been something that's brought me joy."

Kade slipped his hand into his pocket and pulled out a small device that looked like a series of layered discs. "I dabble in engineering a bit myself."

"That's an astrolabe."

"Yes." Kade grinned. "I have more back at my laboratory. Would you like to see them?"

"You have a laboratory?"

He offered her his hand. "The best in Nyumbani. Shall we?"

As charming as their interactions were, I had bigger things to worry about. "Hold on there. Where is Rowan right now?"

"Nowhere," snapped Kade. "You're trouble for him."

I huffed out an angry breath. "That's what your mother said as well."

"She did?" Kade's features softened. "What did she say exactly?"

"That she had visions where I would ensure his death." I couldn't help the sneer that crept into my voice. "She didn't seem too upset about it, either."

"She only ever cared for Storm," said Kade.

Amelia frowned. "What's the story with him anyway?"

"Storm was a great warrior. The man was a folk hero. When he was abducted—"

"Wait," I interrupted. "I thought he ran off."

"When someone like Viktor charms you into leaving your life behind, what do you call that? I think he was taken from us. Mother was always pushing him to be more than he was. I think she hoped Viktor would make Storm all-powerful." Kade's green eyes glazed over with pain. "She supported Viktor's bid to take the throne from our father, you know."

"Yes," I said gently. "She told me about that."

Kade shook his head. "Well, if Mother says you're here to destroy Rowan, then you're quite possibly his only chance to win this upcoming fight. But before I tell you where to find him, I need to know one thing. What are you to my brother?"

An image popped into my mind: my mating band. That was no one's business, though. "I'm a friend."

"You're lying." Kade winked. Evidently, he was the carefree brother. *Why can't I fall for the lighthearted ones?* "And Rowan is most likely in his chambers. The top floor of the castle. Hard to miss."

"Thank you." I heard their happy chatter behind me as I took off.

After talking with Kade and Amelia, I felt even more resolved to fix this. No matter what, I wouldn't stand by while Rowan fought Shujaa.

16

I hiked up the castle's circular staircase. On the third level, I found two guards in red leathers standing on either side of a large wooden door. There were no other entrances around.

I scanned both warriors carefully. Their faces were covered by leather helms; tall wooden spears were gripped in their right fists. As women, the two guards had long and lean bodies. Most likely, they were the wily and fast kind of fighters. That could prove tricky for me, considering how I needed time to pull in magick and speak an incantation. It was true that I still wore Petra's totem ring, but that thing was only loaded with transport spells.

And I wasn't going anywhere. No one could keep me from getting answers now.

Focusing my mage senses, I reached out for Necromancer power. The energy flowed into me, prickling across my skin. I flexed my left hand, ready to focus and cast.

The guards saw my movement and immediately stepped aside. "You may enter," said the first warrior.

I tilted my head. *Things are never this easy for me.* "Wait... You know that I'm the Tsarina, and that's fine with you?"

"We've been informed," added the second guard. "Genesis Rex is inside his chambers right now. He's expecting you."

"Oh." The moment the sound escaped my lips I wished I had uttered a better comment. After all, it seemed like a true Tsarina would have something more formal to say than "Oh." I looked down at the scanty leather scarves that made up my outfit.

Then again, perhaps *this* Tsarina simply said, "Oh" and got out of view as soon possible. I gripped the metal latch and twisted it. The door slid open easily.

I stepped inside.

I didn't know what I expected from Rowan's chambers, but the interior caught me by surprise. The space was as close to being outdoors as possible. All the floors and walls were made of mossy stones that were framed with massive silver trees. Other thinner trunks twisted into furniture shapes. One nest of vines even wrapped about a living fountain. Small and colorful birds played in the waters. More bright-hued flowers decorated the walls, all of them planted to create great swirling patterns.

Warmth filled my veins. This place was lovely.

Rowan stood by a window hole, his body in profile as he stared intently at the castle grounds outside. He braced his right arm against the wall, a movement that also held back what looked like a curtain of living vines. The dying sunlight played across the planes of bare muscle on his chest. Like me, he hadn't changed since the ceremony. There was no missing the long shadows of weariness that darkened his handsome face. Worry weighed down my heart. How long had Shujaa been stealing his power? I forced my face into a mask of calm.

"Hello, Rowan."

"Elea." His gaze stayed locked on whatever was happening outside the window. I stepped up to Rowan's side. Down below in the gardens, Jicho and Kade were crouched beside Amelia, who was building a sundial out of bits of wood and stone. They weren't fighting, which seemed to be a good thing. The shadows were lengthening as the sun set behind them. I hadn't realized how long the ceremony had lasted.

I gestured to the view. "It seems Amelia and Kade share a love of all things mechanical."

Rowan arched his brows. "Give it a moment."

Within a few seconds, Amelia and Kade began arguing over the placement of the sundial. Jicho watched the interplay with a knowing smile. The young boy leaned his head forward. A play of black veins appeared on his chest and shoulders for a moment, and then disappeared. Then Jicho raised his head and replaced the sundial components into what appeared to be the perfect configuration.

"Jicho had a vision of where that should go, didn't he?" I asked.

"Yes. My brother is a strong Seer."

"And your mother?"

Rowan lowered his arm, allowing the vines to swing down and cover the window. He turned his attention to me. "Zoriah is almost as powerful. She could be better, but she's too ambitious. Being a Seer means being open to all future outcomes, without any preference."

A long pause followed. Rowan scanned me from head to foot, but he had his unreadable face on. It was most vexing, especially when there was so much to discuss, I didn't know where to begin. As a Necromancer, I didn't care what most people felt, but Rowan was the exception to every rule. A little hint of his emotions might help here, but it was clear that wouldn't be coming. At least, not right now. I decided to start with my biggest worry.

"I used magick to spy on Shujaa last night. He stole some of your power in order to make one of those golden warriors."

Rowan nodded. "That's been going on for a few months now. Kade and I have tried to track him down, but he's evaded us so far. I'm fairly certain my mother is helping him, but she's been too careful for us to catch her in the act." The muscles in his neck tightened. "The challenge tonight came as a relief. Shujaa can't use Viktor's totem armor on the fighting grounds. We'll end this, one way or another."

"I want to help you fight."

Rowan kept staring out the window, his face in profile. "You know I don't want your life at risk. Besides, Kade will be my second in the battle."

"He'll replace you if you're killed?"

"That's not how it works with Casters. He'll fight at my side. It's already set."

I opened my mouth, ready to say that I wanted to fight at his side. But did I really? Besides, we had other topics to cover first. I decided to go for a general question. "What are you thinking right now?"

Rowan turned to face me for the first time. The intensity in his green eyes took my breath away. "I'm wondering what you thought of the ceremony."

In other words, did I still think he was betrothed to Amelia? Part of me wanted to rail at him for withholding information. But he had tried to explain things to me many times. I was partly to blame as well, so I straightened my back and prepared to own up to my mistake. "I was wrong about your being betrothed to Amelia. I assumed your culture was like mine."

His expression stayed still as stone. "And?"

"Engagements don't mean the same thing to you. I see that now." On reflex, my hand brushed across my neck, where my betrothal ring would normally be hanging on a chain. It was still hidden under my pillow, though. Rowan noticed the movement, and I wondered if he was thinking the same thing I was—the same questions Zoriah posed.

Was ours a false mating? Was it a mating at all?

That conversation felt far too overwhelming, though. I was pleased when Rowan steered our talk onto safer ground. "So, what do you think happened at my engagement?"

"You made a deal with Amelia for the Sword of Theodora."

"That's right." Some of the shadows on his face seemed to lessen. "Viktor is in exile, but I doubt he'll stay there forever."

I nodded. "As much as I hate the fact that you're right? You're right."

"The Sword of Theodora might be the only way to kill him."

"That might not be so easy, at least for me. When we fought Viktor the last time, he showed me that our powers were linked. If he dies, I might die as well."

"I don't know how much value I put on tricks from Viktor. But even if that is true, it's all the more reason to use the Sword of Theodora. It is unstoppable and follows the intent of the bearer. If we want to kill Viktor and leave you alive, then the Sword of Theodora will make that happen." He tilted his head. "So you understand why I need it so badly?"

"I understand. And I spoke to Amelia after the ceremony.

She confirmed that you made it clear that your arrangement wasn't a real betrothal."

He let out a long breath. "Thank you for saying that."

I raised my hands, palms forward. "Wait a moment. You're not getting off so easily."

A small smile curved his full mouth. "I'm not?"

"Four words, Rowan." I counted them off on my fingers. "You. Don't. Trust. Me."

He shook his head. "Elea…"

"You don't. You knew for weeks what kind of deal you'd put together with Amelia. All during that time, you could have told me what you were planning. In fact, I might have even been able to look around for the Sword of Theodora, too." I hated how my voice cracked as I spoke. "Why didn't you tell me?"

Rowan's gaze intensified. "Because of Tristan."

I took a half step backward. Of all the reasons I thought Rowan would give, my one-time best friend wasn't on the list. "Tristan? The man who tricked me into taking on a curse?"

"Yes. And 'tricked' is the right word there. Tristan wanted you to train as a Necromancer."

"I'm not sure what that proves. He told me that himself. He said it was the only way to protect me from Viktor. Once I became trained Necromancer, I could fight off both Viktor and the Vicomte. Otherwise, Viktor would have abducted me, given me his mark, and drained all my power."

"There's more to it than that. All the things you can do with hybrid magick? There are hidden levels to Tristan's motivations, mark my words."

I hugged my elbows. "Tristan visited me last night. He gave me the totem ring that helped me spy on Shujaa."

"All the more reason to suspect him. How many ghosts

hand out totem rings? I'm not even a Necromancer, and I know that."

The old anger coursed through my limbs. "He just keeps lying to me."

"Even worse, he didn't you give you a choice in your life."

"Choice." My gaze locked with Rowan's. "Like the blackbird and the dove."

"Yes. By placing the curse on you, Tristan took away your ability to choose. I won't ever do that."

My mind sifted through all the engagements I'd witnessed in the ceremony. Mated couples always approached the Hadithi together. "All Caster engagements have two sides to the deal. What was your part with Amelia? Keeping her safe?"

"Yes."

"There are also consequences if she gets you the sword and you don't keep her safe. What if she still got hurt?"

Rowan shook his head. "You're too smart, Elea."

I couldn't fight my grin. I was closing in on the truth and I knew it. "Answer the question."

"In that case, I'd suffer her pain for her. I would take on whatever she endured, including death. You saw how the threads of the fabric tie lit up for a real engagement. It's a magickal binding."

"And are Casters' mates are also bound by their engagements?"

Rowan sighed. "Only if they know about the engagement before the magick was enacted."

"So you were protecting me."

"Yes. Trying to."

"But that means you're still making decisions for me. I would still have wanted to know about the engagement."

"If you'd known about the engagement beforehand, there

would have been choice. You would have been involved magically forever. I couldn't risk your life and remove your choices, not in that way. The ceremony with Amelia took place right before the battle with Viktor. I had planned to tell you afterwards."

"But then I wasn't talking to you." I scrubbed my hands over my face. "This is all the blackbird and the dove again."

"This must be your choice." The lines of his face deepened with intensity. This was tearing him apart inside. "There are still things I can't tell you. I wish with all my soul it were different."

I moved so we were standing face-to-face with only inches separating us. "There must be something you can do to move things forward."

Rowan slowly drew his fingertips up my right arm. Wherever we touched, my skin felt on fire. "There is one way."

At last, progress!

"Name it."

He brushed his fingertip along my jawline. "Tell me what you want for your life, Elea."

Yet again, the conversation had veered into unexpected territory. I blinked hard, wondering if I had misheard him. "You want to know my life goals? Right now?"

"Yes. You have your farm back. Is that what you want for your future?"

"Oh, I see what you mean." My shoulders slumped as I thought about my great plan to return to Braddock Farm. "At one point, I wanted to be a farmer. Now, I don't know."

His palm rested against my cheek. "Meaning?"

"That Elea is gone. I gave some of my lands to my tenants, Mabel and Sam. Sometimes I think, maybe I'll give them everything. I don't know."

"Are you serious?"

I nodded. Admitting failure wasn't my favorite pastime.

"That's very brave," said Rowan. He wrapped his arms around me and pulled me in close. Tilting my head, I leaned against his chest. This felt so good. Rowan and me. Together. Why couldn't life be like this between us, only without so many problems? I realized he was still staring at me and waiting for an answer. I inhaled a long breath. This wasn't going to be pleasant to admit.

"I don't want to be a farmer." The words tasted like failure. "For five long years, I'd done everything I could to return to my old life. But when I got there? Maybe I'd changed too much. I mean, I worked the land and all that, but I wasn't doing it out of joy anymore."

"And what about being Tsarina? Is that what you want?"

"Honestly, I don't know that either. Petra wants me to rule." I searched my heart, looking for anything else that could be part of my future.

Was Rowan part of it? I wanted him to be alive and well, but did I really want to share my future with him?

I certainly wanted him to be in my life, but what did that mean? Would I be a queen, a consort, something else? It begged an obvious question. "What about you? Do you enjoy being Genesis Rex?"

"It's not a question of enjoy. It's who I am. I won't leave my people." He rubbed my back in soothing circles. "And I know you, Elea. You won't leave yours, either. At some point, the Necromancers will need you, and you'll heed their call. Petra won't find another Tsarina, and you know it."

I frowned. "Someone else could rise."

"Only if you fall. You brought those mages back from the

dead. As long as you live, you'd be a threat to whoever held the Necromancer crown."

His words made my insides squirm, mostly because they were true. "I could stay here with you until—" I stopped myself before finishing the thought, because the logic was obvious.

I could stay until my people needed me. Then, I'd have to go.

I sighed. "This is impossible, isn't it?"

"Nothing is impossible if you want it enough." He leaned back until our gazes met. The look in his eyes turned intense again. "Why did you want to be a farmer?"

"My parents were farmers. They died when I was an infant, and Braddock was all I had left of them. Being on the farm made me feel close to them."

"And how does casting spells make you feel?"

"Alive." I worried my lower lip with my teeth. "I see where you're going with this. I need to decide what I want, regardless of my parents or Petra or even you." I shook my head. "I wish I had an answer for you right now, but I simply don't know what I want."

His gaze stayed intense, but beyond that, I had no idea what Rowan was thinking. Per usual. "Then we wait."

I tried my best to frown. However, it turned out that wasn't an easy thing to do when Rowan's arms were still around me. "You're still lying to me. Don't think I can't tell. It's a lie of omission."

"Yes." He leaned forward and began kissing my neck. My body instantly heated.

Even so, I was able to keep my focus on the topic at hand. "And these lies of omission, you think they're for my own safety."

"Yes."

"Forget it. I'll find out all your secrets anyway."

"I certainly hope not." He kissed a spot behind my ear. "I've gone to great lengths to keep you in the dark."

"That's why you have Jicho following me around."

He nodded.

"This isn't the way to build trust, you know."

"Oh, I disagree. I think you trust me more and more each day." He kept kissing along my jawline until his lips were only a breath above my own.

"Maybe. A little." I opened my mouth, ready to speak. Instead, I ended up kissing Rowan like my life depended on it. My arms looped around his firm shoulders. Our kiss deepened. Rowan's tongue crossed my lips, and I lost all sanity. Somehow, I got the idea to wrap my legs around his waist.

Great idea, actually.

Rowan started walking us toward his bed. I couldn't help but smile. Few women in their twenties had never lain with a man. I happened to be one of them. Rowan and I came close once, but that was all. If this were to be my first time having sex, then I was glad it would be with Rowan.

He paused by the edge of the bed. "I'm not going anywhere, Elea. You're my heart and my future. I won't ever give you up. I love you."

My eyes widened. Yet another statement I wasn't expecting. "What do you expect me to say to that?"

"Nothing." He leaned forward until our foreheads rested against each other. "I know the truth. You fell hopelessly in love with me the first time fought out on the desert."

"I did, did I?"

"Of course. It's just taking you some time to learn to trust me. Love and trust don't always develop at the same speed. I can be patient." Rowan gazed at me like I was the most beautiful and amazing woman in the world. I leaned forward to kiss him again. Rowan set his pointer finger on my chin, preventing me from moving closer.

"What's wrong?" I asked.

"We need to stop. Someone's at the door."

On reflex, I tightened my legs around his waist. "You're Genesis Rex. Tell them to go away."

"I can't. It's my mother."

"Oh." My verbal skills were back to zero.

I quickly stepped away from Rowan. Thus began a desperate process of trying to realign the scraps of leather that served as my outfit. I wasn't sure if I was making any progress at all. I groaned. "It's going to be obvious what we were up to."

"Don't worry." Rowan straightened out his own leathers. "That's why she's here in the first place. Zoriah doesn't want us together." The muscles in his neck tightened. "It's always been about Storm for her."

Loud knocking sounded at the door. "Let me in." It was Zoriah. "We have much to discuss, my son."

Rowan turned to me. The dark circles under his eyes seemed to visibly deepen. "You can transport away, if you like." He gestured toward Petra's ring that I still wore.

"No." I straightened my shoulders. "I'm staying right here."

Rowan gave me one last gentle kiss. "Good."

For the first time since I stepped into this room, I had the feeling that I'd said the right thing. If only I knew what to say in order for Rowan to fully unlock his secrets.

"Open this door now." Zoriah's muffled voice carried through the room. "Lazy guards."

I stared at the closed door. Maybe I was thinking about

this in the wrong way. Zoriah coming by might not be a bad thing. If Rowan wouldn't tell me the full truth, perhaps she could.

"Right away, Your Majesty," said one of the guards.

The door swung open, and I hoped for the best. One thing was for certain, though. No matter what happened, I wouldn't give up.

17

*R*owan's mother sauntered into the room. Like always, she looked young and perfect with her long brown hair, green eyes, and flawless robes.

All of a sudden, I became acutely aware that I was standing at the foot of Rowan's bed while wearing next to nothing. Sure, the outfit in question had been picked out by Zoriah, but I doubted that she pictured me wearing it with a swollen mouth and mussed-up hair in her son's private chambers.

Rowan gave his mother the barest of nods. "Zoriah."

So, Rowan calls his mother by her first name. Good plan. I wouldn't want to be reminded I had any blood ties with her, either.

She bowed slightly. "My son." Her green eyes locked on me. "And who are you, I wonder?"

Rowan stifled a cough. "You know very well who Elea is."

A small smile rounded Zoriah's mouth. "Do I?"

An itchy feeling crept over my skin. I had the uncomfortable sensation that Rowan and Zoriah were talking about something I didn't know about but probably should. "Care to elaborate?" I asked.

Zoriah shrugged. "I have nothing to say."

Rowan stepped forward, placing his body between me and his mother. I knew Rowan's protective nature. The way he set his fists on his hips, you'd think Zoriah was carrying poisoned darts.

I frowned. Then again, perhaps she was. Every time I thought I had the Caster culture figured out, an unexpected custom popped up out of nowhere. For all I knew, poisoned darts were a common means of greeting.

"So you have nothing to say?" repeated Rowan. "Of course, you do. Out with it."

Zoriah picked invisible bits of lint off her red robes. "I came by to broker a peace. The battle with Shujaa is a week away. Much as I loathe you, Rowan, I don't wish to see you die needlessly."

"You'd love my death, and we both know it."

"I'm here to see if you'll simply hand over the crown to Shujaa. You've been growing weaker for months. You don't stand a chance against him."

"This is excellent news." Rowan's green eyes glittered.

Zoriah stepped closer. "So you'll hand over the throne?"

"Not a chance. I'm pleased because you wouldn't try to broker a deal unless you thought I had a real chance at winning. Thank you for the unintentional vote of confidence."

My own protective nature flared up inside me. Zoriah was only here to try to undermine Rowan. "I think it would be best if you left."

Zoriah rounded on me. "I reached out to your Mother Superior, you know. She doesn't want you here for a moment longer than is necessary. Once Rowan is dead, she expects you back at the Zelle Cloister to rule your people. You aren't staying here to reign over ours."

"Ruling is your dream, Zoriah. Not mine."

"The prophecy will be fulfilled. Shujaa is the true King, and his golden army will take over these lands." She glared at Rowan. "Step down now or die."

"You heard the Tsarina." Rowan's voice took on a deeper tone of menace. "Now, it's time for you to go."

"Remember the prophecy." Zoriah then strode out the door. It slammed behind her with a thud.

Once she was gone, a long silence fell between me and Rowan. "Your mother is scheming," I said at last.

"That's rather typical for her. Some days, I wonder why she didn't drown me as an infant."

Rowan was trying to make light of a terrible situation, but my heart still cracked for him. "I'm sorry you have her as your mother. I didn't know my parents, but at least I could imagine them as kind people."

"Don't pity me too much. My father was a great man. He and Zoriah never got along. When he died...Anyway, he's gone now and I can handle Zoriah." Rowan rubbed his neck. He'd never looked more hollowed out and ill.

"When was the last time you slept?"

The ghost of his crooked smile returned. "Recently."

I pulled him onto the bed. "Lay down."

"This is all rather forward of you."

"I was being rather forward, but that was before your mother stopped by." I tugged on his arm again. "You need to rest, and I'm not going anywhere until you do." I nodded toward the window. "Night is already falling. Time for all good Genesis Rexes to go to sleep."

"If you insist."

His smile widened, and my chest filled with all things warm and happy. "I do."

Rowan scooted onto the bed and raised his left arm. I cuddled into his side, finding his body to be the perfect fit for mine. He kept up a low cough. On reflex, I set my hand on the center of his bare chest.

"How's this?" he asked.

"Perfect, now get some rest."

He pressed me more closely into his side. "That isn't easy with you here, you know."

"Kade said that I could pinch your shoulder and make you fall asleep instantly."

Rowan set his hand on a particular spot on my shoulder blade. The warmth of his skin sent shivers through my insides. "The spot is right here, in case you're wondering. But it only works for a minute or two."

"Really? I thought he was joking."

"Physical force can be more powerful than magick."

"We'll see about that. Try to rest, or I'll cast a sleeper spell on you."

"In that case, I'll do my best." I couldn't see Rowan's face, but there was no mistaking the sound of a smile in his voice.

We lay there for a while, not talking and simply soaking in the sensation of being together. It was all far too exciting. What would it be like to be able to fall asleep at Rowan's side each night? Sleep seemed to be impossible, especially since Rowan kept up his steady cough. After about an hour, my body felt heavy with the need to rest.

As both Rowan and I drifted off to sleep, I thought I saw the veins in my right hand begin to glow red with Caster power. My eyes popped open wide. I'd never summoned Caster power before, at least not without the help of Rowan,

Oni, or Yuri. I turned my hand over, but my skin looked as it always did. With all my focus, I tried to summon fresh Caster power to my right hand once more. Nothing worked. After a few more tries, I started to feel rather foolish.

Me summoning Caster power? It must have been a trick of my mind.

At least, Rowan's coughing had stopped for whatever reason. Now, his chest rose and fell in a steady rhythm. He was feeling better, and no matter what caused the change, I was certainly thankful for it.

With that happy thought, I drifted off to sleep as well.

18

*S*unlight streamed through the vines covering Rowan's windows. The thin lines of brightness shifted across the bed, highlighting how Rowan and I still lay entwined atop the covers. In point of fact, Rowan and I hadn't moved since we fell asleep. Well, not unless I counted how I'd draped my right leg over his.

On second thought, I would definitely count it. The sensation of Rowan's firm thigh underneath mine was pleasant in the extreme.

Rowan's eyes fluttered open. I was happy to see that the dark circles under his eyes had lessened. "Good morning."

"Hello, there."

He reached over and took a lock of my dark hair and rubbed it between his fingertips. "How are you feeling?"

"I should be asking you that question. Did Shujaa summon you last night to make more of his golden warriors?"

"He did not." Rowan kissed my head. "You must bring me good fortune."

"Or scare your brother away." I tried to force a smile, but couldn't. "I hate the idea of him taking your magick."

"I'm fine. Whatever is happening to me, it won't last much longer."

A weight of worry settled onto my shoulders. "I don't like this, Rowan. The battle with Shujaa comes up in just one week. You need your strength. Maybe you should consider postponing it?"

"As I said, it's nothing to worry about. I've always been stronger than Shujaa."

"That's not what I asked." I closely inspected Rowan's face. Although he looked better than last night, there were still lines of weariness across his forehead.

"Look," said Rowan. "If I postpone, that would forfeit my crown. If anything, I should move the date closer." He looked away quickly as he said that last part.

"And have you decided to move the date closer?"

"I'm considering it." Rowan stood up and stretched. I missed the touch of his body the moment he stepped away. "Jicho will be here soon. He's keeping you company today."

I sat up and thought through that last revelation from Rowan about the battle with Shujaa. "You wouldn't move the date closer unless it gave you an advantage."

He flashed me a lopsided grin. "Am I so transparent?"

"To me, you are. Sometimes." *And never when it's truly important.*

A knock sounded at the door. I noticed that the guard's voice was now that of a man. They must have changed shifts. "Your brother is here to see you, Your Majesty."

"Let him in."

The door swung open, and Jicho bounded the room. This morning, he was all knobby knees, bald head, and gap-toothed smile. A long and thin game board was balanced in his arms. "Good morning!"

Rowan stepped over and patted his younger brother's shoulder. Like always, Jicho wore his Seer's robes. "I see you've brought the Jackals and Hounds game."

"Would you two like to play with me?"

"I'm afraid I can't. But Elea may be interested." Rowan turned to me. "What do you think?"

"Certainly." My mind whirred. Too many things were happening at once, and I still didn't have enough information. When it came to getting more insights, there was one person on the top of my list. "Perhaps we could stop by and visit Amelia first?"

Jicho shook his head. "She's over in Kade's laboratory. They've asked not to be disturbed."

I pursed my lips. This was news. *Kade and Amelia are now spending time together in his laboratory?* "What are they working on?"

"Who can tell? It's all little gears and things." A knowing smile crossed Jicho's face. Clearly, Jicho completely envisioned what they were up to. *Clever Seer.*

I folded my arms across my chest. "You're a visionary. I bet you know a lot of things about them."

"Maybe."

Rowan chuckled. "Jicho is a wily one. He won't tell you his visions until you say the right thing."

I decided to try a different tactic. Time to try the second name of my list of people who could give me insights. "How about we visit Philippe then?"

"He's with Amelia in the laboratory. Veronique is, too." Jicho shook the board game. "Come along, Elea. Let's play."

"Perhaps I can help Rowan." With whatever sneakiness he's up to.

Rowan stepped up to me and brushed the backs of his fingers against my cheek. "I wish you could, but it's not right. Please."

Ugh. He always breaks my resolve with that "please."

"Come on." Jicho shook the game again. "I promise. It will be fun." But the way Jicho said those words—*"I promise it will be fun"*—I got the feeling he wanted the same thing I did.

To give me some information. At last.

"In that case," I said, "let's go play."

Hours later, I picked up my carved game piece from the board. Jicho and I now sat on opposite sides of a small table inside my room. We'd been playing Jackals and Hounds all day. Lunch and dinner plates were strewn about, and I'd changed into an extremely comfortable set of Caster leathers.

I scanned the board and considered my next move. Turns out, Jackals and Hounds was a very distracting game that reminded me of chess, something Mother Superior and I would play at the Cloister. Even so, there were only so many hours one could spend playing board games. The sun was starting to touch the horizon line.

And I still didn't have any new information.

Now, I knew Rowan had cast an aegis spell on Jicho, so he couldn't tell me any secrets. Even so, Jicho didn't even seem to be trying to tell me anything. If Jicho's tongue had lit up with magick, I'd know he was trying to break the spell and share a secret. But it hadn't. Not even once. After a full day of this, I was starting to wonder if Jicho wanted to help me all.

I set the piece down on the opposite side of the board. "There."

Jicho grinned. "That's quite a good move."

"Thank you." With a sigh, I rested my chin on my fist. "Is it time yet?"

There was no question what I meant. All day, Jicho had been insisting that I would find out what I needed to know when the moment was right.

"You'll understand it all—" he began.

"When the time is right. I remember."

Jicho bowed his head, and I had to admit, the boy could definitely seem very much the mystic Seer when he wanted to, despite the fact that he was only nine years old. Even so, the day was wasting away, and I'd played more Jackals and Hounds than I ever thought possible.

I leaned back in my chair, my blood starting to boil. My Zuchtlos nature took over. "I'm done with this, Jicho. Tell me the truth, or so help me, I'll cast a truth spell on you, even if you are a sweet boy."

Jicho grinned. "And now, finally, the time is right."

My mouth fell open. "Have you been waiting all day for me to threaten you?"

He shrugged. "I had a vision. Your threat was the start of it." He gave me a gap-toothed grin. "Don't take it personally."

I pinched the bridge of my nose. "You're very much like your brother, you know that? Neither of you will answer a direct question."

"How about this? There are more dresses for you in the wardrobe."

A spark of hope lit in my chest. "Formal dresses?"

"Yes, Zoriah sent them yesterday, but you never know when they'll come in handy."

I drummed my fingers on the tabletop. "Something's going on tonight. A formal ceremony of some kind. That's what you're hinting at."

Jicho didn't answer, but he moved his game piece. I took that to mean *yes*.

"Fine. I'll go. But I'm changing into a fresh set of Caster leathers."

Jicho lowered his head. The veins in his neck turned black for a moment before returning to normal once more. Jicho raised his gaze to meet mine. "You can wear whatever you want tonight. It won't change things."

"Why doesn't your tongue light up when you talk?"

Jicho shrugged. "I had visions that told me what to say. Words to get around Rowan's spell."

"That sounds rather complicated."

"No, it's easy." He moved another piece. "And I win."

"You didn't." I checked the board. He'd won indeed. Jicho was an interesting boy. "Congratulations."

"You better get ready."

"If you say so." The servants had stocked my bureau with plenty of Caster leathers. I took a few steps in that direction.

Jicho raised his pointer finger. "One more thing. Now, listen to me carefully. No matter what happens, you must follow your heart, even if it asks you to do something rather strange."

The hair on my neck stood on end. I had the terrible feeling that *rather strange* would also mean *extremely unpleasant*. Even so, I didn't have much of a choice. "All right. That's what I'll do."

Jicho stood. "In that case, this is where I leave." He didn't say goodbye, but simply walked out my door and closed it behind him. It shut with an ominous thud.

Now, I needed to get dressed and go find Rowan. As I stepped over to the bureau, Jicho's words kept echoing through my mind.

Follow your heart no matter how strange the things it called me to do.

Something told me that life was about to become very strange indeed. Right before I left, I grabbed my mating band from its hiding spot under my pillow. As Jicho suggested, I slipped it on my finger for no better reason than it felt good to do so. Some small part of me knew that wearing the ring was the first step in a huge change.

But perhaps I was ready for a transformation.

19

*E*xiting my chamber, I stepped into the hallway beyond. Distant voices rumbled up the main staircase. My ears perked. I'd heard something similar when I was leaving for yesterday's engagement ceremony. *No question about it.* Another big event was taking place right now. The only question was where everyone was gathered.

Another Caster ceremony filled with surprises? Not an appealing thought. I pulled on the jacket of my leathers. It was too loose, but it covered my skin. I fidgeted with my trousers next.

Long seconds passed before I realized that stalling in a hallway was absurd. *Remember the blackbird and the dove.* Trusting Rowan was something I simply had to try.

Straightening my shoulders, I marched down the winding stairs. Once I reached the main floor, my strength wavered. I'd reached the passage leading to the great hall, but everything in here was dark and deserted.

"Hello?" I called. "Is anyone there?"

No one answered.

With hesitant steps, I moved closer to the entrance archway to the great hall. The place was empty. The voices were louder here, though. They seemed to be echoing in from the window holes by the far wall.

This must be an outdoor celebration. *Interesting.*

Following the crowd's low roar, I marched behind the castle, past the south green, and into the jungle beyond. This was the same path I'd taken with Zoriah in order to reach her greenhouse.

Hopefully, this trip would be more pleasant.

Once again, trudging through the jungle took some time. The bright side was that I wore heavy boots with my leathers, so I could easily climb over fallen trees and under swaying sheets of moss. With every step, the voices grew louder. I couldn't tell if they were angry, cheering with joy, or both.

At last, the rainforest ended. I walked through a wall of palm trees and onto a wide strip of red mud that encircled a small, round, and deep-cut crevasse filled with jungle. Casters were everywhere on this thin loop of red land. Some cheered; others wept. I recognized many of the faces from the engagement celebration—these were the leading families from their respective tribes. Since I was wearing my leathers, I blended right in.

I approached an older woman with a friendly face, browned skin, and long white hair. "Excuse me."

"You're not a Caster." She said the words with a grin, so I wasn't too worried.

"No, I'm here as a guest. I was wondering. What do you call that?" I gestured toward the deep crevasse and jungle inside.

"Oh, that's the Genesis Vale. It's a very old and sacred place for us. Lovely, wouldn't you say?"

I took a few careful steps closer. To my right, the ground ended in a sharp fall-off to a deep valley below. The vale was filled with even more jungle. It filled the view to my right, reminding me of a small green lake. The tops of the trees even shifted with the winds, like a breeze over water. "It is lovely."

"Watch your step now. That's a mighty fall."

"Thank you."

She tapped my shoulder. "And that over there are the three pillars. You've seen the insignia on our guards, yes?"

I followed the woman's point. On the opposite side of the Genesis Vale, there stood a line of three stone pillars. The last rays of the setting sun were dying now, and the trio of white columns glowed with the reflection. The two on either side were lower; the one in the center was the tallest.

That was where I spied Rowan.

Rowan stood on the tallest pillar in his red kilt. Wind rustled his hair and made his long cape billow behind him. Even from this distance, I could see the dark shadows in his cheeks and under his eyes. The planes of his bare chest looked even more hollowed out than before. My throat tightened with worry.

I rounded on the old woman. "What's happening?"

"It's part of our tradition for our King. Genesis Rex makes a new throne here. After the battle, the winner brings it into the great hall."

"But I saw four thrones in the great hall."

"Our Genesis Rex never had a challenger to the throne before, so he never had to make one. He's been using his old throne as Prince. But now, he's making a proper throne for a proper King. You've heard that Shujaa has come back to us, haven't you?"

"Yes." My voice sounded soft and distant. "I have."

"He's fulfilling the prophecy. Our true King has a golden army and everything."

"Maybe he's lying to you." I didn't bother hiding the anger in my voice. "Did you ever think of that?"

She squinted at me. "You look familiar, child. Haven't I seen you before?" She smacked her thin lips. "Ah, I think I have it. Were you at the engagement ceremony yesterday?"

"Excuse me." I pushed off into the crowd. Getting recognized as the Tsarina wasn't a good idea right now. Besides, I wanted to get a better look at Rowan. How much worse had he gotten? The three pillars were on the opposite side of the Genesis Vale. I simply had to get closer.

As I shoved my way along, the crowd kept up their odd mix of celebration and despair. I couldn't decide whether to console them or punch them in the throat. How could they allow this to happen? Rowan was a great King. They should have thrown out Shujaa the moment he walked back into the meeting hall.

Atop the tallest pillar, Rowan raised his right arm. The folds of his red robe billowed behind him. Within seconds, the veins of his hand glowed red with power. His voice was laced with magick; I could clearly hear his incantation.

"Breathe. Live."

The veins in Rowan's right arm flared an even brighter shade of red. Tendrils of crimson mist rose from his palm. The cords of vapor wound up his arm in a way that reminded me of entwined serpents. Rowan spoke again.

"Take the form."

The thin lines of red smoke transformed into a pair of

long winding serpents with red scales and black fangs. The two went in opposite directions. The first serpent slithered up the column to Rowan's left; the second did the same on his right. Once they reached they top of their respective pillars, the two serpents contorted into different shapes.

The first snake glowed with red light before turning into a golden hue. On the pillar to Rowan's left, there now stood a golden throne made from the curling body of the first serpent. The realization smacked into me.

Here was a new throne for a new ruler.

Rowan was about to fight his brother and quite possibly lose. A weight of worry pressed in around me. Rowan looked too sick to fight anyone.

"Finish it," called Rowan.

On the right, the second serpent had twisted itself into a zigzag shape. With another flash of light, the second snake also transformed. This time, the serpent changed into stacks of corded wood. My breath caught. You didn't become a Grand Mistress Necromancer without knowing a funeral pyre when you saw one.

A new throne or a death pyre… Those were his choices.

My insides twisted with worry. In fact I became so caught up, I didn't notice someone was behind me until she spoke.

"You need to leave."

I didn't need to turn around to know it was Zoriah. There were too many people for her to pick me out of a crowd, which could only mean one thing.

"You had a vision that I would come to see Rowan."

"I had such a vision, yes. You came here because you wish to help him."

I turned around to face her. Zoriah was wearing the

Caster leathers herself, only hers had the insignia of the royal guard. She even wore a helm. "Why the disguise?"

"No questions." She gestured toward the jungle. "Walk toward the trees."

I sniffed. "I am not following you into the jungle alone." I scanned the crowd. "It seems as if some people welcome the idea of Shujaa as King, but others don't. Is that why you're hiding and skulking about?" I lowered my voice. "Are you trying to figure out who's on your side?"

Zoriah gripped my wrist. "You need to come with me now."

I broke free from her grasp. "Why are you so set on taking me away from here? What's about to happen with Rowan?" My gaze returned to the tallest pillar. Rowan had his arms raised and seemed ready to address the crowd.

"Away," hissed Zoriah.

I ignored her.

Rowan began to speak. Again, his voice was magickally enhanced, so I could hear very word. "Tomorrow morning, I fight my brother. You knew him as Storm. I know him by his traditional name, Shujaa."

I gasped. *The fight is tomorrow? I thought it was a week away.*

"By the Lady of Creation," snarled Zoriah. "I was supposed to pull you aside and get you out of here before you heard that. Now, I shall have to be obvious. I didn't want to expose our alliance."

I rounded on her. "Alliance? Exposed? What are you talking about?"

"This." Zoriah tapped the totem ring on my finger. The one from Petra.

"Transport," said Zoriah quickly. The word rang with the power of magick.

The world around me disappeared in a haze of blue smoke. My last thought was that Petra could have given any mage the power to activate her totem ring. But it would indeed need to be part of a deep magickal alliance.

Petra was in league with Zoriah.

And now, thanks to that alliance, I was being transported to away from Rowan on the eve of his big battle with Shujaa. My choices were being taken away from me again, and this time, it was by my own Mother Superior. Well, if she thought she could stop me from helping Rowan, she was wrong. I'd made my choice.

I would return to fight, no matter what.

he mist of the transport spell surrounded me. Agony careened through my body; it was like being torn limb from limb. I tried to scream, but no sound escaped my lips. Painful questions overwhelmed my mind. Asking them almost hurt more than the spell itself.

Why had Petra and Zoriah teamed up?

What would happen to Rowan?

And what's about to happen to me?

The next thing I knew, I stood in the center of a small clearing that was high up on a snow-covered mountainside. Chilly air singed my lungs. Above me, thick columns of ice scaled up the mountain, reminding me of so many folds in a great blue curtain. Below me, thin clouds obscured the view. I hugged my elbows. There was no question where the transport spell had taken me.

Zelle Mountain.

That meant my old Cloister wasn't far away. Neither was my Mother Superior.

I cupped my hand beside my mouth. "Where are you, Petra?"

Her voice sounded behind me. "Greetings."

That was the second time someone had snuck up behind me today. Turning around, I saw an elderly woman in long black robes with a shock of white hair to her waist. Petra's features stayed maddeningly calm as she spoke again. "Aren't you going to call me Mother?"

I didn't bother hiding my angry glare. The woman just betrayed me, and now she wanted to play verbal games? I was not in the mood. Instead, I lifted my left arm and began pulling in Necromancer energy. "Here's what happens now. I transport back to Rowan's castle. You *never* interfere with my life again."

Closing my eyes, I pulled fresh Necromancer power into my soul and focused it on my left hand. A chill crept over my skin as my bones glowed blue with magick. I began the incantation for the transport spell.

"From the—"

Pain burned up my arm. The totem ring that Petra had given me now shone with bright blue light. I curled my hand against my chest and hissed in breath. "What is this?"

"I should think that would be obvious."

I gripped the ring and tried to pull it off. The thing wouldn't budge. The pain grew more intense. Still, none of this seemed real. Had Petra booby-trapped this ring so she could control my comings and goings? Perhaps there was another, less awful explanation for what was happening. "This ring won't allow me to transport."

"Obviously." Petra shook her head. "I feared as much.

You've grown sloppy and weak. That ring was my casting. Did you really think I'd give you a transport totem ring and not add in some safeguards to control where you'd go?"

In other words, there was no innocent explanation. The truth hurt worse than my hand.

"No, I didn't suspect you'd give me a booby-trapped ring. I thought—" I bit back a yelp of pain. This couldn't keep going on. There was no other choice. I released every last wisp of magick from my body. The moment my transport spell stopped, so did the agony. The ring quickly returned to a non-glowing shade of silver.

Petra raised her left hand. All her fingers glimmered with totem rings. My heart sank. That many rings meant a lot of spells. She'd been preparing for this moment for some time. I stared down at the transport totem ring. No, I couldn't get it off, but there was a limit to how much magick one of these bands could hold. Most likely, it only contained enough power for two or three transports as well as the ability for Petra to stop me from going anywhere.

That was the dark side of my situation.

The brighter side was that I could still cast anything other than a transport spell.

"You must realize how foolish this is," I said slowly. "I can't transport away, but I can certainly defend myself." No totem ring could block every casting. Only enchanted manacles could do that, and those were extremely rare. "What's your plan?"

"The same as it has always been." Petra's nostrils flared slightly. That meant she was furious. "I am your Mother Superior. You must follow the path I lay out for you. And I'm stronger than I appear. Inevitably, you'll see the wisdom of my advice. Save us both the pain of fighting over it."

I rubbed my neck in a weary rhythm. "Let me guess. You wish me to take my crown as Tsarina."

"It's what you should have done months ago."

"No, Petra."

"I feared you would say such things." She raised her left hand. The rings on two of her fingers shone with blue light.

More spells were coming.

To stop the pain from Petra's ring, I'd fully drained magick from my body. Now, I quickly pulled in a fresh supply. Whatever Petra cast, I had to be ready to counteract it.

The rings on Petra's knobby fingers turned blindingly bright as she called out two words. "Cage! Bindings!"

Two fresh spells were coming.

The flare of blue light died down from Petra's rings. The ground beneath me vibrated for a moment. All of a sudden, a line of teeth burst up from the ground. They were tall and thin, reminding me of the fangs of a giant serpent. The teeth shot up ten feet high, surrounding me like bars in a circular jail cell. I could easily cast a smasher skeleton to take them down, but I needed to focus on pulling in enough power to cast one.

This was Petra's first spell: *"Cage."* The bone jail looked fearsome, but I could break through it easily enough.

But Petra's second spell had been *"Bindings."* That magick would far more worrisome. Petra was summoning enchanted manacles. I'd run across these beauties before at the Midnight Cloister. They were hefty iron handcuffs that contained both Caster and Necromancer magick—hybrid items created by none other than Viktor himself. They'd block my ability to cast anything at all.

I didn't know how Petra got her hands on these things, but that didn't really matter at the moment. She had them, and she was casting a mini transport spell to place them on my wrists.

That wasn't something I could allow her to do.

With all my will, I drew fresh power into my body. Sure enough, wisps of smoke quickly appeared around my wrists. The magick wasn't mine. Petra's spell was already transporting the enchanted manacles onto my arms. Good thing I'd pulled in some serious power. I spoke the words to summon a few useful friends.

"My Brothers and Sisters
Born of bone and night
Appear to me now
Feast on my plight"

The moment my incantation ended, my left palm glowed with blue light. After that, a dozen ghosts appeared around me, their translucent bodies having the same dull gray hue. All wore Necromancer robes as they hovered around me. These were hungry ghosts. In life, they were Necromancers who'd become twisted by magick and still craved it in death. I didn't summon them often, but this was the kind of casting where they were ideal.

The ghostly figures stared hungrily at the haze of magic around my wrists. "What are you waiting for?" I asked. "Eat it up."

They flew down onto my wrists, their ghostly hands tearing off bits of Petra's power and stuffing it into their mouths. Their gray bodies lit up as they ate up every bit of the spell. It took an effort not to smile. Petra had taught me everything I knew. Hungry ghosts were one of her favorite spells.

Within seconds, all the magick from Petra was gone from

my wrists. The spirits all turned to me, their faces tight with craving for more power...And I had plenty in my soul. If I didn't send them away, they'd tear me apart. I had saved some magick for this, though. I spoke the words to partial dismissal spell.

"Leave me now
The danger had ceased
You may only return
For the very same feast"

The hungry ghosts vanished, but if Petra tried another mini-transport spell like that last one, they'd reappear and start feasting once more.

There were no manacles on my wrists, but my body felt drained. Casting hungry ghosts was no easy thing to do. Still, I was far from giving up. I began pulling more power into my body, and since this was the Zelle Mountain, there was magick everywhere. Taking in the fresh energy felt like drinking a cool glass of water on a hot summer's day. *Delicious.*

Petra stalked closer. "You can't cast a transportation spell, but perhaps you'll be tempted to break through my cage and escape on foot."

I raised my hand. My bones glowed blue. "You wouldn't be wrong."

"Think, Elea. It's a long way to run down the mountainside. That's tiresome enough, but you'll be casting against me all the way. And if you do get free from me, where will you find a mage strong enough to transport you to Nyumbani? Be reasonable. I only ask for a minute to make my case properly. I'm afraid we've gotten into a deep misunderstanding."

My chest tightened with longing. How I wanted to believe this was all some simple mistake. Unfortunately, that wasn't possible, and I couldn't take any risks with Rowan's life. I must return for his fight with Shujaa. Anything else was a distraction.

"You broke my trust, Petra. That means you don't get a chance to explain yourself. I'm leaving."

Petra raised her left arm again. More rings glowed with sapphire light. Her voice cut through the chill air. "Craniant!"

The word made my insides twist with fear. I'd heard about the craniant—they were fearsome bone monsters—but I'd never actually seen one of them get cast. All of a sudden, being stuck in a cage felt like a very bad place to be.

An entire sheet of snow undulated above my head. Great rumbles sounded as the packed ice started to splinter. The wall of snow burst, and out stepped a massive monster made of thousands of skulls. The thing took a humanoid shape with gangly limbs. A great club was held in its fist. The weapon was also formed from skulls.

A craniant. This wasn't good.

The monster leaned back, making its long arms sway behind it. The creature opened its mouth and let out an ear-splitting roar.

"Craniant," called Petra. "Show my Novice some manners."

The monster crouched down beside my cage. Its head was as tall as my entire body, and all the skulls that made up its face chattered and twitched as it spoke. "Heed your Mother."

Petra stepped closer, stopping just outside the circle of bones that acted as my cage. A fresh ring glowed on her hand. She was ready to cast yet another spell.

"Fine," I said. "You win. I'm listening." I didn't hold out much hope for Petra to make any sense, but I did need some extra time to pull in more magick. Fighting a craniant would not be easy.

"Will you be our Tsarina?" asked Petra.

"No."

She shook her head. "Then there's another way to end this madness. If you won't become Tsarina, then you must give up your powers. Go where they mean nothing."

I stared at her, my features slack with shock. "You want me to join the Sire of Souls?"

"Yes, leave this realm. That's what you did to Viktor, didn't you? Cross a gateway. If you enter in that manner, you won't become a ghost. Imagine. You'll be able to enjoy all the intellectual pursuits of the palace of the Sire of Souls. There will be nothing but quiet study for all eternity."

There were so many flaws with her plan, I didn't know where to begin. I started with the most obvious. "It's not that easy to cross over. Rowan helped me send Viktor away. Before that, we got a special spell for Oni and Yuri."

"How little you know. Viktor left behind totems. I've been able to acquire one that can help in this area. I can easily open the gateway to the Eternal Lands."

My eyes widened. "I know where you got those totems. You're in league with Zoriah."

Petra blinked. "I'm sure I don't understand what you mean."

"Viktor left some totem armor behind. Zoriah's son Shujaa has been using it." I didn't add in that he'd been employing it to create golden warriors.

"If I made a trade with Zoriah, then I did nothing wrong."

I knew Petra well enough to guess the kind of agreement she'd made. "You promised to keep me away from Rowan when the time came, and in return, you received this gateway totem to send me away if I wouldn't become Tsarina." My heart sank. "And then you cast a transport ring to drag me back when you wanted me."

"Those were last options," said Petra. "Failsafe plans, as it were. Honestly, I don't know how Rowan has lasted this long. Based on the power Shujaa is pulling out of him to create those warriors, Rowan should have been dead weeks ago."

A chill crept over my skin, and it had nothing to do with the weather. "You've gone mad."

Petra huffed out a frustrated breath. "What a child you are. As I told you, I have Seers now. I know many new things, and yes, that has opened my eyes. But that's not important. All that matters is that I can help you to cross over to the Eternal Lands. Once you're gone, a new Tsar or Tsarina can safely be named."

"Name one now, Petra. You have my blessing."

"Nonsense. Until you are gone, the Necromancers won't follow another mage." She waved her hand dismissively. "Let's not pretend you want to be here. The Seers have told me that you're done playing at being a farmer. Your choices are to become Tsarina…Or move on and let someone else lead us."

There was something wrong with her logic, but I couldn't quite put my finger on it. "I could hide from you all."

"But not from your true nature as a Necromancer." Petra stepped closer to my cage. "The Seers have shown me what happened to Viktor. He was powerful like you, but unable to control it. In the end, it drove him mad. You can't be off on your own, causing trouble."

I set my hand on my throat. "I'm nothing like him."

"The Seers don't think so. You're choices are simple. You must stay here and become Tsarina or cross over into exile."

I hugged my elbows. Over the years, I'd learned a lot about

the court of the Sire of Souls. It was a peaceful place with meditation, books, and learning...But no magick. That was only possible in the mortal realm. I closed my eyes and searched my soul.

Did I want to give up my powers? It would mean leaving everything behind for a life of eternal tranquility.

There would be no more battles.

No more spells.

And I'd never see Rowan again.

From the deepest parts of me, the answer was instantly clear. No, I would never give up my magick. It was part of the fabric of my very soul, and its energy tied me to Rowan in ways that went beyond the mating band. Losing it was turning away from the most central part of myself.

I locked gazes with Petra. "I don't care what the Seers say. I am a Necromancer and a strong woman. I can handle this power. I won't be Tsarina, and I won't be sent off into exile. Do you have any other choices to offer?"

Petra whispered the words to a fresh incantation. Smoke appeared around her left hand. A moment later, the enchanted manacles were in her fist. "You can stay here and wear these."

I rolled my eyes. "So, no additional choices." Eye-rolling was a flagrant break with Necromancer ways, but at this point, I didn't care. All I could focus on was what I had to do next.

Looks like I'm breaking free and speed-casting my way down the mountain.

Petra stepped back. "You're as weak and emotional as a Caster." She waved her arm, and the craniant rose to its full height and lifted it cudgel. The thing was about to attack.

I'd been pulling in Necromancer power for some time.

Now, I sent it rushing to my left arm. A good shatter spell would take down that craniant. I started the incantation.

"Power and light
Bone and—"

Petra raised her left hand and spoke two words. "Bone dart." One of her rings flared with blue light. A hail of tiny white needles flew off her palm and straight at me.

Bone darts.

They'd paralyze me and put me to sleep.

Suddenly, I had a much bigger problem than the craniant.

I refocused my energy, switching my power from the shatter spell to an incantation for protection.

"Shield my—"

The first dart hit me before another word left my mouth. A dozen needle-like projectiles struck my torso. The magickal poison stopped me instantly. I curled over and fell into the snow as my visions began to blur.

Petra stepped right up to the bars of my bone cage. "Don't worry. When you wake up, I'll have a visitor for you who will change everything. I can still convince you to become Tsarina."

My last act of consciousness was to growl my displeasure. It was another kind of emotional display that Necromancers loathed, and I couldn't help the small sense of triumph as a muscle ticked along her jawline.

21

When I woke up, I found myself deep inside the Zelle Cloister. There was no mistaking the energy signature – this was the place where I'd trained for so many years. The chamber was new to me, however. Like most of the Zelle, it was a small room that had been scooped out of the mountain. In fact, the rock wall above my cot still held scratch marks from where skeletal servants had originally dug out the room.

I tried to move on my small wooden cot. Not happening. Heavy ropes bound me in place. Plus, someone had changed me from my Caster leathers into my Necromancer robes. For some reason, of all the things happening right now, that change of outfit bothered me the most.

Petra sat on a tall wooden chair by my bedside. Beside her, a small wooden table held a single candle. It was the only illumination in the room.

Petra leaned forward. "You're awake. Are you feeling better? I had our healers cast spells on you to reverse the effects of the battle." In other words, my needle marks were gone. I supposed she wanted a thank you.

She wouldn't get one.

I was in no mood to chat with my old Mother Superior. Closing my eyes, I reached out for Necromancer power instead. Try I might, I found nothing. No magick. No energy. My skin turned slick with sweat. Not being able to access magick was trouble, pure and simple. Either I was very tired, or there were enchanted manacles on my wrists. Whoever had tied me to the bed had done so where I couldn't see my torso easily. Curling up my body, I tried for a better look at my hands.

Sure enough, a heavy loop of iron surrounded each of my wrists. Enchanted manacles. *By the Sire.* My powers were blocked. Even worse, the last time I removed these manacles, Rowan had to help me, and the whole process almost killed me.

Petra's features stayed still as a stone wall. "You should speak when you're spoken to."

"How about this? Let me out of here."

Petra straightened her back. "You'll be happy to know we received a message from Rowan. He understands that you've chosen to take your role as Tsarina and wishes you well."

I twisted under the coil of ropes. "You told him *what?*"

Petra gave me the barest of shrugs. "Do you think this is easy for me? I'm the one who has to guide you into claiming your rightful role. One day, you'll thank me."

"That won't happen, I assure you."

"There's much I haven't told you."

"So you keep saying. Please, just stop all this and let me go."

Petra leaned back in her chair. I'd seen this movement

before. It was what she did when she about to give me a lesson. "This is what you need to understand. For centuries, our people have been growing weaker. Necromancer magick is becoming too much for them. Many Necromancers stopped casting and simply let the power consume them. That's why you were able to summon those hungry ghosts. There are countless more where they came from."

For years, there had been stories about the Necromancers growing weaker. I'd been happy on my farm, so I hadn't really paid much attention one way or another. And when Viktor had killed off the last Tsar, I was more worried about my curse than anything. I certainly never wondered why one mage was able to take down the old Tsar.

"That's all the more reason to hate Viktor," I said. "He used the weakened state of the Necromancers to take over. And it's why you shouldn't be using his totems." I rattled my manacles for emphasis.

"You may not believe this, but Viktor wasn't always evil."

"You're right, I don't believe it."

"Use your mind and move past emotions, Elea. The fact is, Viktor was sent to our lands for a reason. He was supposed to strengthen the Necromancers, but he wouldn't follow his destiny. Instead of helping us, he murdered the Tsar and began killing and draining his own kind. Now you have his same gifts and strength. That is nothing less than a boon from the gods. You must use that power to fulfill Viktor's life path and rejuvenate our people."

I couldn't believe what I was hearing. *Petra is delusional.* "And the fact that I'm not agreeing to this plan means nothing to you?"

"Not yet."

"Ah, that's right. You expect some mystery visitor to

change my mind." Those were the last words Petra had said to me after her bone darts had knocked me unconscious.

"I most certainly do." Petra rose, picked up the candle, and strode across the room. The space was larger than I'd initially thought. As she neared the opposite side of the room, I could see four gleaming spikes has been set into the wall. The metal shone with a purple sheen. These were more of Viktor's totems, and if they worked anything like what I'd seen with Shujaa, then they only needed a magickal source to get them activated.

Petra set her palm flush against the rock wall under the gateway. She began whispering an incantation under her breath. The bones of her arm glowed blue. Power streamed out from her palm in four neat lines, one headed for each of the spikes. The metal glowed bright purple before a door-shaped hole appeared in the wall.

My breath caught. Petra had said she could help me go live in the palace of the Sire of Souls. Had she just created a gateway to the Eternal Lands?

I forced my breathing to slow. *Stay calm, Elea. Think.*

My logical side pointed out a few facts. I'd been through situations like this before, and it had all been a matter of perspective. Take Rowan, for example. Everything had seemed horrible with him being engaged to Amelia. However, once I found out more, it all had made sense.

My emotional side pointed out that Rowan hadn't tied me down and blocked my powers with enchanted manacles in order to make his point.

I had to admit, my emotional side was making more sense right now.

A figure stepped up to stand in the darkened doorway. I blinked hard, not believing what I saw.

It was Tristan.

My one-time best friend appeared as when I'd last seen him. He was all pale skin, high cheekbones, and jet-black hair. He still wore his Necromancer robes, but now they were paired something I'd never seen before: a circlet of white gold atop his head. That could only mean one thing.

Tristan hadn't been human. Ever.

I'd heard stories of the members of Oni and Yuri's court. They were descendants from the dark days when gods mated with humans. The result was part human, part immortal.

The small chamber took on a dreamlike haze as I realized one simple fact: Tristan had lied to me more than I'd known.

He was a godling.

Tristan stepped into the chamber. "Someone summoned me." He squinted. "Elea, was it you? I wasn't expecting it so soon." He scanned the darkness but didn't step any farther into the chamber.

Petra stepped forward. "I'm the Mother Superior of the Zelle Cloister, and Elea is my charge. I brought you here to talk some sense—"

There was no way I'd listen to this speech again. "She's got me tied up over here, Tristan."

"What?" Tristan snapped his fingers, and a ball of blue light formed at the center of the ceiling. So Tristan could still do magick. I thought that was impossible once you crossed over.

I shook my head. Tristan was a godling. They could do whatever they liked.

Tristan spied me on the cot, and his handsome face drooped into a scowl. "Petra did that to you?"

"Of course, I did," offered Petra. "I had to. My Seers showed me what her life path is. She needs to follow it."

"Not like this." Tristan snapped his fingers once more. The ropes that bound me fell apart.

Thus far, my encounter with Tristan was going pretty well. I was now no longer tied up, and I was pretty certain I had an ally against Petra. Sure, Tristan had lied to me about being human instead of a godling, but all of that felt very secondary to him being my ally right now. I simply had to return to Nyumbani.

Without my help, Rowan could die.

I gingerly sat up. My muscles ached from being held in one position for so long. I lifted my wrists, showed the manacles to Tristan, and spoke in my most casual voice. "Take these off while you're at it."

"I'm afraid I can't do that just yet." Tristan gave me his sad puppy look, which always used to work when I thought he was alive and mortal.

Not so much now.

My blood heated with anger. "Why are you here? And why did you never tell me that you're a godling?" I raked my fingers through my hair. "You know what? Forget I asked. This is our second useless conversation in as many days. You're a liar."

Tristan rounded on Petra. "What have you done? This is precisely how Viktor went evil. You can't force her."

I set my hand on my throat. Tristan now knew about Viktor being groomed to run the Necromancers? It took some effort, but I forced myself to stand. "Someone tell me what's going on."

But Petra and Tristan were staring at each other. At last, Tristan broke the silence. "Do you have any idea of my role in the Sire of Soul's court?"

I raised my hand. "I'd like to know that actually."

Petra began to tremble slightly. She held her hands up, palms forward. "I can explain."

"You shouldn't have summoned me with Viktor's totem. She's clearly not ready." Tristan sighed and turned to me. "First things first. You must want answers, Elea."

"Yes." *Finally.*

"I'm not dead. And I'm not a ghost."

"Guess what? I figured that out already. You're a godling of the Sire's court, and you tricked me into getting a curse."

"Please understand," said Tristan. "Despite the mistakes" — here Tristan glared at Petra— "everything can still go to plan."

I folded my arms over my chest. What I wouldn't give to cast a bone melter spell right now. "There's a plan?"

Tristan gave me a sly smile. "Someone always has a plan."

Sly smiles. How did I ever let that work on me?

"Let me make one thing clear," I said. "I can't cast spells, but I can slam these manacles right into your throat. Stop playing around."

Petra stepped between us. "Consider this, Elea. I have Seers now. I know everything. You have a special role for our people. Look at Tristan. He's a godling from the court of the Sire of Souls. And he cares about you and our work here. Isn't that exciting? Doesn't that change your mind?"

"It's doesn't, and I loathe you both." I started toward the door, but Petra stepped into my path. She raised her hand high, and I noticed she had a new set of totem rings on all her fingers.

Escape wasn't going to be easy.

"I'll be fully honest with you," said Petra.

"I'm listening."

"According to the Seers, the problem is Rowan." She lifted her chin again, and the movement was starting to annoy me.

"You will accept your destiny once Genesis Rex is killed. They've confirmed this."

My throat tightened with dread. "So that's another reason why you and Zoriah are working together. You both want Rowan dead."

Tristan started talking to Petra like I wasn't there. "The mortal's death might work; it might not. Seeing is not an exact art. Still, this Genesis Rex won't last much longer. We'll know the outcome soon enough."

Worry bit into my temples. I'd forgotten that Rowan's battle was due to begin this morning. "Has the fight with Shujaa started?"

Tristan nodded. "It began a few minutes ago." He reached into his long coat and pulled out a small polished stone. "This is a scrying stone. It will show you how it ends."

"Good." I marched over to Tristan and held my hand out in a gesture that said, *Place that right here.*

Tristan started to set the stone on my palm, but paused. "Once this infatuation with Rowan is over, I humbly beg you to summon me once more. I'll return and explain everything. You can be Tsarina, or you can cross over to the other side with me. Whatever you want."

I couldn't help but notice these were the same two choices that Petra gave me. "And what about staying here as a magick user?"

Tristan's shoulders slumped. "It's not ideal, but I'll see what I can do."

"And if I want a life with Rowan?"

"He's not an option at all." Tristan's face hardened with something close to rage. "I had no idea that things between you had gone so far, but then, we can't see everything from the other side."

I scooped the stone from him and raised my wrists once more. "Take these off and let's talk right now."

"How I wish I could." Tristan stepped toward the gateway, stopped, and then turned back to face me once more. "I know you. You'll need to see firsthand that this is over before you can move on."

I gripped the stone so hard, my knuckles turned white. "Everyone seems to have plenty of ideas about my life."

Tristan shook his head sadly. "Just summon me again when it's over." He stepped through the new door-hole in the wall. Once Tristan was out of view, the wall sealed over again like nothing had happened.

Petra sped to my side. "Isn't it exciting? That was a godling, right here, in my Cloister." Her eyes glittered with excitement before she schooled her features again. "You should be honored you were given such a gift over hybrid magick."

"You've mentioned that before." I wanted to toss my new scry stone at her head. Instead, I sat back down on my cot and inspected Tristan's gift. It was a small flat rock the size of my palm. The stone's surface was covered in carving of Necromancer runes. As I stared at the surface, the lines expanded and rearranged themselves until I could see the image of Rowan and Kade. Both were in battle leathers. Kade was gripping a short sword in each hand. Rowan's right arm was raised as he prepared to cast a spell. My breath caught. The battle had indeed begun.

Next, Shujaa and Wren appeared on the surface of the stone. Rowan was still casting his spell, which meant he was vulnerable. Shujaa was brandishing a long sword while Wren held massive stingers in her fists. They were both heading toward Rowan.

I clenched the stone so tightly, I almost expected it to crack.

Not Rowan, please.

My wish was answered in the most horrible way possible. At the last second, Shujaa and Wren turned away from Rowan and descended on Kade. Wren jammed her stinger-daggers into his shoulders. Shujaa thrust his long sword into Kade's side. Rowan's hand became encircled with tendrils of mist as he released his spell.

After that, all images from the stone disappeared.

I tapped the scrying stone, held it up to my eye, and even shook it a few times. There was nothing.

Petra sat down beside me on the bed. "He's dead then." Her voice was carefully gentle. "Are you ready to discuss your role as Tsarina? That's what I want." She gestured to the door. "It's what all the Necromancers want."

I clenched the scrying stone to my chest. Petra's words whirled through my mind.

"That's what I want."

A realization crept across my consciousness. For so long, I'd heard one version after another of that phrase.

Petra wants.

Tristan wants.

Philippe wants.

Even Zoriah wants.

Yet, there was only one person who has always asked me what I want. That was Rowan. And it seemed, he'd endured a lot of pain to give me that choice. And now, he was fighting Shujaa and Wren alone.

I had to help him. Now.

The glitter of the metal spikes caught my eye. An idea formed. Enchanted manacles were made with hybrid magick.

So were the spikes that opened the gateway to the Eternal Lands. Could I somehow harness power from one to destroy the other?

It was the best chance I had.

Only, I couldn't play around with spikes and manacles with Petra sitting beside me. Fortunately, my Mother Superior was a true Necromancer. We had our rituals for the dead, and I could only hope she hadn't gone so crazy she wouldn't honor them.

Petra patted my hand. It was an awkward tap, as Necromancers never touched. For years after I joined the Zelle, I craved any kind of touch or physical affection. Now, the feeling of Petra's papery skin against mine made me ill.

"It's over," I said in a low voice. "I hereby request a minute for the Sire." This was an old ritual where the person closest to the deceased spent a minute alone with the dead body. Everyone had to leave the room. It was one of our oldest traditions.

"But there's no body," said Petra.

"I have the scrying stone. In cases where the body cannot be found, it is allowed for the primary mourner to use an item from the deceased."

"We should summon Tristan first."

"That breaks tradition."

Petra pointed at the wall. "But he said for you to summon him right away."

"One minute for the Sire. That's all I ask of you." I made sure to sniffle loudly. "I'm sure it will help me accept this loss gracefully."

Petra nodded toward the heavy wooden door. "I'll stand right outside, if you need me."

I could have danced for joy. "Thank you."

Petra stood. "A single minute, not a second more."

"I ask nothing more than what tradition demands."

"As is just and right." At last, Petra stepped away and closed the massive wooden door behind her. That meant I had a minute to figure out how to break these manacles. My plan simply had to work. Shujaa was winning the battle. Without my help, I knew one thing for certain.

Rowan was good as dead.

22

*B*efore me, the heavy wooden door slammed shut with a spine-rattling thud. I exhaled a long breath.

Petra was gone.

Once more, I sat alone in my prison cell. Lines of frost crisscrossed the dark stone walls. My small wooden cot creaked as I shifted my weight. The stump of a candle flickered on a nearby table, its flame whipping about while it struggled to stay alight.

One minute.

Petra promised to give me that long to mourn the *supposed* death of Rowan. Much as I wanted to obsess over all that had just happened with the gateway and Tristan, I had far more pressing worries.

Like Rowan and Kade.

I rushed over to the back wall and pulled at one of the metal spikes. The thing wouldn't budge. Normally, I'd simply pull some Necromancer power into my arm, gain magickal energy, and yank the thing out. But the manacles made that impossible.

So, I did the next best thing. The spike stood out about six inches from the wall. I jammed the spike between my left wrist and the manacle. It was a tight fit, but possible. Both the manacle and the spike were filled with magick. Whichever totem was more powerful would shatter the other.

Once I was certain the spike was well inside the loop of manacle, I pulled with all my strength. A long crack sounded as the spike tore through the metal manacle like it was paper.

Thank the gods. Maybe they were on my side, after all.

"Elea? Are you all right?"

I didn't answer. I jammed the same spike between my right wrist and the manacle that encircled it. Once again, the spike tore through the loop of metal.

I was free.

The door slammed open. Petra stood at the threshold, her face pale. "What are you doing?"

I glared at her. "Leaving."

Petra raised her left hand. Blue light blazed from all her totem rings. "Stop this nonsense. Don't you see my totems? You're not enough of a Necromancer to win against them."

My stomach sank. She was right.

All of a sudden, Rowan's advice came back to be. *"Physical force can be more powerful than magick."*

"No, Petra. I'm *not* a strong enough mage."

But I may be a powerful enough woman.

Leaping forward, I grabbed Petra's shoulder and pinched hard, right on the spot where Rowan had taught me. She collapsed onto the floor.

By the gods. I knocked her out.

My little prison cell took on a surreal haze. At this

moment, my old Mother Superior lay curled up on the floor. This was the woman I'd trusted for five long years.

My movements felt dreamlike as I scooped up Petra, set her on my cot, and carefully checked her breathing. She'd wake up again and soon.

That meant I needed to quickly cast some additional spells. I'd pull Petra's totem rings off her fingers, but without knowing what was loaded on them, I couldn't activate the magick. And casting a detector spell on each ring? That would take up too much time.

It was down to me.

Closing my eyes, I pulled in fresh Necromancer magick. Energy careened through me; I stifled a gasp. After the manacles had blocked me, it felt amazing to have magick wind through every corner of my body. I drove it into my left hand. The skin on my arm chilled over; the bones there rapidly glowed blue. The strength of the spell became so potent, the temperature in the entire room dropped. My breath appeared in puffs of white as I began casting a series of spells.

First, I placed sleeper spell on Petra. I didn't need her waking up any time soon.

Second, I set a ward against further visitors to this prison cell. It would last for at least a few hours. In other words, this way I wouldn't have anyone *else* waking up Petra, either.

All in all, I'd bought myself some time. There were many more protections and spells that would help, but I couldn't wait any longer. Hopefully, a few hours would be enough for my needs.

Finally, I began the incantation for my transport spell.

> *"Magick is the tie that binds*
> *The hunter that tracks*

The child that follows
Now send me back"

With any luck, this spell would make me appear right beside Rowan. I'd have used it before, but Petra had been so obliging with her transport rings. *What a disaster that had turned out to be.* I crossed my fingers.

Please, let it work now.

Wisps of blue smoke wound around my left arm. Icy bolts of power darted through my chest. I hissed in a pained breath. The sapphire-colored haze poured off my fingertips and onto the floor.

My transport spell had begun.

The magickal haze whirled up my body. Blue smoke clouded my vision. After that came nothing but bone-crunching pain. Agony pressed in as magick transported me to Nyumbani.

The next thing I knew, the blue haze disappeared. Pain vanished. I found myself standing on the lip of red mud over-looking the Genesis Vale. Once again, Casters packed the space between the jungle and the vale below. They were dancing and cheering in the rain.

This wasn't a battle scene. It was yet another Caster cele-bration. Where was Rowan? Had something gone wrong with my transport spell?

Someone gripped my wrist from behind. I spun about to find Jicho. My pulse sped.

Dropping to my knees, I met his gaze straight on. "Where is Rowan?"

A boom of thunder sounded. Jicho didn't flinch as rain-drops streamed down his smiling face. "I knew you would make it." His gaze dropped to the scrying stone in my hand. "Where did you get that?"

I stared at the stone and shrugged. Through everything, I'd still held on to my only connection to Rowan. I handed the disc-like stone over to Jicho. "Someone gave it to me."

Jicho turned it over. "I never thought I'd see one of these."

My voice lowered with desperation. "Please. I need to find Rowan."

Jicho bounced on the balls of his feet. "That's why I'm here. Shujaa cheated. Someone hid extra supplies for him in the jungle to help him."

"Was it Zoriah?"

Jicho nodded. "We can't stop the fight just because Shujaa cheated, but then Kade got hurt. Shujaa stabbed him."

"You said he's hurt...Is Kade's alive?"

"Yes, he's with the healers."

A spark of joy lit in my heart. "Oh, thank the Sire."

"And since Shujaa cheated, Kade has named you as his replacement to be Rowan's second. Kade even gave me the incantation to give you so you can join the fight. Isn't that great?"

I'd never felt more relieved in my life. "Where's the battle?"

Jicho pointed to the Genesis Vale. "There."

I must have misunderstood. "The jungle?"

"That's where all our official battles take place." He nodded toward the three pillars. "That's why Rowan built the throne and pyre here. Whoever wins, they take the throne back to the Genesis Hall and get crowned."

I rubbed my neck as I tried to process this information. In the scrying stone, I'd only seen people, not their surroundings. I'd just assumed there was some kind of neat and formal battlefield.

Then again, knowing Nyumbani, the jungle made sense.

"How do I enter the vale?" I asked.

"There's a line of white stones by the lip of the crevasse," said Jicho. "They keep everyone out except the combatants and their seconds. The stones are hard to see in the rain and mud, but they stop people from breaking into the battle. You just say the incantation to make yourself the second, and then you can join the fight." Jicho had a boy's excitement for all of this.

I gave him a wobbly smile. "I'll transport over."

Jicho frowned. "No transporting in the Genesis Vale. Not until the battle is over."

"Fine. I'll figure out something else. What's the incantation?"

"Speak these six words: my first, my captain, my one."

"That's it?" Caster incantations were too short to be believed.

Jicho nodded. "Only, I can't see if you two win or not…You know…In case you were wondering."

"That's fine, Jicho. Rowan and I only need a chance. Thank you."

With that, I rushed over to the edge of the crevasse. The Genesis Vale loomed below me. It was an impossible labyrinth of jungle. Rowan was down there somewhere.

No question about it. I would find him.

23

I kicked the ground near the lip of the crevasse. Rain pelted me from every direction. Sure enough, a line of white stones lay under the mud. Each one was about the size of a robin's egg. I pulled some Necromancer magick into my body so I could cast right away.

A few Casters bumped into me as they danced on by. They must have been celebrating all night. Everyone was so drunk, no one seemed to notice I was back wearing my Necromancer robes. It was probably for the best. I had enough to worry about without answering a lot of questions.

Closing my eyes, I spoke the words Jicho had given me.

"My first, my captain, my one."

Straightening my shoulders, I stepped forward and crossed the line of stones. I exhaled. The spell worked.

Now it was time to fight.

Raising my left arm, I focused the Necromancer magick that I'd pulled into my body before. Sure, I couldn't use a transport spell to reach Rowan, but I knew the perfect alternative. Power built up in my left arm until my bones vibrated with energy. My hand glowed a searing shade of blue as I spoke my incantation.

"Life from death
Movement from stone
Bring me a winged rider
My mount alone"

The ground trembled with the force of my spell. The Casters nearby let out a drunken bellow of glee. Below me, chunks of stone and red earth tumbled from the cliff side down to the jungle floor. For a moment, everything went silent once again.

Then, a skeletal horse burst from cliff.

Dirt and rock went shooting in every direction as the mare flapped its bony wings and circled the sky. I grinned. *What a beautiful casting.*

The horse hovered before me. The sight seemed to stop the revelry from the nearby Casters, which was an unexpected benefit. Gripping its neck vertebrae, I hoisted myself onto the mount's back and gave my next command.

"Take me to Rowan."

The beast tossed its head and neighed. It was a ghostly noise that reminded me of a thousand spirits speaking at once. Flapping its skeletal wings, my horse rose higher in the sky. Magick made the beast fly, but there were still scraps of flesh on the bat-like wings. As we sped toward the warriors, I cast another quick spell.

"Point and target
Power and bone

Create a weapon
Strong as stone."

Blue smoke wound up my arm as the spell's power grew. A second later, the haze solidified into the shape of a long javelin in my left hand. Up close, the thing was made from hundreds of tiny white bones, each one as delicate as a bird's. Together they created a javelin that was almost as tall and deadly as I was.

Almost.

As we swooped down over the rainforest, a massive explosion sounded.

BOOM!

Just ahead, a column of red fire shot up from the rainforest and disappeared into the clouds. Thousands of birds took to the skies, darkening the landscape below my mount. Fresh plumes of red smoke rolled up in the rain. My skin warmed with a familiar kind of magick. I'd felt that signature before.

That was Rowan's spell.

And I could determine even more than that: this was a sun surge spell. These were incredibly exhausting to cast, but could destroy almost anything. I remembered the strange pattern I'd seen in the scrying stone before. It had looked like everyone disappeared, but that could certainly have been a sun surge spell at work instead.

Up on the lip of the crevasse, the Casters cheered. The explosion had taken place close to the cliff wall. Now they could see something actually happening.

I wanted my horse to land, but I couldn't make out anything on the ground below. Although I was impatient to help, I wouldn't do Rowan any good with a broken neck.

"Fan your wings."

My horse obeyed the command and drove the smoke away. Soon, I could see the ground below me. Where there had once been trees, the space was now a flattened-out clearing. Small fires burned in spots on the now-swampy ground. Three warriors stood in the center of the clearing: Shujaa, Wren, and Rowan. They were all alive, although even from here, I could see how pale Rowan looked. His skin seemed to hang from a far bonier frame than I remembered.

The crowd let out another massive shout. They could see the fighting now, too.

"Down," I commanded.

My horse swooped toward the trio of warriors. Shujaa and Wren stared at me, open mouthed, while Rowan positively beamed in my direction.

I grinned. For another look like that one, I'd do this all over again.

Raising my javelin to shoulder-height, I aimed it straight at Shujaa's chest. I wanted this fight over and quickly. With all my focus, I poured extra magick into my throwing arm, giving my volley even more power. My arm glowed as I finished the throw. With the extra magick from my arm to power it, the weapon sped through the air.

Shujaa only stared at me, his golden face still slack with shock. My heart beat faster.

This was it. I would finally take down Shujaa.

At the last possible second, Wren pushed her master out of the way. Shujaa tumbled onto his face as my weapon speared straight through Wren's chest. My horse whisper-neighed, and I fought back a groan.

It was a miss, but at least I got Wren. She was now tacked to the ground like a bug with a pin. And Shujaa had evidently scuffed his chin, as he now cradled it with both hands and moaned.

Couldn't happen to a nicer pair of Changed Ones.

Far off on the lip of the crevasse, the Caster mob cheered. I was fairly certain that by this point, they were too drunk to care who won, so long as they saw a good fight.

I shook my head. There was no time to worry about the Casters right now. I needed to take down Shujaa. I summoned a new javelin and set my heels into my horse's sides.

"Swoop in after the one in the white leathers." I fond it oddly satisfying to say those words. After all, Shujaa couldn't wear his purple armor on the battlefield.

"Elea, wait!" Rowan raised his right arm. Magick glowed in his veins.

Some small part of me said it was wiser to wait and move into battle as a team with Rowan. But more of me was simply excited to take down Shujaa. I kicked my heels into the horse's sides once more. "Go!"

My flying horse beat a steady rhythm as we winged toward Shujaa. He'd recovered from his shock and was now running across the clearing in a zigzag pattern. Watching Shujaa hightail it across the burned-out ground…all while still cradling his bruised chin? This battle was becoming downright enjoyable.

I gripped my javelin more tightly and sent fresh magick into my arm. With Shujaa moving so much, I'd need to be pretty close in order to ensure that I hit my mark.

Not a problem.

My horse flew faster than ever before. We skimmed along the burned-out ground as we closed in on Shujaa. Suddenly, my mount began swaying from one side to another. *Strange.* If I didn't know better, I'd say it was drunk. Sure, if I got too close to Shujaa, it would make me disoriented. But my horse and I had enough distance. We shouldn't be affected. *Unless Shujaa's power works differently on a creature created with a spell?*

That was when my mount went berserk.

My skeletal horse sped toward the clouds, neighing and coughing the entire way.

Wait, coughing? This horse didn't even have lungs.

That settled it. Shujaa's disorienting spell had a greater effect on magickal animals than mages. I was in deep trouble.

Leaning forward, I grabbed on to my horse's neck for balance. My javelin dropped. From the corner of my eye, I watched Shujaa race into the cover of the rainforest.

Damn. He escaped.

I could cast another kill spell on him, but my horse was going berserk. It was all I could do to use my power not to fall off. I laced my words with magick.

"Set me down by Rowan."

That was what I ordered, but my horse decided to fly higher instead. If I thought it had been pumping its wings quickly before, that was nothing compared to what my mount did now. We quickly sped far above the clouds.

Not good.

Using the last bit of magick I has stored up, I laced my final command with ultimate power.

"Down!"

The moment that instruction left my lips, I knew it was a mistake. The horse flipped directions, pumping with all its speed toward the ground. Even worse, it was heading straight for Rowan, too.

Nothing like killing the both of us at once. *Great work, Elea.*

Rowan stood his ground like some kind of statue on the burning mud. Even from this distance, I could feel his green eyes locking with mine. He raised his arms, and his right hand glowed with power and magick. The request was obvious and unspoken.

Jump.

He didn't need to ask me twice. Rowan was a powerful mage. If he had enough magick stored up, the man could catch the moon.

I leapt off my horse, but my robes got caught on one of its skeletal ribs. The pair of us got snarled as we tumbled through the sky. My stomach turned woozy as I tried to tear my skirt free.

And we were still headed toward Rowan.

One thought crystallized in my mind.

What an incredibly stupid way for a Grand Mistress Necromancer to die.

At the last second possible, I tore my robes free from the horse, but we were still far too close to Rowan. I tried to push the horse away from both of us, but the thing was way too strong and insane.

What happened next took place in seconds, but my mind followed each fraction of time as if it lasted for hours. In one smooth movement, Rowan caught me in his arms, rested his weight on his right foot, and kicked the horse straight in the skull. The thing skidded away to get half-buried in the mud. The thought occurred to me that Kade was right again. Sometimes physical power was a good thing to develop.

If I ever lived through this, I vowed to ask Rowan for fighting lessons.

A moment passed as I lay in Rowan's arms. Our gazes locked right before he curled me against his chest, leaned in close, and nuzzled my neck. "You shouldn't have come."

What a Rowan thing to say. "You know, that thought had

occurred to me." I wanted to sound sassy, but my voice cracked too much for that. I was simply overjoyed to be near him again.

I shook my head. *Overjoyed?* That emotionality was the kind of nonsense that got me in trouble. As in, being friends with a manipulative man like Tristan who was really a godling. But Rowan and I had other matters to worry about right now. "Where's Shujaa? Aren't we in a battle to the death?"

"Zoriah left him little caches of supplies in the jungle. My guess is it's some kind of healing plant."

"That's the cheating Jicho told me about."

"It was. And it appears his treachery ended up in my favor. I take it Kade was able to name a replacement for himself."

"I prefer to think of it as an improvement."

"Quite." Rowan stared off into the jungle. "Under normal circumstances, I would chase Shujaa down. But now that you're here, we can enjoy a few moments to plan."

Part of me noticed that I hadn't asked Rowan to set me down. I decided that it must be the shock of my spell going wrong and rested my head against his shoulder.

"Shujaa has a magickal aura around him that disorients people." Rowan sighed. "I didn't realize it could affect my magick so strongly, though. Most of my castings simply go wrong when they get too close."

"Let me guess. Sun surges are the exception."

"Correct." Rowan's arms trembled as he finally set me onto my feet. "But those spells cost a lot of energy to cast." Rowan looked worse than ever. Up close, his body seemed almost skeletal. Deep bruises marred his skin, and his leathers were seeped in blood.

He needed some healing.

I scanned the clearing. Wren was still stuck in the mud. I'd say she was dead, but her body was vibrating, and the low sound of insect buzzing filled the air. I'm guessing she still had a few tricks left, unfortunately. As for Shujaa, he was still off sneaking healing spells in the rainforest. Rowan and I had a few moments, so I could certainly cast a healing spell. My heartbeat sped up at the thought.

Maybe this spell could do more than heal Rowan. I remembered the fountain in Zoriah's greenhouse. True mates could share power on a circuit, making each other stronger than ever before. Perhaps this spell could start the same process for Rowan and me. We'd become true mates and heal in every way possible.

It was worth a try.

I raised my hand. Magick welled inside me. Power and brightness glowed from my arm. The raindrops reflected the light as they cascaded past my palm.

"Bone and blood
Spirit and skin
Heal this mortal
Without and in"

I set my palm onto the center of Rowan's chest and watched. With all my heart, I wanted to share magick and healing with him in the way that true mates did. Rowan deserved nothing less. I pictured how the blue lines of my power could expand across Rowan's body, making him healthier and stronger. That's what I wanted to happen.

It didn't take place.

In the end, I was only able to conjure a pale puff of blue mist that soaked into Rowan's chest. There was no circuit, though. And there was certainly no massive healing. Still, some of the shadows lifted from Rowan's face. That was better than nothing, I supposed.

I dropped my hand.

Rowan set his knuckle under my chin, guiding my gaze back up to meet his. "Thank you."

I nodded, not trusting my voice.

Rowan must have sensed what I was trying to do. "Zoriah told you about true mates."

"Yes." I hated how my voice cracked.

"I don't need our powers to connect in order to win this battle, or to know that you're my true mate. The circuit will form when the time is right. I can be patient."

I cleared my throat, trying to hide the rasp that was still in my voice. "It looks like Wren is about to get up again. We should prepare to fight."

"Agreed."

I glanced over to where Wren sat pinned to the earth. Her body vibrated violently before transforming completely. Where Wren had once been flesh and blood, she changed into a humanoid form made completely of wasps. The insects flew off in a hundred directions at once. I was guessing they had some kind of preset recovery spell. The wasps would meet back up at a distance so Wren could safety retake her human form at that spot.

It was an impressive trick, I had to admit.

"How long before she returns, do you think?" I asked.

Rowan pursed his lips. "I'd say we have a few more minutes. Hopefully enough to deal with my brother."

"Quick," I said. "We need to cast a kill spell."

Rowan raised his arm and closed his eyes. "It will have to

be another sun surge. It doesn't kill him, but it does slow him down."

My brows lifted. "Just slows him down?"

"That's all. I'm working on another plan to actually destroy him. Turns out, Shujaa is rather hard to kill. The disorientation magick that Viktor placed on Shujaa? It's more powerful than anything I've ever seen before. And as long as Wren stays somewhat near him, she enjoys the same protection as well." He shook his head. "Did I mention that I didn't want you to come here?"

"Don't worry. We'll figure something out."

At that moment, Shujaa sauntered out from the jungle. He wore white battle leathers with a matching helm. Shujaa brandished his long sword, and I could have sworn I saw the gleam of purple light on the metal. Had he swapped out his normal weapon for one that was laden with Viktor's magick? I wouldn't put it past him.

"Do you see that long sword?" I asked.

"I do," says Rowan. "I know what you're thinking, and the answer is yes."

"He's cheating again. We should call off the battle."

"I've already gotten a replacement for my second. If this is reported a second time, I'd forfeit my crown. As King, it was my responsibility to clear the vale of any contraband. I'm sure Zoriah found a way around our wards." He closed his eyes again and focused on pulling in magick.

Meanwhile, Shujaa march closer, all while swinging sword in a great figure eight. The crowd roared with glee. It was getting harder and harder not to hate Rowan's people.

I drew in more Necromancer magick, but my reserves were still far too low. There wasn't enough energy yet for me to start a spell. I glanced over to Rowan. "How long until you can cast another sun surge?"

Rowan opened his right eye a crack. "I just pulled you out of the sky and kicked a horse in the face. I need at least two minutes here."

"Fine." I winked. "Baby."

While Rowan pulled in his own power, I stored up more Necromancer energy. My kind didn't have any equivalent spell to a sun surge. Unfortunately, the most I could do was keep doing healing incantations to keep Rowan going.

That wasn't exactly a winning plan.

Something itched at the back of my mind. I recalled Shujaa's perfect face at the engagement ceremony. Now, his white battle leathers didn't have so much as a spatter of mud. This was all part of a bigger realization, but I couldn't quite reach it.

The crowd broke out into chants of "Shujaa! Shujaa!"

Beads of sweat rolled down Rowan's cheeks as he struggled to pull in fresh magick. Before my eyes, his body turned even more skeletal. With every breath, his chest gurgled with blood.

Rowan was dying.

I gripped Rowan's hand. All the color had drained from his face. He wobbled a bit from foot to foot. "What's wrong?" I asked.

"That sword…" Rowan's voice came out as a croak. "The closer it gets, the more I'm drained."

My heart cracked. Viktor created Shujaa's armor in order to drain Rowan's spirit and create a golden army. It makes sense that Viktor would also create a sword to drain Rowan's body, too.

By the gods. As bad as I thought things were, they just got worse.

The cheers from the crowd grew deafeningly loud. "Shujaa! Shujaa!" I'd never wanted to cast a silencer spell more in my life.

Meanwhile, Shujaa waved to the mob and strutted about. After that, he pulled off his helm. Once again, I saw the man's face: he had tanned skin, green eyes, and golden-blond hair. He was perfect. The realization that had eluded me for so long finally came closer.

Shujaa was actually too perfect...just like those apples I'd seen with Lizzie and Gail.

Memories appeared in my mind, like pages of a book turning on their own. I thought about Zoriah and her greenhouse. I pictured Shujaa at the ruined Caster village. At that time, my bone bomb had barely scratched him, but Shujaa had screamed as if he'd lost a limb. And just now, he almost lost his mind over simply bruising his chin.

It was true that Shujaa raced off into the woods for a weapon. But Rowan said he'd also gone there for Zoriah's healing spells. In a flash, I knew exactly what kind of supplies Zoriah had left for Shujaa.

She'd left fruits that had been struck with freeze blight. Somehow, the freeze blight was protecting Shujaa. Every shielding spell had a weakness. If freeze blight was being used to somehow protect Shujaa, then it could bring him down as well.

And since I was a farm girl, I knew the exact thing that liked to nibble on freeze blight.

I turned to Rowan. "Do have enough power to cast an animal?"

He gave me a shaky nod. "A small one."

"I need you to cast crimson mites."

"The ones who bother cattle?"

"The same. Cast as many as you can and send them at Shujaa."

"Why—" began Rowan.

"There's no time to explain why."

"That's not what I was going to say." Rowan closed his eyes and raised his right arm. The veins there soon glowed red with power as he spoke his incantation.

"Live and bite."

A red mist appeared and enveloped Rowan's hand. A second later, it solidified into a handful of tiny red insects. They dropped from Rowan's palm and sped over the muddy earth toward Shujaa.

Rowan turned to me. "Why didn't I just make you my second from the beginning?"

His words made my eyes sting with held in tears. "You're a little overprotective."

"I'll make a point to work on that."

"Not too hard, though."

Shujaa spotted the red insects as they sped toward him. "What's this? Has my brother resorted to using bugs against me? How very sad."

Moving in a small red wave, the insects sped up Shujaa's legs. Their tiny red bodies stood out clearly against his white leathers. Shujaa clawed at his chest. "Get them off me! They bite!"

Atop the lip of the crevasse, the crowd grew quiet.

Shujaa stripped off his upper leathers, exposing how the mites were biting through the shell of his skin, exposing the milky goop underneath. This was freeze blight, the same as the apples, but some kind of twisted version that Zoriah had created for Shujaa.

I thought back to Wren's story at the burned-out village. How did a scrawny boy miraculously turn into a perfect-looking warrior overnight? Magick, pure and simple.

And all magick has its weaknesses.

Speak of the Caster. Zoriah now stood at the lip of the crevasse, staring down at the battle in horror.

The white substance oozed off Shujaa's body, leaving behind a gray and shriveled up figure. He wasn't old; he wasn't young. Shujaa appeared to be trapped somewhere between being formed and destroyed. A few sickly yellow hairs stuck to his gray head. His eyes were milky white with drooping lids. Shujaa's sword fell from his ruined hand. Shujaa kicked himself toward us on small, misshapen legs.

"Rowan, my brother, you must bring Mother here. She can cure me if she arrives quickly enough."

Rowan's face was still as stone. "She can't cross the barrier into the battle, not until it's over. Not even Viktor can break that magick."

"What about Wren?" asked Shujaa. His voice was starting to crack and fade as well. "She can resign as my second and allow Mother to help me." His skin began to shrivel before our eyes. "Ask your witch to help me, then. Her hybrid magick may have a cure."

I knelt down so I could be eye to eye with him. "The gods themselves could order me to help you, and I wouldn't lift a finger." It was against Necromancer training to feel extremely satisfied in this moment. I decided that I could forget my Necromancer training for today.

Shujaa's body now began to visibly wither. He swung his arms toward Rowan. "Please, brother. Do something."

"I will. I'll watch you die while looking you straight in the eye. This is a situation you created. You wanted this throne. You asked for this battle. And you cheated every way you could in order to drain me so you could achieve your malevolent aims. This death is no more than you deserve." Rowan gently guided me to stand at his side. "And this is the woman I love. She is under my protection. You will never speak to her again."

I leaned in closer against Rowan. Even though he was thin and weak in body, Rowan's spirit had never been stronger.

Shujaa then swung his gaze toward the crowd. "Mother, help me."

Zoriah merely glared at Shujaa and then stepped away into the mass of bodies. Unbelievable. Zoriah had cast a freeze spell on Storm to give him the appearance of strength and beauty. That had turned him into Shujaa, a warrior who was more illusion than reality—a twisted being in a perfect shell.

Before our eyes, Shujaa's body turned into an empty gray husk. A gentle breeze came by, and what remained of Shujaa collapsed into a pile of dust.

Atop the lip of the crevasse, all the Casters stayed silent. Everyone was watching Rowan, waiting to see what he would do next.

"They want you to proclaim victory," I said. My gaze rested on the golden throne that still sat atop its pillar. "You can then officially ascend to your throne."

"We all know that's a lie," said Rowan. "This battle isn't over until Zoriah's dead."

I looked up at the Caster's expectant faces. "Are you going to say something?"

A muscle twitched along Rowan's jaw. "Not today. At this moment, I'm not feeling very Kingly."

"I don't blame you for that." I held my thumb and pointer finger an inch apart. "I came this close to casting a silencer spell on all of them." Rowan gave me a sly smile, and that made my heart soar. I wound my arm about his waist. "Let's get you some rest."

As Rowan and I limped off the battlefield, I knew one thing for certain. This wasn't a victory. It was the first battle in a war we didn't even have a name for yet.

24

*M*oonlight streamed through the windows in Rowan's chambers, casting odd shadows on his bed. I lay atop the covers beside him. Kade, Amelia, and Jicho stood nearby, along with a small horde of healers. They'd been working on both Rowan and me ever since the battle with Shujaa ended. As far as I could tell, they'd been at it for about eight hours or so. I'd been passed out for part of it. By the time I woke up, someone had washed us and stitched us up. That was when family had been allowed into the room.

Kade, Amelia, and Jicho had a never-ending list of questions for me. In some ways, I wished Rowan would wake up so I wouldn't have to field all their queries alone. I explained about the battle and about Storm and Wren. They said Zoriah had left right before I transported us back to the castle. No one had seen her since.

I leaned back on the pillow. It had been an hour of answering questions, and I was ready to sleep. "Thank you for coming by," I said.

Amelia was now washed and coiffed in a fresh pink gown. "Is that your way of asking us to leave?"

I grinned. "In a word, yes."

Kade crossed his arms over his chest. He was back in his red guard leathers and looking fit. "I won't leave my brother."

"The healers say he's fine," I replied. "And we both could use some rest."

One of the young healers stepped forward. "We can escort you to your chambers now, Tsarina." They'd tried to keep me and Rowan apart during the healing process, but one of us always pitched a fit.

"No, I'll stay here. Rowan felt better the last time we slept close by."

Jicho nodded vigorously. "That's right. You're good for each other."

I tried to keep my eyes wide open and failed. "Thank you, Jicho."

They all slipped out of the room as I fell into a deep sleep.

When I woke up again, it was still night. I wasn't sure if it was the same night as the battle or another evening. It was hard to tell when you'd been magickally healed. I rolled onto my side and propped my head on my hand. For a time, I watched Rowan's chest slowly rise and fall. Moonlight shifted over his handsome features. He looked better, but still not back to full strength.

He cracked open his right eye. "I can't sleep with you staring at me."

"I'll look away." I didn't, though.

Rowan opened both his eyes and stretched his arms over his head. "How long have we been asleep?"

"I'm not really sure."

"I had a dream you talked to Kade, Amelia, and Jicho."

"It wasn't a dream. We did speak. They're safe and healed."

Rowan frowned. "What has you worried?"

"Shujaa is dead, but your mother escaped. She'll try to cause trouble."

"Doubtless." He scrubbed his hands over his face. "Perhaps Jicho has some kind of vision that can help us."

I stared at Rowan's handsome face in the moonlight and then did what was possibly the most Zuchtlos action of my life. I leaned over and kissed him. Rowan's mouth was as soft and delicious as I remembered. I suppose my impulsivity could have ended there, but it didn't. I rolled atop him so our bodies lay flush against each other. Our kiss deepened. Rowan's warm hands slid up my back. Words started tumbling from my mouth. "I've never slept with a man before."

Rowan narrowed his eyes. "What's this about?"

I moved to straddle his waistline. "You know what I mean."

Rowan's gaze turned intense. "If we have sex, you're as good as married to me. We'd share any engagements I make in the future."

My eyes widened. "Like the engagement to Amelia."

Rowan nodded. "You have to choose this, Elea."

"I do. Really."

"Our bodies say otherwise. We haven't shared energy."

A shiver of doubt moved up my spine. "Maybe we can't."

"We already did. With Viktor."

"Zoriah says t's not possible for the energy to go both ways. You can only give me your power."

"In that case, we definitely can. If something is good for me, then she goes out of her way to ensure it won't happen."

"She also says I drain you."

A muscle ticked along Rowan's jaw. "That's my choice."

"What do you mean? Please tell me."

"When you're ready, we will bond. I have no doubt of that. And I want a real mating. One that changes everything. A true mating transforms how we kiss, how we fight. It's worth waiting for. You're worth waiting for."

My eyes stung with held-in tears. "How do you know that?"

"You've been in love with me from the first time you saw me, same as I fell in love with you."

"That's not possible."

"We're both people with heavy burdens who carry them for others. We give much to our people, but for ourselves? We have only each other."

My hands were splayed on Rowan's chest. I stared at my mating ring. "Then why can't I share energy with you?"

"For some of us, love is easy. But trust? That takes longer."

A chill crept over my skin. His words hit the mark inside me. When I spoke again, my voice was a rough whisper. "Trust does take longer. Tristan betrayed me."

"With the curse."

"There's more. He's actually a godling. I saw him with Petra and…He said you and I can't be together. That our relationship is impossible."

Rowan wrapped his hands around mine. "What do *you* want, Elea?"

"I want to sleep with you."

A small smile rounded his full lips. "No."

"You're a damned noble menace, you know that? Why can't you take advantage of a girl like a normal person?"

"You know why. And if the situation were different, you wouldn't take advantage, either."

"Maybe I would."

"Then take me. I won't stop you."

I reached toward the waistline of his leathers and stopped. "But you want to wait."

Rowan arched his brow. "You see? Pleasant as this would be, I know you too well. You're only trying to prove that I'm as evil as everyone else. I take advantage and I lose you." His gaze turned intense again. "And I won't lose you."

All of a sudden, voices sounded from the courtyard outside the window. People were yelling. I rushed to the window and looked outside. Casters were scurrying about everywhere. Bells began to ring.

Someone pounded on the door. "It's Kade. Is Rowan awake?"

"I'm up," called Rowan.

"You're needed for a diplomatic summit." Kade's voice shook with anger. "Let's refuse, or better yet, we should—"

"You know we have to respect a request for diplomatic parlay. I'll be right out."

I turned away from the window. "Let me guess. Your mother has returned."

"That would be a safe guess." Rowan cracked his neck from side to side, stepped over to a cabinet, and began refilling all his scabbards with weapons. "No doubt, she's rallied the golden army and plans to march triumphantly into the castle in the name of her favorite son and true King."

"And the fact that Shujaa died as a shriveled-up old blob of gray on a battlefield in front of everyone?"

"That would be why Zoriah is going to march in with a golden army and a great story that she tells under cover of parlay. No doubt, this is all my fault somehow. It will be interesting to see what kind of lie she spins."

"Let me guess. Whatever she says, it will all end with *and that's why I need to be Genesis Regina.*"

Rowan grinned. "You were always a fast learner."

I pulled at the neckline of my jacket. "I'd like to change into some fresh Caster leathers."

Rowan paused. "There's no point asking you to stay out of the battle, is there?"

"Is there going to be a battle? I thought this was a diplomatic parlay."

"Theoretically, it could be a peaceful parlay. She might even release the Casters trapped as enchanted members of the golden army." Rowan shrugged. "But most likely Zoriah will show up, parade around, tell her story, and ask me to resign my crown."

"So why don't you? I mean, your people are rather fickle."

"They have good hearts, Elea. This prophecy is something they've hoped for over a thousand years. If I walk away now, I leave them to tyranny and torment. If the situation were reversed, could you walk away from your Necromancers?"

I pictured the same scene, but with my mages in the place of Rowan's. "No."

"And I won't either. So, I'll tell her I won't resign, and that's when the battle begins. Which brings me back to my previous statement. There's no point asking you to stay out of this fight, is there?"

"Not at all."

"Good." He winked. "We make a good team."

That was one more revelation in a long list of things that I needed time in order to fully process. However, it didn't seem like that was possible at this point. I shook my head. None of this situation seemed real.

Right now, Rowan and I had to go fight his mother.

The gods help us.

25

I stood in Rowan's chambers and pressed my palms against my eyes. Despite the jungle heat, a chill crept over my skin.

This couldn't be happening, could it?

Rowan's mother Zoriah—along with her golden army—were heading straight for this very castle. And although this was supposed to be a parlay, it would most likely end with Rowan and I fighting his only living parent. A heavy sense of dread pressed in around me, tight as a vise.

Surprisingly enough, it had nothing to do with Zoriah.

Every time I closed my eyes, I saw the same face. Viktor. Although I knew more about what was really happening, there were still so many things that didn't make sense, and most of them had to do with him. It made sense that Viktor would have made the armor for Shujaa. Rowan's evil brother had been thin-skinned in the worst sense. The same was true for the disorientation spell: that also kept Shujaa safe. By all accounts, Shujaa had been using both of those protections for years.

Not so with the golden army.

For some reason, Shujaa only started making the golden army *after* Rowan and I sent Viktor into exile. The timing couldn't be more suspicious.

My throat tightened with worry. Petra always said, *"Never enter a battle where you don't fully understand your enemy."* Sadly, I had no idea what Zoriah was truly capable of, let alone Viktor. And yet, Rowan and I would soon face Zoriah along with her golden army.

And Viktor was most likely behind it all.

I straightened my back. *Nothing for it but to move forward.* Lowering my hands, I opened my eyes. Another shock awaited me.

Rowan was naked.

I tried to look away, but my eyes weren't obeying my brain for some reason. Possibly this disobedience was due to the fact that Rowan's bare backside was in full view as he changed into his battle leathers.

Now, Rowan had certainly lost weight. His coloring was pale. A rough cough racked him from time to time. Plus, his skin was even bruised in places. But none of that made any difference. This was Rowan. *My Rowan.* His naked backside was still a beautiful sight.

All of which made me wonder what his front looked like as well. A blush crawled up my cheeks. I was becoming more Zuchtlos by the minute.

"You'd better change," said Rowan. There might have been a bit of a smile in his voice, but I was too distracted to know for certain. "Did you hear me?"

"I, uh, what?"

Well spoken, Elea.

Rowan called over his shoulder. "You'll find battle gear in the chest under the window."

Finally, the words *"battle gear"* snapped me out of my reverie. Once Rowan and I finished this fight against his mother, I could go back to staring.

If we lived through the fight, that is.

Tearing my gaze away, I stepped over to the chest, opened it, and gasped. The wooden box was packed with leathers of every kind, including a set in Necromancer black. All of them were in my size. I turned to Rowan, who had pulled on his breeches. *What a shame.*

I managed to make a single sound. "Huh."

"Didn't you find anything?"

"Let me run through this for a moment." I pointed to the opened chest. "You just so happen to have a trunk filled with leathers for a lady Caster."

"Right."

"And they're all in my size."

"Right again." Rowan pulled on his jacket. "The green bureau is filled with formal dresses for you as well." He winked. "What can I say? I'm a confident man." He raised his right hand. Our mating band shone on his finger.

Confident. I was glad one of us felt that way. I wasn't sure either of us would live to see another day.

Even so, I couldn't stop my smile. "Thank you."

"Any time."

Returning my attention to the trunk, I picked up the black leathers. They were incredibly soft and made with meticulous stitches. A pang of guilt moved through my stomach. Rowan had trusted in us so completely, he'd gone ahead and filled his chambers with clothing for me. And yet, I didn't fully return

the confidence and trust, and so, we were unable to truly activate our bond. I was a failure.

Keep your mind on the battle, Elea. Worry about the rest later.

Shaking my head, I refocused on changing into my
fighting gear. Rowan's eyes followed me as I pulled on the
trousers and slipped into the jacket. Unlike my other set of
leathers, these fit perfectly. Rowan stepped around me slowly.

"Shouldn't we be going off to parlay with your mother?"
I asked.

"In a moment. I've spent a lot of time imagining you
wearing these leathers."

I spun about to give him a better view. It was still night
outside, so I took care to stand by a candle. "And does the
view match your expectations?"

"Exceeds." He took my hand in his. "Now, let's face my
mother."

"I can't wait."

Rowan and I stepped out of his chambers to find Kade
waiting for us in the outer vestibule. I scanned the small space
and frowned. "Where is everyone?" Typically, there were at
least two guards present at all times. The space looked especially dark and lonely, even for nighttime.

Anger tightened Kade's features. "All the castle workers are
outside, per Zoriah's mandate."

I turned to Rowan. "But you're Genesis Rex. How can your
mother order anyone around?" I raised my arm palm forward
and took a deep breath. "Forgot I asked that. The better question is, what lies has Zoriah been telling the crowd?"

Kade frowned. "She says it's all your fault, Elea. You're a
powerful witch whose evil spell made Shujaa wither up
and die."

"I am not a witch. Why does everyone keep saying that?" I

took in another calming breath. "You don't need to answer that, either. Where is Zoriah right now?"

"Waiting you and Rowan outside the castle's drawbridge. All the Casters are waiting in the gardens to watch what happens."

Rowan gripped the hilt of his short sword. "Elea and I will speak with Zoriah." He rounded on Kade. "But I want you, Amelia, Veronique, and Jicho to leave the castle immediately. Hide out in of the tree bases in the Genesis Vale."

Kade jutted out his square chin. "Absolutely not. I'm your second. I won't leave you to face Zoriah alone."

"I won't be alone. Elea fights at my side now." Rowan lowered his voice. "And that wasn't a question, Kade. It was an order from your King."

Kade frowned. "As my Rex commands." After giving us a quick bow, he sped down the shadowy staircase. His footsteps and outline were quickly swallowed up by the darkness.

Rowan turned to me again. "This is your last chance. You don't need to face down my mother."

I set my fist on my hip. "But I'm doing it, and there's no stopping me."

Rowan took my free hand; I loved the warmth of his touch. "As my Regina commands." Together, we descended the castle staircase. With every step, I questioned my advice to Rowan. Was it really a good idea for me and Rowan to face down Zoriah and her entire army?

Whether it was or not, we'd find out soon enough.

26

*R*owan and I made our way to the castle's entrance. Every step felt like I was slogging through chest-deep water. I still hadn't fully recovered from the battle with Shujaa. Meanwhile, Rowan didn't look much better than I did. His breathing was labored, and the bruises along his neck were deepening.

In other words, we weren't ready for a fight.

As we stepped through the empty corridors, muffled voices echoed in through the open window holes. Some were even raised in song. The people were doing more than watching a moonlight parade of the golden army; they were having a grand old time.

I shot Rowan a questioning glance. "That sounds like quite the celebration on short notice."

"Always." He shrugged. "We're Casters." He paused by the castle's main entrance. The huge wooden drawbridge was pulled up tight. "Besides, we've been without mages for a long time. Now the golden army has arrived, and all our troubles will supposedly be over. People like an easy answer."

"But you don't."

"Oh, I *like* the idea of easy answers well enough." He shot me a side-eyed glance. "I just don't believe they work."

"Your people should have more faith in you." The moment the words left my mouth, I wished I could take them back.

Wasn't that true for me as well? I still held back my faith and trust in Rowan.

Rowan met my gaze straight on. Somehow, he knew exactly what I was worried about. "There are no easy answers, Elea. That means waiting when it's important, and as I said, I'm a patient man." He ran his fingertip along my jawline. My chest heated with warmth and affection. "Now, are you ready?"

"After that touch? I can do anything."

Rowan gave me a crooked smile. "The same is true for me." He gripped the rotary wheel and slowly lowered the bridge. "Let's meet my mother."

Moving together, Rowan and I stepped across the threshold. Here, the castle's drawbridge spanned a moat. Beyond the water, a wide pathway led into the gardens beyond. A full moon cast the entire scene in a bluish light. Every inch of the castle grounds seemed to be packed with Caster families in traditional leathers.

These must be the clan leaders and their families, coming for the celebration just as Zoriah requested. Some of the revelers held gourd-lanterns. Others played flutes or beat on small drums. Children ran through the sea of bodies while waving tall sticks topped with ribbons. Throughout the crowd, Zoriah's golden warriors stood still as statues. I scanned them carefully. Some of the Casters were dancing around their own lost family members, only they didn't know it. The Shadow Family were here, too. That led to one conclusion.

I couldn't wait for this fight to begin.

Zoriah stepped out from the throng of revelers to stand at the spot where the drawbridge met the other shore. She wore her black Seer robes and a look of total triumph on her lovely face. The moment we opened the front doors, she raised her arms.

All the revelers fell silent.

"Rowan," declared Zoriah. "How brave of you to face your people after your lying witch killed your brother."

Rowan lifted his chin slightly. "Greet the Tsarina properly."

Zoriah widened her eyes as if seeing me for the first time. "Elea. You're still here."

Rage burned through my soul. "I'm hard to move."

"Obviously." Zoriah sniffed. "My son, our people accept that you've been bewitched by this, ah, Tsarina. They are willing to allow the both of you to leave in peace as long as you hand your throne over to me. I shall rule in place of our lost hero, Shujaa. What do you say?"

"No," said Rowan. The word echoed in odd ways through the darkened gardens.

"But everyone is ready to start this new age of Caster power." Zoriah gestured to the crowd behind her. "You can see how the people already celebrate my future rule."

"Leave now," said Rowan carefully. "And you'll be allowed to live."

Zoriah took a half step backward. "You can't threaten me. I'm your mother."

The crowd quieted. A thick sense of tension filled the air.

Rowan unsheathed a short sword and raised it high. "Leave or die."

"How dare you?" Zoriah set her fists on her hips. Black veins lit up in her neck as she gave a magickal command. "My army. Stand at attention." Moving as a single unit, all the golden warriors shifted to stand facing me and Rowan. I fought back a gasp.

If Rowan was shocked by this, he didn't show it. He simply raised his arms and addressed the crowd. "My people, I stand before you as your rightful King. Beside me stands Elea, my true mate. Zoriah has told you nothing but lies. Shujaa made his own magickal pacts in the hopes to gain power. He died in a trap of his own creation. And this golden army you admire so much? They are the Shadow Family that you've all lost, only twisted by stealing my own magick. I have waited months for my chance to stop this atrocity, free my people, and make those responsible for your torment pay the penalty. That moment has come. As such, I command you to depart the castle grounds immediately."

The people only stared at him, open-mouthed.

Rowan raised his right hand. His veins glowed red with Caster power. "Act as your Rex commands."

They still didn't budge.

This wasn't good.

I addressed the crowd as well. "You really need to leave." My words didn't help at all. Rowan's people wanted to believe Zoriah's story. It would be funny if it didn't mean that we were about to fight Zoriah with a crowd of innocent families standing by.

Zoriah lowered her arms while whispering a fresh incantation. This time, the black smoke poured off her palms and spread across the moonlit grounds. Small bits of red lightning sparked in its depths.

Zoriah's voice grew louder as her incantation took hold. The language wasn't one I knew, but the results of her spell were obvious.

The golden army began to melt.

Or, it only *looked* as if they were melting. In reality, some of the tiny golden beetles on their bodies were crawling away. After that, the insects disappeared onto the fog-covered ground. Between the smoke and darkness, it was impossible to see anything else that was happening.

Rowan and I exchanged a confused look. What was Zoriah doing? She couldn't be giving up. Every instinct screamed for me to start casting a spell, but I didn't know what to cast. And the few incantations that I thought might help could easily end up injuring an innocent bystander.

All of a sudden, screams sliced through the night air. Finally, moonlight reflected off the Caster populace. Now, golden beetles were crawling up the bodies of every man, woman, and child in the gardens. Just like I'd seen with Shujaa in the burned-out village, the beetles melted down into smooth metal coating. It only took a matter of seconds before all the Casters were frozen in place.

I blinked hard, not believing what I saw. The gardens appeared to be filled with golden statues, all of them in different stages of screaming or running away. It was horrible.

Zoriah grinned. "Dear people, as you've now discovered, my son was indeed telling the truth. My golden army isn't made up of magickal warriors. They are Casters just like you who were transformed with hybrid magick from Viktor."

"Release these people," said Rowan, his voice deep with rage. "Now."

"Why? I've given them exactly what they wanted: to be part of a golden age of Caster power. And as you can see, I have kept my word. They're all perfectly encased. They aren't good enough to be golden warriors, but it's time we cleaned up the unworthy."

I scanned their faces in the moonlight. Despite the fact that these people couldn't move, the terror shone in their poses. When I spoke again, my voice was barely a whisper. "You're suffocating them."

"Yes." Zoriah rounded on me. "And you're next."

Quick as a heartbeat, golden beetles sped up my legs and encased my body. I frantically tried to pull in air. There was nothing. I couldn't move, let alone breathe. Panic twisted through my soul.

Although I was encased in gold, I could still make our Zoriah's muffled voice. "Ask me what I want, Rowan. As you know, we Seers always hold our engagements."

"Fine, Zoriah. What do you want?"

"Since you won't step down peacefully, I ask you to accept my engagement to challenge your rule."

My lungs burned for air, but breathing wasn't the only thing I was worried about. How I wished I could warn Rowan right now. Zoriah was setting up some kind of trap. I still had Necromancer magick stored up in my arm, but it took longer to cast a spell without being able to speak.

Much longer.

Possibly too long.

"Set everyone free," said Rowan. "And I will accept your challenge."

Zoriah tapped her chin. "And who will be your second in our fight? Your little Necromancer?"

"Her name is Elea, and yes."

"Then it's agreed," said Zoriah. "I will free our people." She put special emphasis on the words *our people.* I didn't like that part at all.

Inside my rib cage, my lungs convulsed for air. At last, I managed to clearly think through the words to an exploder spell. My hand glowed blue as the gold burst off my body. At last, I could move again. Meanwhile, the metal casing that had trapped me turned back into golden beetles again. The insects now crawled back across the drawbridge and disappeared into the black cloud that still covered the castle grounds.

The golden beetles slid away from the crowd as well. The moment they were free, the mob began a mad rush for the gates. I felt sorry for the frightened children, but the adults didn't upset me as much. They should have listened to Rowan. Even I trusted him enough to run when he told me to.

Usually.

Zoriah raised her arms once more. "Let the challenge begin!"

I still had some magick left over from my last spell. Even though I was still gasping for breath, I cast a quick incantation over me and Rowan. Blue smoke danced across our skin and soaked into our souls.

Rowan leaned over me. "Elea, are you all right?"

"Fine." I finished the protection spell as I sucked in more air. "Now we won't...Get caught...Under golden beetles again."

Zoriah clapped her hands. "Pay attention, children. I'd like you to meet my second."

A huge form rose out of the black smoke that covered the castle grounds. It was a massive warrior made entirely of wasps. My mouth fell open.

Wren had returned.

"I'd hoped she'd stay away a little longer." My voice came out as a murmur. "And now, we have to fight both your mother and a wasp monster."

Rowan gave me a dry look. "That sums it up pretty well."

"You mother really is horrible." Which reminded me of Rowan's family members who weren't here. I could only hope that Kade, Amelia, Veronique, and Jicho got to safety.

The Giant-Wren turned to us, roared, and raised her huge booted foot. The ear-splitting done of wasps broke the still night air. Hundreds of stingers glinted in the moonlight. There was no question about it: Wren aimed to squash both me and Rowan.

Now, there's nothing like a massive waspy boot coming toward your head to put priorities in order.

For a massive monster, Giant-Wren moved quickly. Her boot was only inches above my skull when I moved into action and leapt off the left-hand side of the drawbridge. Rowan jumped alongside me.

Giant-Wren's boot slammed down through the front of the castle. Stone shards flew in every direction. Where there had once been an entryway, now there was nothing but a pile of rubble.

She had barely missed us.

Rowan gripped my hand. "We need to make for the Genesis Vale." Like me, Rowan had been banged up and cut from the rubble, but he was still in one piece.

We raced toward the back of the castle. From there, we broke into the jungle beyond. Behind us, I could hear the thud-thud of the Giant-Wren as she tracked us through the darkness. As we sped through the undergrowth, more of Zoriah's golden army chased us through the rainforest that separated the castle from the Genesis Vale. Everywhere we turned, there were more of their blank faces and grasping arms.

Wren may have been Zoriah's second, but we weren't in the Genesis Vale yet. That meant we were fair game to whatever Zoriah sent in our direction.

And she had an army.

We kept dodging through the undergrowth, racing toward the edge of the crevasse. We leapt over a nest of vines, releasing a swarm of bats into the sky.

The sight gave me an idea.

"We need to even the playing field," I said. "Now that Shujaa is gone, we can cast a whole new set of spells on Wren." Shujaa's protection from spells had been extended to Wren. Now that Shujaa was dead, Rowan wasn't limited to sun surges any more.

Rowan leaped over a moss-covered log. "Go on."

"Do you have enough power to summon bats?"

"Easily." Rowan led us through a dense thicket. Behind us, the ground shook with every step that Giant-Wren took. I glanced over my shoulder. Moonlight reflected off the metallic bodies chasing us through the heavy ferns and vines. The golden army was tracking us down.

"Bats eat wasps," added Rowan. "Is that what you're thinking?"

"Exactly. That should kill Wren once and for all. Can you cast and run at the same time?"

"One of my specialties." As we rushed through the darkness, Rowan raised his right hand and bellowed out an incantation.

> *"Wing and night*
> *Take your flight."*

Red mist appeared on Rowan's palm. A second later, the haze quickly solidified into the shape of a red bat. The animal flew off into the night sky. Then, a second bat appeared and a third. Soon, the air was darkened with hundreds of crimson bats. They converged on Giant-Wren, swooping around her in a loose column.

Wren screeched with rage as she kept racing toward us. The bats kept up their furious attack, gnawing at the bugs that made up Giant's-Wren's limbs. Her right leg buckled; Giant-Wren fell to the ground with a great thud. Rowan's bats swooped in and covered the body. Within seconds, they flew back off into the night sky.

I didn't look back again after that. There was no need to; Wren was dead.

Finally.

That was when a dozen golden warriors broke free from the rest and lunged at us from behind. Metallic fingers scratched along my spine as Rowan grabbed my waist with one hand, a vine in his other palm, and scaled us both up a tree. We stood on an upper branch, catching our breath. I stared down at the moonlit jungle floor below us.

"Where did you learn to do that?" I asked.

"Climb trees?" He arched his brows. "I grew up in a jungle."

The branch we stood on shook violently. I almost fell over. Looking down, I saw that the golden warriors were now tearing through the trunk with their metal fingers. We needed to get out of here.

"I need a minute to reload my magic," said Rowan. "How about you?"

"I'm good." While we'd been running, I had built up a reserve of magick in my soul. I now focused it into my arm until my bones shone bright blue in the dark night. I spoke one of my favorite incantations.

Another skeletal horse burst out of the jungle floor and swooped up under the branch. The entire tree was swaying from side to side now. The golden warriors were making good headway with tearing it down. Just as the horse got close enough to mount, the tree moved us in the opposite direction.

My skeletal horse came around for another pass. This time, the tree swayed in an obliging arc. Moving in sync, Rowan and I leapt off our branch and onto the horse's back. Rowan sat behind me, I gripped the horse's reins. The steed beat its great wings until we rose above the canopy of trees. I couldn't help but smile. I did so love to cast spells. How could I ever return to farm life?

Rowan's chest pressed against my back. "Well done, Elea."

My heart swelled with pride. "Thank you. How much farther to the vale?"

Rowan pointed to a spot just ahead. "It's just past that line of trees."

A sense of relief eased my shoulders. We were so close to the Genesis Vale. Once we were inside that protected valley, it would be the two of us against Zoriah. The golden army couldn't get to us there. We would be back under the protection of the same magick that prevented outsiders from breaking into our fight with Wren and Shujaa.

This time, it would be two against one. That was a fight we could win.

Rowan and I flew over the last line of trees and undergrowth. The edge of the crevasse to the Genesis Vale lay below us.

Unfortunately, Zoriah was there as well. My skin prickled over with fear as I commanded my horse. "Wait."

Rowan and I hovered above the cliff wall that led to the Genesis Vale. Rowan's mother stood at the top edge of the crevasse. While Rowan and I looked cut up and had half a jungle stuck in our hair, Zoriah's black Seer robes still fell in perfect folds from her shoulders. Moonlight shone from behind her, outlining her slim frame with a pale blue halo. Simply put, the woman looked like a goddess. Beside her, hundreds of golden warriors stood in neat formation around the lip of the crevasse. And before them all stood Kade, Jicho, Veronique, and Amelia, all frozen in metal. Their faces were trapped in silent cries of pain and fear.

We were in deep trouble.

"Land now." Zoriah pointed to a spot before her. "Or I'll keep them encased until they suffocate."

I'd thought we had a chance to win this fight. But now, the idea of living through this battle seemed far off indeed.

"*D*own," I said to my horse. Moments later, Rowan and I stood before Zoriah, right where she wished us to be. All around the edge of the crevasse, hundreds of faceless warriors watched our every move.

Escape would not be easy.

Rowan glared at Zoriah. "We had a bargain. You said you'd set all my people free...And Seers always keep their word."

"I said *people*," countered Zoriah. "Not *family*." She stared at Amelia and Veronique with distaste. "And certainly not a pair of nobodies from the Necromancer lands."

"Free them." Rowan's eyes darkened. "Now."

Kade, Amelia, Veronique, and Jicho stood in their frozen poses of terror. My mind spun through any spell that could help them.

Sun surge.

Bone knives.

Cutter hawks.

Death melter.

Zoriah held up her hands, palms forward. "I can see the two of you planning to cast. You've convinced me. I'll save you the trouble and free these four right now."

"So, you're letting them go," repeated Rowan. The tone of his voice said he didn't believe her at all. I didn't either, for that matter.

"Please." Zoriah fluttered her lashes. "I give you my sacred word." The veins in her neck turned black as she spoke. "That's a bond I cannot break. Once these four are free, then we'll all go down to the vale and kill each other like family. Agreed?"

Rowan folded his arms over his chest. "Go on and cast your spell."

"Thank you, my son." Zoriah's eyes instantly turned all black. Flashes of red lightning appeared in her pupils while more dark veins crawled up her neck. Black smoke encircled her hands and then poured off her palms. The dark cloud flickered with red lightning as it slowly surrounded Jicho, Amelia, Veronique, and Kade.

A second later, the metal that encased them transformed into golden beetles. A strange whooshing noise filled the air.

I stared at Zoriah, dumbfounded. "You freed them?"

"Of course." Zoriah snapped her fingers again. With a flash of red lightning, Amelia, Kade, Veronique and Jicho were bound and gagged inside a large bamboo cage. "And now they're trapped." She blinked to excess. "What? I didn't say that they'd stay free. I merely wanted to distract my son."

Her word sent chills up my back. *"Distract my son."* That strange whooshing noise? Zoriah had done something to Rowan.

Little by little, I turned to examine Rowan. He hadn't looked fit before. Now, long shards of bamboo had impaled him like so many knives. Long cuts sliced across his body. All his leathers were soaked with blood. I gasped as the realization set in.

Unless he got help and fast, Rowan was going to die.

As I stood in shock, Zoriah waved her arms. Another dark haze of magick appeared. Wind roared as the black cloud transformed into a cyclone of power that slammed into Rowan, knocking him over the edge of the crevasse and into vale below.

I gasped.

Zoriah rounded on me. "Be thankful that Petra insisted that I spare you. Otherwise, you'd be as dead as Rowan."

Her words echoed through my mind.

Rowan was dead.

It couldn't be true. Sobbing, I stumbled up to the edge of the crevasse and stared down. In the moonlight, I could clearly see Rowan's body at the base of the cliff side. He wasn't moving.

Black mist surrounded my legs. In the back of my mind, I knew Zoriah was casting a spell. I turned to her and pumped fresh power into my arm. Blue light brightened my bones as I shot a raw bolt of Necromancer energy into Zoriah's stomach. There wasn't any form to my spell. I'd spoken no incantation. It was merely a thrust of light and power that slammed Zoriah back against the ground with a thud.

Zoriah didn't move.

It wasn't in me to care.

I didn't remember casting the spell, but I must have created a bone rope because the next thing I knew, I was using it to rappel down the cliff. Tears streamed down my cheeks as I closed in on the jungle floor.

"Rowan!"

He didn't answer.

Once I reached the lower ground, I sped over to kneel at Rowan's side. He looked so still and peaceful, he might have been sleeping. I pressed my hands against his bloody chest. There was no heartbeat. My eyes stung with fresh tears.

I pulled out every bit of bamboo from his body while casting one healing spell after another. I even tried an incantation to raise him from the dead like I had all those Necromancers.

Nothing worked.

At some point, I became aware of high-pitched moaning from the top of the crevasse. Zoriah was waking up.

In my mind, I knew I should avenge Rowan. I could cast another skeletal horse, fly up the cliff, and strike Zoriah down for good. But that would mean leaving Rowan's side. Whether he was alive or dead, I couldn't bring myself to move away from him.

Not yet.

My hand still rested at the center of Rowan's chest. My palm was sticky with what was now cool blood. How long had I been here, trying to heal Rowan? It couldn't have been more than a few minutes.

Still, Rowan was gone.

With that realization, something deep inside me snapped. Memories of Rowan flashed through my mind. I recalled how he found me in the desert...The moment we shared our mating bands...The battles against Viktor...And always, how he waited so patiently for me to learn to trust him. After what happened with Tristan, it wasn't easy to have faith in anyone again. But in this moment, I knew the truth.

There was no comparing Rowan to anyone else. Knowing that, some hidden pieces of my soul realigned. Fresh magick thrummed through my veins. I focused all my energy on Rowan, one last time.

Closing my eyes, I spoke a version of the Caster mantra that Rowan has said to me when he'd healed me after I escaped the Midnight Cloisters, six months and a million years ago.

"Hear my truth. You always gave me a choice and had faith in my judgment. And so in return, I give you all of my heart. Rowan, you are my mate, my history, my future, and my world." I gently brushed the backs of my fingers against his cheek. "Tonight, I truly understand the meaning of faith, because I believe in you, Rowan. I trust you to come back to me. I love you, Rowan."

Leaning forward, I gave him the gentlest of kisses.

Suddenly, my right hand warmed. Opening my eyes, I saw that my mating band now glowed with purple light. *Hybrid magick.* Excitement sparked in my rib cage. I pressed my palm harder against the center of Rowan's chest.

"Live," I pleaded. "Come back to me."

Rivulets of violet light poured off my hand and across Rowan's chest. Hope sparked in my soul.

It was working.

The lines of brightness soon encircled Rowan in an intricate web. His chest heaved. He took in a breath. Fresh tears streamed down my face, but not from sorrow.

Rowan gripped my wrists. *He moved!* I laughed and cried at the same time. Fresh lines of light whipped up his arms. These weren't purple, though, but red. Caster red. Rowan's power. The streams of crimson brightness crossed over from Rowan's hands to mine.

We were sharing power, just like true mates.

Now blue light and energy poured down my arm and into

Rowan. Our magick formed a circuit between our bodies. This was just what I'd seen in the fountain. Our magick was merging.

Rowan's power slammed through my soul. His heat and strength infused every corner of my consciousness. After that, I sensed the cool strength of my Necromancer energy moving into him, combining further with his Caster powers. The lines of blue and red magick between us quickly merged into a single shade of violet.

All hybrid magick.

Next, Rowan's body healed itself. His wounds closed up. Color returned to his skin. Every bruise disappeared. My own body grew stronger as well. My bones stretched as my magick expanded. I became physically taller. The Caster leathers I wore now pulled on me more tightly.

We'd shared power.

Grown stronger.

Truly mated our souls.

Rowan awoke, looked into my eyes, and grinned. I smiled back. He sat up and pulled me into his arms. His voice sounded low in my ear. "So worth it."

And he was right.

For a long moment, we only embraced each other. I opened my mouth, ready to say all sorts of romantic things. *You're my life. I love you beyond compare.* Instead, I could only manage a simple word. "Hello."

But this was a greeting.

A new beginning.

It was everything.

Rowan ran his finger along my jawline. "My bonded mate."

A loud crack of lightning sounded. Looking up, I saw a

dark sphere of smoke and red lightning speeding straight for us.

It was a kill spell.

Zoriah now stood on the top edge of the crevasse, a smug grin on her pretty face. If the fact that Rowan was alive upset her, she didn't show it. No, her only reaction was to send a lightning bomb our way.

How perfect.

My gaze locked with Rowan's. "Reflector?" This was my way of asking if we could cast a joint reflection spell on her sphere, which would send the orb right back at her.

"Reflector," repeated Rowan solemnly. "Our incantation is 'stop, reverse, soar.'"

How I loved the simplicity of Caster incantations. "Understood."

Moving together, we stood and lifted our right arms up, careful to keep our palms flat and facing toward the oncoming spell. As the sphere sped closer, I could tell it was larger than both of us.

Zoriah wasn't holding back.

We wouldn't either.

Rowan and I both focused our new hybrid magick into our casting hands. A spider web of violet lines glowed along our arms. One second later, Zoriah's black spell slammed against our palms.

It didn't get any farther than that.

Even though the spell didn't touch me, I could still feel the power inside it. The churning energy made the bones in my entire arm vibrate. Rowan and I spoke the incantation in unison.

"Stop, reverse, soar."

The orb stayed flush against our palms for a heartbeat or two. Its inner core of red lightning glowed more brightly. After that, it ricocheted back in Zoriah's direction. Another thunderous boom sounded as the spell made impact. A long pause followed.

"Do you think we got her?" I asked.

"No, I believe she's playing dead. Let's see what she's really up to." Rowan reached toward my back. "May I?"

I had no idea what Rowan was planning, but I didn't need to. I trusted him. "Go on."

Rowan set his hand flush against my back and between my shoulder blades. Magick and warmth from his palm flared as he spoke a one-word incantation.

"Fly."

A strange sensation unfurled along my shoulders as the bones there realigned and my muscles expanded. I glanced over my shoulder and gasped in awe. Rowan had given me a pair of black raven's wings. I smiled and ran my fingers over the edges of the feathers. "They're beautiful."

"We need to return to the upper ground in order to see that Zoriah is doing. This way, we'll be able to stay out of the reach of golden warriors." Rowan shifted so his back now faced me. "My turn."

There was no question what I'd cast for him. Setting my palm right between his shoulder blades, I spoke the same short incantation.

"Fly."

Great bony wings instantly rose from Rowan's shoulders.

They reminded me of those on my skeletal horse, only these were fuller and filled with incandescent blue skin like a bat's. Rowan looked up as his own wings unfurled. "Perfect."

The magick knew what needed to happen, so we both let the power take on its own path. My wings began beating a steady rhythm, as did Rowan's. We quickly rose up the side of the crevasse until we reached the upper level. What we saw made both of us gasp.

Zoriah was wearing the helm to Shujaa's old armor, and she was using it on Kade, Veronique, Amelia, and Jicho. This wasn't like before, when Zoriah simply commanded the golden beetles to encapsulate and suffocate them. No, Zoriah was using far stronger magick now.

Zoriah was transforming Kade, Veronique, Amelia, and Jicho into golden warriors.

The image was one I'd never forget. Zoriah standing behind the bamboo cage, her arm looped through the bars so she could grasp Kade's throat. For his part, Kade thrashed against his bindings, but it was no use. Zoriah's grip held firm against his neck. Tiny golden beetles appeared on Kade's skin. They swarmed over him, encasing his entire body. After that, they smoothed over into metal. Silver beams of moonlight glinted off the gold.

My heart cracked. Kade was now a faceless golden warrior.

"No!" Rowan howled with rage, arced his wings and swooped in toward Kade.

Zoriah gripped Amelia's throat next. A heartbeat later, Amelia stood upright beside Kade within the same cage. She, too, had been transformed into a faceless golden statue. Cords of grief and rage tightened about my throat. I was losing too many people I cared about.

My gaze locked on Rowan. He was still speeding toward the ground. His path was headed right for Zoriah.

And she was smirking.

This was yet another trap.

Panic tightened every muscle in my body. Pumping my own wings, I changed my path so I could intersect with Rowan's flight. Whatever Zoriah's scheme was, Rowan and I needed to carefully think through our next steps. I swooped in closer to Rowan and grasped his hand. "Please, stop!"

Rowan paused, his wings beating a steady rhythm. "I want to kill her," he growled.

"I do too. But we need a plan."

By this point, Zoriah had already transformed Veronique as well. The third golden statue now stood in a row. Next Zoriah reached for Jicho. Leaning over, she wrapped her fingers around his thin throat.

Something deep in my heart broke clean in two. "No!" I cried.

"Don't worry," called Zoriah. "You're next."

At these words, an idea appeared. I turned to Rowan. "I think I know what we can do."

"Name it."

"She wants golden warriors? She can have us next. How about you let her grab your throat? I'll take the helm."

Some small part of me said this was a terrible plan. I'd just saved Rowan, how could I place him right back in harm's way?

But all I could do was focus on was Jicho's tear-stained face while Zoriah clasped his throat.

This nightmare needed to end.

"It's a plan," said Rowan. He swooped down to land before Zoriah. "You want a golden warrior? I'm right here."

Zoriah looked up. Despite wearing the helm, the grin on her face was still clear. She reached for Rowan, wrapping her long fingers about his neck. The golden beetles erupted over Rowan's skin, encasing him almost immediately. I leapt straight for Zoriah, allowing my new wings to bring me speed. I dove in over her head and plucked the helm away.

Then I placed it on myself.

All the while, two thoughts echoed through my mind, over and over.

Destroy the golden insects.

Set every Caster free.

My wings beat out a steady rhythm as I hovered above the jungle. The helm weighed heavily against my brow. Power unlike anything I'd known coursed through my mind. It felt both searing hot and bone cold.

I spied Rowan below me. He was now a golden warrior. Rage heated my blood.

There was no thought to my spell, only instinct and emotion. And that feeling was anger. How dare she hurt my Rowan? Wrath poured into my soul from the golden warriors as well. Through some magick of the helm, I could feel their rage and torment. My stream of anger quickly turned into a tidal wave of fury. Magick consumed my mind. The helm glowed with bright purple light. On pure instinct, I cast some kind of spell.

Suddenly, the upper jungle erupted with golden beetles. The tiny insects covered every leaf and twig. My wings beat a regular rhythm as I stayed above the treetops. A shifting sea of golden insects moved below me. The reality hit me like a fist.

If I wanted to free Rowan and the others again, this wasn't the way to do it.

Rage and magick weren't delivering the right spell. This

helm had been created with hybrid power. In order to control it, I needed to use both logic and emotion. Right now, I was allowing my heart to rule everything.

I needed my mind, too.

With all my will, I forced my thoughts to calm.

Closing my eyes, I went back to the old breathing exercises I did as a Novice.

In.

Out.

Life.

Death.

Focus.

At last, I clasped some semblance of balance within me. Using both logic and determination, I commanded the magick to set everyone free. A specific incantation came to me in a flash.

> *"Gold and bite*
> *Hale and blight*
> *Free my loved ones*
> *Turn evil right"*

Another blast of power moved through my soul, stronger than ever before. The light from the helm became blinding. When I opened my eyes again, all the beetles were climbing down from their perches on the leaves and trees. Moving in a great wave, they burrowed their way into the earth. More of them melted off the hundreds of golden warriors.

I whipped off the helm and swooped back to the place where I'd last left Rowan and the others.

All of them still stood in a neat line: Rowan, Jicho, Amelia, Veronique and Kade. Only now, they were back to being human once again. Hope and fear battled it out inside me. The five of them looked whole and healthy. Even their bindings were gone. They stared at me with a combination of relief and shock.

They were free? It seemed too wonderful to be true.

I rushed over to Rowan, brushing my fingers over his face and arms. There were no insects anywhere on his skin. Joy sparked in my soul.

"It's over," I murmured. "The magick is really gone."

Rowan pulled me into a hug. "Yes, you did it." The press of his firm body against mine was everything that was beautiful in my life, rolled up into one moment. "You're one of a kind, Elea."

"Hey," I countered. "All I had to do was wear the helm. You were the one who got turned into a metal warrior." I leaned back, met his gaze and winced. "Was it terrible?"

Rowan pursed his lips. "As horrors from my mother go, it wasn't too awful. One moment, she was grabbing my throat and golden beetles were everywhere. The next second, you were running toward me and all the insects were gone. I don't remember anything in between."

"That's a relief."

"Still, Zoriah didn't have me trapped for very long. It could have been different for the others."

I nodded. "When I was wearing the helm, I felt connected to them. There was so such rage coming from the golden warriors."

"They were angry?"

"Yes, it was like they were all their own people on the inside, but they were being moved around like puppets by Shujaa and Zoriah. Their fury at being confined—" I let out a rattling breath. "I'd never felt anything that horrible. The emotion was so strong, it was partly why my first casting got out of control."

Rowan stepped back. "It seems they've all returned to normal now."

For the first time, I took a good look at the red earth encircling the Genesis Vale. The place was packed with people. Although they all still stood in their ranks, only they were no longer metallic warriors or cursed beings, but hundreds of actual *people*—young, strong and healthy. And there was no mistaking the rage glittering in their eyes. Every bit of it was directed at one person.

Zoriah.

While the freed Casters were angry, Zoriah remained haughty and cool as ever. She raced up and down the neat lines of bodies, scanning the faces in dismay. "How did this happen?" She plucked at the blonde hair of one girl. "Not gold enough." She set her hands on her hips. "Someone here must be left in gold. I cannot take my rightful place in the castle without a golden army." She waved her hand dismissively. "You're all dismissed. I'm through with you. If there are any golden ones left, they can stay."

Rowan and I shared a long look. We didn't need to say a word. Both of us knew how this was going to end. "What do you want to do?" I asked.

"Enjoy the view." Rowan turned to Kade. "Although perhaps Jicho might do well to visit the castle. What do you say, Kade?"

Kade looked around with a glassy-eyed stare. "What happened? I was tied up."

"Me too." Jicho blinked. His eyes looked almost as glossed over as Kade's. "What happened to the ropes around my hand and feet?"

Veronique stared blankly ahead. She was quiet, for once. I took that as a good thing.

I turned to Amelia. Thank the gods she looked rather sane. "Things might get ugly here. Don't you think Jicho should leave?"

Amelia glanced over to Zoriah, nodded slowly, and then took Jicho's hand. "We're all going back to the castle now." Without any further ado, she simply walked off into the jungle with Jicho. Kade and Veronique followed along behind her. I was never more proud to be Amelia's friend.

The moment the four of them disappeared into the rainforest, Zoriah started to lose her mind. "Why aren't you all leaving? Didn't you hear what I said? You are dismissed. I only want my golden warriors. Where are you? Come here this instant!"

All the freed Casters slowly turned toward Zoriah. White-hot rage poured off them in waves. For a moment, everything was still.

Then they pounced.

Zoriah was still screaming for her golden warriors while the freed Casters dragged her off into the jungle. Her cries grew louder and then fell silent.

I gave Rowan's hand a squeeze. "What would you like to do next?"

"I'm King. I'll go and see what my subjects have done."

"And I'll join you."

Hand in hand, we walked into the jungle. The hundreds of freed Casters were crowded around a figure lying in the mud. Most of them held clubs or stones. A combination of agony and triumph now lit their eyes.

The true battle was officially over.

Zoriah was dead.

*R*owan and I spent hours helping the newly-freed Casters. It seemed they'd been completely aware of what was happening to them even though they'd been trapped inside those golden shells. Other family members began showing up soon after the golden warriors had been freed. It was that innate magick all Casters wielded. It did my heart good to see how deeply Casters loved each other.

The reunions began to take on a similar routine. The family would stumble into the jungle behind the castle. Often, it was one or two people. They'd find their loved one and hear the tale about Shujaa and share tear-filled embraces. After that, everyone pledged their undying devotion to Rowan for saving them.

That last part was my favorite of all. Rowan deserved all that praise and more.

It was late morning when Rowan and I decided to return to the castle for some much needed rest. In fact, we were halfway across the upper jungle when we felt it.

The ground shaking beneath our feet.

Rowan leaned down and rested his palm against the ground. "This is magick."

I frowned. "Where is the source?"

"Genesis Vale."

It had already been a surreal couple of days. Rowan's brother and mother had died. We'd fought down a golden army. And both of us still had wings attached to our backs. We held each other's hands as we headed back to the Genesis Vale.

With every step closer to the valley, the ground shimmied more violently beneath our feet. At length, we stood again at the edge of the vale. The crevasse opened up before us. The sun was rising in the sky. The red muddy earth around the lip of the circular vale was empty. No Casters celebrating, for once.

The world turned quiet. The crickets, monkeys, and birds all ceased their constant low chatter. Sunbeams broke out through the clouds and sent long beams of light onto the emerald-bright palm leaves. For a moment, the Genesis Vale became so quiet, the silence was suffocating in its completeness.

The center of the vale erupted.

The ground broke open, and a tall column burst up from the earth. I'd seen this happen before, back at the Havilland mansion. This time, a metal column stretched into the sky. It was a writhing thing made entirely of golden beetles. Atop the column stood an archway. Again, this structure was made from the same writhing insects as the rest. Under that gateway, there stood a solo figure. My heart sank.

It was Viktor.

The man looked the same as always. He was taller than

most men with a lean and sinewy body that was accented by his black robes. His long dark hair was tied back at the nape of his neck with a leather strap.

My knees turned rubbery beneath me. Viktor had opened another gateway to return to our world. His other gateways had used Bone Crawlers to hold hybrid magick and open the passage. This time, he'd stored the power in the helm.

My stomach sickened with nausea, and it wasn't from all the flying that I'd done today. I felt ill because when I released so many golden beetles, I was the one who made Viktor's return possible.

By the Sire.

Rowan and I locked gazes. Determination shone in his eyes, same as mine. We were about to head into another battle, and this is one we simply had to win. If there was any consolation in the upcoming fight, it was that Rowan and I would face Viktor as true mates. We were both stronger than ever before, both physically and in terms of our magick.

Perhaps we could send him back again.

I stared at the writhing gateway of golden beetles. The last time we'd sent Viktor away, I'd shoved him through an obliging gateway. But that was when the gateway was made of stone. This new one didn't look nearly as stable.

I couldn't send Viktor away without a gate to put him through.

Atop his golden pillar, Viktor slowly turned around, surveying the landscape. He stopped when he spied Rowan and me. From the moment I saw Viktor on that pillar, I'd begun gathering Necromancer power into my body. There was no reason to ask Rowan if he'd been doing the same. The resolute look on his face had told me that yes, he was getting ready for battle as well.

Viktor scanned the lip of the crevasse. "Come forth, Shujaa. It is time for you to claim your promised reward for freeing me."

Now, I could easily correct Viktor and explain that Shujaa was dead, but I decided that the safer course of action would be to continue focusing on drawing in new power, so that was precisely what I did.

"Shujaa is not here, then." Viktor tilted his head. "Show yourself, Zoriah. I wish to bestow my gifts on you instead. Clearly, you followed my instructions to the letter and made it possible for me to return. Your diligence shall be rewarded." He scanned the jungle for a moment. "No Zoriah, either." His gaze rested on me and Rowan. "that leaves the pair of you. I should have guessed. You were the ones to free me, eh?" He closed his eyes and both his palms lit up with violet light. If I had to guess, I'd say he was casting an insight spell.

I was planning a few incantations of my own, and I'd come up with the perfect option to help us end our Viktor problem. Maybe.

"My magick shows me that you are indeed responsible for my escape," said Viktor. "And for that, I shall grant you the same reward I had planned for Zoriah and Shujaa: a slow and painful death in celebration of my new role as Genesis Rex. Congratulations on achieving such a coveted honor."

Every bone in my body felt weighed down with dread. Didn't we just get rid of not one, but two insane mages who wanted to rule Nyumbani? And in trying to fix one problem, we somehow unleashed far worse trouble.

Perhaps the idea of giving up on magick did have some merit, after all.

"Before we begin, there is one thing I must do." Viktor waved his arm, and the gateway of golden beetles sunk back into the pillar beneath it. "See? You can't push me back through a gateway unaware ever again. I'm clever in such matters."

I lowered my voice to a whisper that only Rowan could hear. "I know how to get rid of Viktor. I'll need to transport away for a few minutes."

Atop the golden pillar, Viktor raised his arms. Both the bones and veins in his hands glowed with purple light. He was getting ready to cast a spell. Next, Viktor's voice echoed across the vale.

"Crawler killers."

Five massive creatures appeared in the morning sky. They had the bodies of vultures with the long bony tails of snake skeletons. Crawler killers. Yet another spell I'd never seen in real life before. Time was, I used to read about such exotic magick in the Zelle and wish I wasn't cursed so I could go experience it.

Now, I was starting to wonder if my desires had cursed me in a different way. It seemed I was now doomed to encounter unusual battle spells.

Rowan's arm glowed bright red. Crimson mist appeared on his palm. The haze instantly solidified into a massive fireball. Rowan spoke a single word.

"Strike."

The fireball sped off Rowan's hand and slammed into the first crawler killer. "You'd better hurry, if you're going. I can't hold off crawler killers forever."

"Don't you want to know what I'm about to do?"

"No, I trust you." He winked. "Surprise me."

I tapped the transport ring from Petra. "Take me to the last place I stood in the Zelle Cloister." The ring flared blue, and I was off.

Like always, transport hurt like anything. However, knowing Rowan was back there fighting Viktor made it easy to focus past the pain. A second later, I stood in the same prison cell I'd been in before. Petra was gone, which was fortunate. I rushed to the back wall, my heart thudding at double speed.

Were they still there?

Sure enough, the four metal spikes were still stuck in the stone wall, just where Petra had left them when she'd opened the portal for Tristan.

If my plan worked out, Tristan would be getting a visitor of his own: Viktor. If I could get these spikes back to the Genesis Vale, then I could activate the gateway and send Viktor back where he came from.

That was the plan, anyway.

It was worth nothing that, in my life, things rarely did go to plan.

I pumped fresh energy into my arm. The bones glowed blue. I gripped onto the first spike and channeled the magick to my hand. With the extra power behind me, I found it easy to pluck the metal spike from the wall. I grabbed the second, third, fourth and I was ready to return to the battle, except for one thing.

Petra had returned.

She stood framed in the doorway, a skeletal and shaky figure whose inner spirit was anything but. She exhaled a long sigh. For Petra, that was as good as a cheer. "The Seer said you'd return. You've come back to be our Tsarina."

"Honestly? I've come back to steal your portable gateway." I raised the four spikes, two in each hand.

Petra shook her head. "You aren't going anywhere. Have you forgotten? You wear my totem ring."

I allowed myself a big smile, mostly because I knew how much it would Irritate Petra. "And have *you* forgotten that I escaped from here even though you had me trapped with enchanted manacles?" I slammed my hand onto the top of one of the spikes, careful to make sure that Petra's totem ring crashed onto the hybrid metal. The ring broke in two and tumbled to the stone floor of my one-time prison. My grin widened. "Goodbye, Petra."

While holding the spikes, it was even easier to wield magick. With only the barest thought about casting my next spell, I found power flooded my arms. My veins and bones instantly glowed with purple light. I spoke a single world aloud.

"Transport."

The next thing I knew, I was back at the Genesis Vale, only I waited at the base of the writhing column of golden beetles. High above me, Viktor still stood atop the pillar, watching Rowan as he swooped through the sky. Beside him, there flew a great lioness with skeletal armor and huge red wings. Together, Rowan and his magickal lioness were taking out the last crawler killer. Viktor's arms were lit up with power. He was about to cast another attack spell. That meant one thing.

It was time for me to use my wings too.

Gripping the four spikes in my hands, I started a low flight around the base of the pillar. Every so often, I'd pause and set one of the spikes into the ground. It wasn't as neat as the way

Petra had set them into the wall, but this wasn't the time to be artistic. Once all four were in place, I needed to speak an incantation. Trouble was, I'd never heard what Petra had said when she opened the gateway for Tristan. There was no getting that information from her now, so I made up my own wording instead.

"To mountain to valley
From water and sands
Send this Caster
To Eternal Lands"

A great rumble shook the earth. Rowan stopped mid-fight. Viktor leaned over the edge of the pillar and looked down. Even the crawler killers paused in the sky, their massive vulture wings beating a worried rhythm.

For another moment, everything was still.

Then the bottom of the Genesis Vale fell out in a huge and somewhat lopsided sinkhole. The pillar tumbled into the ground. The golden beetles chittered and writhed as they sped downward. I didn't focus on them though. My gaze stayed locked on Viktor as he tumbled past me into the earth. His elegant features were twisted with rage. I found it to be a flattering look on him, and I took care to wave him a hearty goodbye.

The moment Viktor was through the gateway, I yanked the four spikes out of the earth. The channel to the Eternal Lands closed. The sinkhole disappeared. There was a normal swath of jungle once more.

Rowan swooped down to land beside me. He wrapped me in his arms and kissed me deeply. Now that our souls had mated, Rowan had extra height and strength to match his inner beauty. He was also a far better kisser, although that could just be other things as well. I opened my eye a crack.

Sure enough, wherever Rowan and I touched, our skin flared with purple light. That meant life was about to get rather interesting.

"When you said before that a true mating changes everything—"

Rowan cut me off. "Yes."

"Does that mean it changes how we—"

"Yes."

A cloud of red and blue smoke whirled around us. This wasn't magick that I had summoned, so I knew it had to be Rowan. Between kisses, he said one word.

"Transport."

There was no question where we were going. I trusted him in that, too.

30

*T*he next thing I knew, the Genesis Vale was gone, and I found myself on Rowan's bed. My wings were gone, as were Rowan's. Instead, my body had returned to normal, or as normal as I could be these days.

I now lay on my back with Rowan above me, his arms braced above my shoulders. Our mouths met in kiss after kiss. With each touch, magick flared between us, turning every sensation more potent. I ran my hands over the hard planes of his chest and pulled off his upper leathers. Rowan gripped my jacket at the neckline and slowly tore it open. I couldn't help but grin.

"That's wasting perfectly good leathers," I said.

"You'd outgrown them anyway."

He finished ripping my torso bare when I heard it. People were chanting outside the window. I paused. "Do you hear anything?"

"I do, and it's lovely music." He kissed the base of my neck. The touch of his lips made me shiver. Both of us were only wearing our leather trousers, and I suddenly felt that was some kind of tragedy. Even so, I couldn't help but wonder what was happening outside.

"What are they saying?"

"Regina. Regina." He arched his back so his shaft rubbed me in perfect ways through the leather that separated us. "They want you to be my Queen."

"I'd like that very much."

A fresh rush of energy moved between our bare torsos. The feel of his warm skin was so intense, I couldn't wait another moment. I suppose Rowan felt the same way, because we both pulled off our trousers at the same time.

Rowan and I were completely bare against each other, and it was perfect. At last, our bodies matched our souls. He pressed himself inside me, and we were joined as one. It was perfect. And we stayed that way, moving together and sharing bliss, throughout the night. All the while, the Casters chanted outside our window.

I would be their Queen. For the first time since I'd been struck by my curse, I knew exactly who I was and precisely what I wanted. Forever.

e didn't leave Rowan's room for days. Servants brought us food, and Rowan's chambers included an excellent bath modeled like a waterfall. I could have stayed there for another month at least.

But Rowan was still King, and I was soon to be Queen. Eventually, one of had to leave and face the general populace. When Rowan volunteered, I didn't complain. Instead, I decided to transport back to Braddock Farm and check on my family, namely Sam, Mabel, Lucy, and Smokey. Now that I'd truly mated with Rowan, transport spells hardly tickled.

When I arrived in the old farmhouse, Sam and Mabel weren't home, so I headed to my old bedroom in the barn. If felt like I different lifetime when I'd slept in the loft and tried to be a farm girl. The place was neat and well kept as always. Thin fingers of sunlight poked through the cracks in the walls. Clean hay covered the floor. It all smelled like sunshine and comfort. I gave Smokey a fresh bucket of oats and tried to lure Lucy over so I could pet her. Like always, my so-called cat couldn't be bothered with me. That said, she did seem to watch me for an extra-long spell before stalking away. After years of living near each other, I thought perhaps she was starting to form a true attachment.

I was about to transport back to Nyumbani when a ticklish feeling crawled up my arms. Someone else was here. I scanned the barn to find Tristan standing by the door. He gave me a shaky smile. "Hello, Elea. I see you've new clothes these days." Rowan had a new set of black leathers made for me. I wore them constantly, when I wore anything.

I folded my arms over my chest. "What do you want?"

"I came because I owe you an explanation."

I tilted my head. "Just one?"

"Fine, I need to clarify a number of things with you. Here's the truth. I am a godling. I was sent here to help guide you toward Necromancy. The curse was a painful way to do that. I should never have extended my curse to you. Believe me, that didn't mean it didn't hurt me every time the fires burned off my flesh."

"Is that supposed to explain away why you lied to me? Do you have any idea how deeply that injured me?"

"I experienced my own pain, Elea. Believe me, if I'd had any sense of self-preservation, I'd have gone back to the Sire of Souls and left this world to rot. But I endured it all for you."

I'd seen him suffer, night after night. My soul ached for his pain. Still, this godling wasn't Rowan. I didn't trust him. "Tell me. Did you endure the curse for me...Or because you were under orders from Oni and Yuri. Did they send you back here again today?"

"That's not fair. I came here of my own volition in order to warn you. Petra's very angry with you. She's not the only one, either."

"That's fascinating. Now, leave."

Tristan shook his head. "You shouldn't have bonded with Rowan. Oni and Yuri don't know this yet, but when they find out? Let's just say that they won't be pleased. And Petra will find a way to tell them. Mark my words."

I narrowed my eyes. "What about you? Will you tell them?"

"No, I wouldn't do that."

I considered his words before shaking my head. "Why would the gods care about me and my life? So, I can use both kinds of magick. Rowan can do the same now."

Tristan's face darkened. "And *that* would be why they care. Didn't you ever wonder why there are two continents and two such different ways of casting? It was all crafted to stay in a careful balance. Left and right. Flesh and bone. Animal and skeleton. You're mixing everything up. That's not what you were meant to do."

"Maybe they should have discussed their plans with me."

"They tried that already and it failed."

"You mean with Viktor."

Tristan raked his hand through his dark hair. "I'm not supposed to talk of such things."

I took a hesitant step closer. "How can I trust you when you won't tell me the truth?"

Tristan huffed out a long breath. "Viktor is much older than you are. He can wield both kinds of magick, and that makes him strong. You know the Necromancers had been a shadow of what they once were. That's been going on for a long time."

"And Viktor was supposed to change that."

"Yes. His job was to lead the Necromancers back into glory."

"But it all went wrong. How?"

"Viktor fell in love with a Caster."

My head felt wobbly on my shoulders. I stepped over to sit down on a nearby bench. "Was she his true mate?"

"I don't know if it even got that far. At the time, Viktor was young and foolish."

I tapped my chest with my pointer finger. "I'm young and foolish, you know."

"Well, Viktor couldn't have her. At first, he seemed to accept that fact, but over time, he became bitter. He saw the gods as having a great conspiracy to keep him away from what he wanted to do. So he decided he needed to consolidate magick in his own person."

I slumped against the wall. "That's why he drained all those Necromancers. He wanted to make himself strong enough to fight the gods."

"Clearly, Viktor was a mistake. But the Necromancers remained weakened. So the gods decided to try again with this great gift of hybrid magick." Tristan shook his head. "You were supposed to be different."

"I am different. I'm just not what *they* wanted."

Tristan let out one of his beleaguered sighs. "Listen to me. If you love this man and his people, then you'll walk away right now. Tell him about Oni and Yuri. He'll push you out the door."

Anger heated my veins. "I'll tell him everything, but I know his reply already. Rowan won't want me to walk away. He'll ask me to trust in him. No, in *us*." I looked around my old barn. Tristan and I used to chatter in here by the hour. Now, even being in this place without Rowan felt wrong. "And that's what I'll do: have faith in our bond. Which is why you have to leave. You've delivered your message. Now run back to Oni and Yuri and tell them what I said."

"Don't get crowned Genesis Regina. The gods will see you as an abomination who is trying to upset the very fabric of our world by handing out your own gifts of hybrid magick. Neither of you will live out the year. Oni and Yuri will destroy you, body and soul."

"Duly noted. Now if you don't mind?" I pointed toward the door.

"It would have been so much easier if you'd fallen in love with me, you know."

"I suppose even godlings don't get everything they wish, do they?"

"Evidently, they don't." He tipped his tri-cornered hat. "Until I see you again." He walked out the door while slowly vanishing from view.

With that, Tristan simply disappeared. I only wished that his words would vanish from my mind as easily.

That night, I'd tried to sleep, but I was still churning through Tristan's warnings. Rowan pulled me more tightly against his warm body. "Ready to talk about it yet?"

I leaned my head back against his chest. "Sorry I didn't say anything earlier."

"I knew you'd tell me when you're ready. Are you ready?"

"Tristan visited me again. He asked me to return to the Eternal Lands to keep you safe. If Oni and Yuri find out about us, they'll be angry. We shouldn't be mixing magick."

"I doubt the gods care much one way or another."

"That's what I told him. But I think they do care, Rowan. This is very dangerous. Tristan thinks I should go to the Eternal Lands and never become crowned Genesis Regina."

His fingers absently toyed with the ends of my hair. "And what did you say to that?"

"I'd relay the message, but I was certain that you'd want would me to stay as your Queen."

"Quite right." In one smooth movement, he flipped me onto my back, positioned himself above me, and grinned. I could see the outline of his face in the faint moonlight from the opened window. "And what does my future Queen demand of her King?"

"I think you know that."

Rowan leaned and kissed me fiercely, proving that indeed, he did know exactly what I needed.

I pulled on the scraps of leather that served as my formal gown. No matter how I tugged, they only seemed to cover less skin, not more. I began scouring Rowan's chambers for another bureau or hidden closet. The fight with Zoriah and her golden army had taken place a month ago, and now Rowan and I had our first formal celebration to attend. Not our coronation; Tristan's warning was still too fresh for that.

No, this was something just as important. I simply had to go. Only, I wished there was something else I could wear.

A whirlpool of purple smoke formed on the floor nearby. Within a few seconds, Rowan appeared in the spot. I caught my breath. Seeing that handsome face always took my breath away.

Rowan offered me his hand. "Are you ready?"

"Not really. Are there other things I can wear?"

"No."

"And you're certain?"

A crooked smile rounded his mouth. "What do you think?"

I shrugged. There was no point in answering that question. It was obvious that this was a traditional "dress" for Caster Royalty, and I'd have to adjust to things now that I'd agreed to become Genesis Regina.

"You look lovely, by the way."

"You're…" I eyed him from head to toe while tapping my chin in mock-consideration. "Fine. I suppose."

Rowan laughed. He knew how much I adored his official garb of a leather kilt and long cape. "Then we should depart."

"True." Even though I wanted more of my skin covered, I didn't want to be late. Today's celebration was an important one. I got misty just thinking about it.

The mating ceremony for Amelia and Kade would take place any minute now. I'd go naked if I had to.

I glanced at my reflection in the smooth stone that served as Rowan's full-length mirror. I supposed I was attending their mating ceremony pretty much naked. Ah well. I'd faced far worse.

"I'm as ready as I'll ever be," I announced. "Lead the way, Genesis Rex."

Once again, Rowan and I stood onstage at the meeting hall. The last time we were here, it was for the engagement ceremony. Although that event took place less than a week ago, it felt like we were now entirely different people.

Perhaps we were.

Rowan and I stood hand in hand at center stage. To be honest, I was still adjusting to the idea of holding hands at all, let alone in public. Necromancers avoided touch, as a rule.

But this was Rowan. Although it felt odd, I wanted everyone to know what he meant to me. So, I gritted my teeth and held on even more tightly.

Amelia stood on the left-hand side of the stage. Kade waited on the right. My friend looked beautiful a Caster gown, only she'd found someone to dye hers bright pink. It perfectly complemented her long red hair, which hung in loose waves down her back. Across the way, Kade wore the traditional garb of the Caster Imperial family: a leather kilt and long cape thrown over his shoulders. Both Amelia and I wore crowns of white flowers in our hair. Kade and Rowan wore fresh laurel wreaths.

Before us, the meeting hall was filled with Casters sitting cross-legged on the floor or kneeling in small groups. Many new and smiling faces beamed at us from the crowd. A palpable sense of joy filled the air. There was no question why, either: so many of these families had recently been reunited with loved ones. My chest swelled with pride. Rowan and I helped to make that joy come to pass.

In moments like these, the pain of leadership was worth it and then some.

Rowan raised his arms; the hall fell silent. The front row before the stage was for immediate friends and family. I counted Jicho, Veronique, Mabel, Sam, and their new baby girl, Daisy. One benefit of being able to transport without pain was that I could now bring people to Nyumbani without hurting any of us. It warmed my soul to see them together, happy and healthy. On the day that Daisy was born, I'd given them the deed to all of Braddock Farm. It felt just and right. It also threw Wyatt into a rage, which was an added bonus.

"Greetings to you all, Casters and honored guests." Rowan smiled toward Mabel and Sam. "It's a honor to have you here today for the mating ceremony of my brother, His Imperial Highness, Prince Kade Kivuli of the Clans Kazi and Dunia, to the Esteemed Lady and Inventor, Mademoiselle Amelia Masson." Rowan turned toward Kade. "My brother, you are a fierce warrior and bright engineer. Your loyalty is beyond question. For years, I have wished with all my heart that you find a mate who shared your good judgment, open mind, and deep capacity for love." Rowan glanced toward Amelia. "My brother believed that affairs of the heart were impossible for him, my Lady. I'm glad to see him proven wrong." At the same time, Amelia and Kade blushed and stared at their feet. It was adorable.

I raised my voice and focused on my friend. "Amelia, you are one of the smartest, most driven, and strongest women I know. When others would cower, you calmly planned how to succeed. Where some might see bits of metal, you picture elaborate devices that rival any magick spell. You've wanted security and protection from someone else, and yet in the end, you found love and strength by sharing yourself equally with a man who matches your intelligence and passion. I am honored to be part of your mating ceremony today."

Rowan raised his right fist. "Here I hold the mating ring of Imperial Prince Kade. Come forward."

Kade stepped out from the side of the stage to stand right before Rowan. It was my turn next.

I raised my left fist. "Here I hold the mating ring of Lady Amelia Masson. Come forward."

Amelia now stepped to center stage and stood toe-to-toe with Kade. Their gazes met, and the pair shared a shy smile. All kinds of happiness sparked in my chest. It was wonderful to share this moment with my friend. And I was excited to also perform my first official ceremony with Rowan as his mate. One day, Rowan's new throne would be added to this stage, and another created beside it. These would be our places of honor as Genesis Rex and Regina. Until that time, I was happy to share in these ceremonies as nothing more than the woman who held Rowan's love. After all, that's what was most important.

Rowan opened his fist and handed the mating band to Kade. "You know what to do," he said with a wink.

Kade nodded, took the ring, and set it on Amelia's finger as he spoke the same incantation Rowan had once said to me.

"My bond, my life, my one."

I offered Amelia her ring as well. "Now you," I said with a smile. Amelia's dainty hands trembled as she lifted the band from my palm and set it on Kade's finger.

"My bond, my life, my one."

So far, the bonding ceremony had followed the Caster traditions precisely. This was the point where one of them would take power from the other. True matings—like what happened to Rowan and me—were very rare and only experienced by the most powerful mages. Amelia had some untrained Necromancer abilities. Kade could cast a little magick but nothing more. Neither of them expected to be able to share a true mating.

But this was where Rowan and I had decided to change the traditions. I supposed we might be upsetting the balance, as Tristan had put it. We could even be angering the gods. Neither of us was worried. Other people who loved each other deeply should be able to share the same kind of connection as a true mating.

And since we had hybrid power, we could easily make that happen.

Once their mating rings were in place, Kade and Amelia joined hands and met each other's gazes.

Rowan and I had decided that would be our cue.

I set my palm on the back of Amelia's neck; Rowan did the same with Kade. It was a shadow of the gesture that Shujaa had done when he'd transformed unwilling Casters into golden warriors. Today, we would turn that movement into something else entirely.

Rowan and I looped our free arms across each other's shoulders. Our gazes shifted between Kade and Amelia as we spoke in unison. "By the power in our souls, we bestow on you the magick and connection of true mates."

Kade and Amelia shared a long look. They didn't appear upset so much as slightly confused. They'd see the truth soon enough.

Rowan and I sparked up the hybrid magick between us. Lines of purple power streamed over our connected arms and across our chests. Again, it was just as what Shujaa had done before. Only now, for a far better purpose. The hybrid energy rolled into Kade and Amelia. Their skin lit up with a violet hue.

And then their connected hands lit up as well.

I'll never forget the moment when their eyes sparked with the understanding of the new power of touch and intimacy they now shared. Sure, the magick we'd given them wasn't enough for them to cast any spells, but it would always make their physical and spiritual connection greater. I couldn't think of a more fitting gift for our friends.

Rowan and I dropped our arms. Kade and Amelia stayed hand in hand. The audience had been quiet all this time. Now they broke out into loud cheers and dancing. People shouted about the new Genesis Rex and Regina and how we'd truly brought a golden age of power and light to their people.

In all the cheering, Kade focused his attention on me. "Thank you, Elea. I know I wasn't always very kind to you."

"You were protective of Rowan," I said. "I respect that."

His green eyes brimmed with tears. "After what you've done for Amelia and me, I can only hope you'll become our Genesis Regina…Officially."

I shared a long look with Rowan. He knew the truth. Petra had been sending me one threatening messenger after another. She wanted me to officially take my role as the ruler of the Necromancers. I was specifically forbidden to even discuss becoming Genesis Regina.

Amelia bobbed a little on the balls of her feet. "You should take the throne here. You'd be a wonderful Queen."

I fought back a frown. There were those words again.

"You should."

Maybe it was our new connection, but Rowan sensed my sadness instantly. He gently set his knuckles beneath my chin, guiding me until our gazes locked. "There are many things people say you should do. What do *you* want, Elea?"

A sense of warmth and rightness filled my heart. "To stay here and be your Queen."

I didn't think I'd ever seen a wider smile on Rowan's face. "And why is that?"

"Because I trust us to handle whatever comes our way."

"Good."

I wrapped my arms around his neck and pulled him in for

such a long and deep kiss, all the Casters began to whoop. I didn't care.

Love and trust. There was no better reason to celebrate.

—The End—

~

The adventure continues with CROWNED, Book 4 in the Beholder series. Read on for a sample chapter!

ALSO BY CHRISTINA BAUER

CROWNED

The adventure continues with CROWNED, Book 4 in the Beholder Series.

CLICK TO ORDER

ANGELBOUND

The kick-ass paranormal romance with more than 1 million copies sold!

CLICK TO ORDER

FAIRY TALES OF THE MAGICORUM

Don't miss these modern fairy tales with sass, action, and romance that *USA Today* calls a 'must-read!'

CLICK TO ORDER

DIMENSION DRIFT

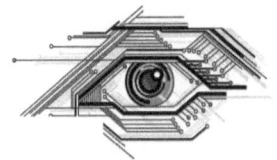

DIVERGENT meets OCEAN'S EIGHT in this dystopian adventure!

CLICK TO ORDER

*I*t was never a good idea to spy on the gods, as a rule.

That said, I was never one to follow the rules.

All of which was why I now stood in a hilltop ringed with skulls, staring out over a deserted landscape. A shiver of foreboding rolled across my shoulders. This place gave new meaning to the word bleak. Ashen soil stretched off in every direction. Charcoal-colored clouds wheeled overhead. A freestanding archway made from chipped stone loomed nearby. The thing looked like a ruin, but it was actually a magickal gateway called the Skullock Passage. Soon, this archway would also serve as my supernatural keyhole for spying on the gods. Quite possibly, I'd be killed in the process.

Considering my situation, it was a risk worth taking.

I glanced up at the darkening sky.

Almost time to begin.

Any minute now, a slash of blood-red light would appear by the horizon, marking the arrival of the Martyr's Comet, a heavenly body that showed itself once every two thousand years. Unfortunately, the Martyr's Comet had all sorts of dark legends surrounding it, such as the prophecy that whoever was the strongest Necromancer alive when the comet appeared, then that same Necromancer had to die when the comet vanished.

This particular legend had changed my life from bad to worse.

First, the bad part. About two months ago, my one-time Mother Superior, Petra, informed me of the Martyr's Comet prophecy, including the bit about the strongest Necromancer dying. That was certainly bad news; some poor mage was supposedly doomed.

Second, the worse part. Then Petra shared that I was the strongest Necromancer alive and she planned to end my life when the comet vanished. In other words, about three days from now. As I said, worse.

Of course, I'd no intention of dying any time soon. I just needed more information so I could foil Petra's schemes— hence my spying expedition.

A flicker of light appeared at the horizon. My gaze locked on the spot. Was that the Martyr's Comet?

I squinted into the darkening sky. The brightness clearly shone white, not red.

Only a shooting star, then.

A weight of disappointment settled on my shoulders. In some ways, I was looking forward to the comet's arrival. With it, there came additional powers over gateways, especially for mages like me. Tapping into those extra abilities, I'd turn the Skullock Passage into my personal spy-hole.

Take that, Petra.

A small cloud of dust began spinning on the ground nearby. The particles whirled in curlicue shapes that were too perfect to be natural. Magick. My heart lightened. Perhaps my mate Rowan was arriving. I had expected him to magickally transport here any second.

Sadly enough, blue lights sparkled deep within the haze. A weight of dread settled into my bones. Someone was casting a transport spell, only it wasn't Rowan. My mate was a Creation Caster, so his power came from life and his magick glowed red. This brightness shone blue, which meant the visiting mage was a Necromancer like me.

Damn.

Most likely, Petra was sending yet another messenger my way, asking me to fulfill the Prophecy of the Martyr's Comet and die willingly on the comet's last day. Meeting these messengers was never pleasant, but it wasn't particularly dangerous, either. Petra wouldn't try to kill me until the Martyr's Comet was just about to disappear.

Small comfort, really.

Within seconds, a wisp of a girl materialized beside me. She looked about sixteen years old with large brown eyes, pale skin, and raven-dark hair. The image of her skull had been magickally marked onto her face in dark tones. Her clothes were long black robes decorated with a few ties, which was the formal dress for a Sister, the lowest level of initiated Necromancer.

The girl spied me, gasped, and fell to her knees. A small puff of dried earth flew up where she landed. "Greetings, my Tsarina."

I pinched the bridge of my nose. All Petra's messengers fell on their knees when they first laid eyes on me. It was rather unsettling. I wasn't this girl's Tsarina, and even if I were, bowing and scraping weren't my idea of fun.

"I'm Elea. Just Elea. What's your name?"

The girl clasped her hands under her chin. "I am called Petra's Echo."

Not again. Petra was forever renaming her followers. So far this week, I'd met Petra's Consolation, Petra's Light, Petra's Patience, and now, Petra's Echo. It was demeaning to steal away someone's identity in such a manner. My one-time Mother Superior was turning crueler by the day.

"What's your real name?" I asked.

"I gave it to you. Being called Petra's Echo is an honor for me."

It was an effort not to roll my eyes. Should I fight her on this point? Perhaps. This girl seemed more open and innocent than my past messengers, so I might be able to break past Petra's brainwashing. Plus, I did have some time before both Rowan and the comet arrived. I decided to test the waters. "How about I call you Echo?"

"Whatever you wish, Tsarina."

I fought the urge to smile. None of the other messengers had allowed me to de-Petra their names. Maybe I could help this girl.

Echo glanced nervously around, as if Petra might be lurking under a nearby rock. "But make no mistake. Everything that I am today comes from Petra and Petra alone. I owe her my life."

I sniffed. "That's not how I remember it happening. As I recall, there was a great battle. On one side, there was the evil mage Viktor. On the other side, there was me and my mate Rowan. During the fighting, I summoned an army of Necromancers back from the dead to help win the day. You have my skull-mark on your face. That means you were one of those mages. Petra played no part in it."

"Oh, how disrespectful I have been to you, my Tsarina."

Echo leaned deeper into her kneel, stopping only when her forehead slammed against the ground. "You did indeed raise my physical body from the dead. However, Petra has since renewed my soul. I beg you to forgive me. Hear my vow: I promise to worship you as well, my Tsarina."

"That's not what I meant." I knelt beside her. "I wish you wouldn't worship Petra or me. When you regained your mortal body, it's true that my death magick reached out to your spirit. But never forget—it was your will that tapped into my spell. You hauled yourself back into the realm of the living. On its own, my skills couldn't have done that. Power and light dance inside you; those are yours alone. Don't ever give credit for them to someone else. Not even me."

Echo angled her head against the dusty earth, stopping when her gaze met mine. "This is all a trick." Her voice quavered. "You are testing my faith."

"No, I'm trying to help you. How about we both stand up?"

"As you command." Echo hopped upright and stared wide-eyed toward the horizon. When she spoke again, her voice held the singsong notes of a trained speech. "My name is Petra's Echo. You are our Tsarina, born Elea of Braddock Farm. You raised my body from the dead, and now my soul is led by Petra, the Most Holy Messenger of the Gods."

"The list of Petra's titles grows by the day." With slow movements, I forced myself to rise once more. "You'd best share what you came to tell me." I glanced up at the sky. No red slash of light; the Martyr's Comet had yet to arrive. There was still time to convince this girl.

Echo kept speaking in her singsong tone. "Petra is the Mouthpiece of the Gods, and she has a request for you. Our people believe you are our Tsarina."

"I'm aware." When I refused to take over ruling the Necromancers, Petra simply told everyone I was leading them from afar. It was most annoying.

"The Mouthpiece of the Gods has trusted me with a great secret." Echo lowered her voice to a whisper. "You are not truly our Tsarina. You haven't completed the sacred rites."

I sighed. "I'm aware of that as well."

"Don't you want to be Tsarina? You'll be hailed as the strongest Necromancer alive."

"That's precisely why I don't want the title. Right now, being confirmed as the strongest Necromancer isn't exactly a good thing." I shook my head. "Not that you'd know that. The messengers never receive all the necessary information."

"That doesn't make any sense. The Divine Petra has told me everything I need to know. Her message to you is this: complete the rituals and take over your true mantle as our Tsarina. Cease your pointless refusals."

Here we go again. Every missive from Petra was the same, as was my response, which always came in the form of a question. "And has Petra told you why I refuse?"

"Not specifically."

Because she never does. I'm sure Petra wouldn't find so many willing messengers if they knew the truth. No one wants to tell someone powerful that they must die soon. "Did Petra give you totem rings, by any chance?"

"Two of them. It is an honor." Echo lifted her dainty hands. She wore two silver thumb bands carved in skull patterns— the classic sign of Petra's totem ring creations. The reason for the bands was simple. Necromancer spells required exceedingly long incantations. Grand Mistresses could load magick onto rings and activate them with a single word.

"She always sends one messenger and two totem rings." I shook my head. "Those bands aren't a gift; they're a means of controlling you. Petra has loaded that first ring with a memory wipe spell. It will activate once we're done talking, usually when you speak the formal Necromancer farewell, valedictions. The second band is loaded with a transport spell to bring you back to Petra's side. That one will launch when you say the word transport."

"You're wrong about the totem rings, you know." Echo lifted her right hand. "This isn't a transport spell."

I narrowed my eyes. "What is it then?"

"A secret."

"I see." This girl was proving tough to reach. It was time to call in my best weapon. "You never answered my question. Do you wish to know the truth about why I refuse to become Tsarina?"

Echo hugged her elbows for a moment. Then, she nodded.

"Good." I gestured to the rickety arch behind me. "This is a gateway. Have you seen any before?"

"Yes, there's one hidden in our Cloister. It leads to another world—the Eternal Lands of the Sire and Lady."

"Quite right. The Sire of Souls and the Lady of Creation fashioned all the magickal arches in our world. Most of them lead to the Eternal Lands, but some connect elsewhere instead. In fact, legend tells of a place called the Meadow of Many Gateways where the arches link to nothing but other worlds." I gestured to the night sky. "Every two thousand years, the Martyr's Comet appears and weakens these gateways. Since our world has been magickally tied to so many others, we can't risk those arches falling apart. The very foundations of this world would collapse."

Echo popped her hand over her mouth. "Is that true?"

"Unfortunately." As if to highlight the point, a low rumble shook the earth. These quakes were becoming more and more common. "Up until this point, Petra and I believe the same things. But what I'm about to tell you next? That is where we differ. Petra also believes that the Martyr's Comet carries with it a prophecy. Have you heard of it?"

Echo frowned. "A prophecy related to the Martyr's Comet? Never."

"I hadn't heard of it either until a few months ago. This prophecy states that when the Martyr's Comet arrives, the greatest mage must sacrifice their life and power into one of these very gateways. The arch will then soak in their magick, distribute it to the other gateways, and maintain our world. The most powerful Necromancer alive is supposed to rule our kind. As a result every two thousand years, our Tsar or Tsarina always sacrifices themselves to the gateways."

Echo blinked. "I don't understand. You need to die?"

"The Martyr's Comet will appear any minute now. It will then cross by the horizon and vanish in three day's time. At the end of the third day, Petra plans to kill me and toss my body onto one of these gateways. But I won't let it happen."

This last part was a bit of a lie. I'd cast vision spells, pored over ancient texts, consulted Seers, and hired legions of mortal researchers. All of them confirmed that some unlucky Necromancer always died to fulfill the prophecy of the Martyr's Comet. According to every vision spell and Seer, the next sacrifice would never be Viktor, a homicidal mage who was my preferred choice for the job. No, all the scholars and visionaries agreed: the sacrifice was likely to be me.

I could see the logic, sadly enough. Viktor was also locked off in exile. Even if he could be set free, I'd need the Sword and perfect timing in order to have him be the sacrifice. It was far better for all of us if I had a back-up plan.

Echo's pretty features fell slack with chock. "Everything

will fall apart without the gateways having magick. You said so yourself. Don't you want to save our world?"

"I do, but there's always more than one way to accomplish any task. In my case, I am mated to Rowan, a Creation Caster. We've shared our Necromancer and Caster energies to create a new kind of hybrid magick. It's incredibly powerful. In fact, I think it could fix these gateways. But Rowan and I need access to the gateways in order to test out our spells." We also needed to spy on the gods for more information before the testing could begin, but I didn't volunteer that fact.

"Oh, that won't happen. The Sire and Lady have warded every gateway. You can't even approach them safely, let alone cast a spell."

"I've noticed." I scanned the dark sky again. "Once the comet appears, that will change. I'll be able to cast a spell or two."

"And the Sire and Lady will allow that?"

"No, unfortunately. I've pleaded with them for information about the gateways and hybrid magick. They've refused. They won't even lower the wards so I can test out a few minor spells. Don't you think that's suspicious? Shouldn't I be allowed to try something else before giving up my life?"

Echo stared at her totem things. "This is all very confusing. I'm failing at my task."

Poor Echo. She seemed so deflated and miserable. "Look, you've failed at nothing. Petra has no real verbal message for me today. She merely sends Sisters like you to show me that she can get to me whenever she wants to...And she plans to find me at on the third day of the Martyr's Comet."

Echo twisted her totem rings in a nervous rhythm. "The Mouthpiece of the Gods warned me that you wouldn't agree. But I'm not to transport back to her like the others. I'm to activate this totem ring, bringing the Divine Petra here to speak to you directly."

I frowned. This was different for Petra, and with the Martyr's Comet about to appear, I didn't like things changing, especially with someone as young and inexperienced as Echo around.

"Listen to me carefully, Echo. Do not speak the word to launch that ring."

Echo went on anyway. "Possession!" With that word, Echo's totem ring flared with blue light. Instantly, an indigo haze enveloped the girl. Her eyes took on a glazed and empty look. When she spoke again, Echo's voice had a distinct monotone. "I have taken control of this lesser mage. Now I give my true message to you, Elea."

I'd heard that voice many times before. Petra. She'd cast a spell of possession on young Echo. A chill of fear crawled up my limbs. This wouldn't end well.

I cupped my hand by my mouth. "If you can hear me, Echo, you need to stop speaking."

On reflex, I reached out with my mage senses, getting ready to cast a counter-spell. Necromancer power lay all around me, resting heavily in the bones and fossil-laden rocks under the earth's surface. I drew that energy into my soul. Magick flowed into my limbs, making the bones in my arms glow blue with power.

When Echo spoke again, it was still with Petra's voice. "You'll never pull in enough power in time to help this lesser mage. You must stop fighting me and pay attention. You have forced me to possess this girl's body because I must teach you a lesson. When you disobey the gods, this what happens to those you love."

Blue light flared once more from Echo's totem ring. More

possession spells. With unnatural speed, Echo turned to face the deadly gateway.

I gasped. "No!"

Without so much as a glance in my direction, Echo rushed toward the magickal arch at a supernatural pace. I quickly glanced upward. The Martyr's Comet still hadn't appeared. Echo was headed toward a gateway that remained fully warded and absolutely deadly. I simply had to stop her.

I raced toward the girl. "Wait!"

But Echo didn't seem to hear my words. Just as Petra had predicted, there wasn't time for me to cast a spell or catch up by running, especially considering Echo's magickal burst of speed. I could only watch in horror as the young girl stepped under the arch. For a moment, Echo stood frozen in place. After that, her body took on a glass-like sheen, like she was made of porcelain instead of flesh and blood. Blue light illuminated her from within. Dark fissures formed along her skin and robes. My heart cracked as well.

The gateway's magick was about to pull Echo apart.

With a great boom, Echo shattered into a thousand glowing shards of blue light that flew into the illuminated stones of the gateway. For a moment, the arch's rocks flared with such a bright shade of blue, they almost looked white. A weight of sadness settled into my soul. There was no coming back when you were obliterated by a gateway.

Echo was dead.

Around me, everything reverted to its non-magickal state. The gateway's stones returned to being non-illuminated blocks of gray. I stared down at my arms. Blue light still shone in my bones. There's still so much power in my body, all of it ready to cast a counter-spell. Plus, if Rowan had been here, we could have brought hybrid magick into the mix as well. That was even more energy.

And yet, I couldn't save that innocent girl.

Echo was gone, but her words—or I should say, Petra's—reverberated through my soul: "When you disobey the gods, this is what happens to those you love."

Petra kills them.

Meaning I should sacrifice myself or she'd take those I cared about.

Waves of rage tightened up my rib cage. Petra had moved on from sending threatening messengers to murdering mages before my eyes. My one-time Mother Superior had made her point: she would do anything to force my sacrifice, one way or another. And there was no question who she planned to go after next.

Those I love.

Rowan.

If Petra's intention was to frighten me into submission, it didn't work. With each passing moment, more of my will hardened into stony resolve. I would still spy on the gods and get some answers. Then I'd use that information to learn hybrid magick and fix the gateways.

And after all that, I'd make Petra pay for what she'd done to Echo.

—The End—

❧

To find out more about CROWNED, visit:

http://monsterhousebooks.com/books/beholder/crowned